TO: Granddaughter,

MW01099140

Anna's Legacy

Mickey Cook

Love, from

aka Marlene K. Yandt

Mickey Cook

Anna's Legacy

MOSCOW. SPOKANE. VERNONIA.

TATE PUBLISHING & *Enterprises*

Published by Tate Publishing & Enterprises, LLC
127 E. Trade Center Terrace | Mustang, Oklahoma 73064 USA
1.888.361.9473 | www.tatepublishing.com

Tate Publishing is committed to excellence in the publishing industry. The company reflects the philosophy established by the founders, based on Psalm 68:11,
"The Lord gave the word and great was the company of those who published it."

Cover design by Kellie Southerland
Interior design by Stephanie Woloszyn

Published in the United States of America

ISBN: 978-1-60696-316-6
1. Fiction / Christian / Historical
2. Family & Relationships / Life Stages / General
09.03.16

Dedication

I would like to dedicate this book personally to my late Swedish grandmother, Anna. This story is dedicated to her life and family. I would also like to dedicate it to my late Swedish grandfather, Adolph, who emigrated from Sweden to the United States; to my mother who filled me in on the necessary details of Anna's life; to my late father who was the family patriarch, a leader in the Civilian Conservation Corps and in everything he joined; to my brother Keith, who surprised us all with his extraordinary underwater photography with the Navy Seabees and Bikini Atoll at the end of World War II; to my sister-in-law, Geraldine Cook, who provided Keith's story from her press release.

Without the unique experiences of their lives, there would be no *Anna's Legacy.*

Acknowledgments

A special thanks to…

- *Oregon Christian Writers* for their excellent speakers, workshops, and insights for teaching and inspiring me.
- *Christian Writers Guild* for training me in the necessary skills of how to write and my excellent mentor, DiAnn Mills, who encouraged and persevered with me every step of the way.
- *The Writer's Critique Group* to whom I am grateful for not always allowing me to have my way with words and who told me how to make it sound better.
- *Billie Reynolds and Crystal "Chris" Ortmann* who invited me into their critique groups and showed me the art of editing.
- *Editor David Kopp*, who taught me the joy of writing and inspired me to write in the journalism class from Multnomah Biblical Seminary.
- *Tate Publishing* who gave me my first chance at being the author of a book.
- *Chad McComas*, editor of *Christian Journal* in southern Oregon, who gave me my first opportunities to be a published writer.
- *Mark Mehall*, the "computer guy" who helped me put it all together technically.

Table of Contents

Foreword

Mickey Cook's heart is to use her writing skills to honor her God. She has generously written and given her articles to Christian publications to reach out to a reading audience with stories of love, courage, and hope in God. Now Mickey has written her book, *Anna's Legacy,* to share through Christian fiction a story of hope and courage in a young woman's life. Mickey has weaved throughout the chapters insights of God's love and leading. The reader will walk away with a strengthened hope in God and courage to face life and all its challenges.

Chad McComas, Editor
The Christian Journal
Medford, Oregon
June 2008

Mullan Burns

Crackle. Crackle. Crackle…

Anna opened her eyes to the brightness of the morning. Was it the heat of an August morning that had awakened her from a restless night's sleep? She rubbed her bloodshot eyes and listened to the baby's coughing. Slipping out of bed, her toes touched the hardwood floor. She nearly tripped on her clean white linen nightgown. What was that sound she heard? A crackle. The smell. It was stinging her lungs. She coughed in unison with the baby. Where was Adolph? He had said he did not work today. The heat. It felt so intense. Baby Phyl reached for her momma and coughed again. Anna scooped up Phyl and cradled her in the crib-side rocker. Why was it so unusually hot this early in the morning? What was that flash of light? She nursed and fidgeted. Panic began to fill her being. Something was just not right.

She continued to rock Phyl, trying to comfort her while her own fears were anything but calm.

Crackle. Crackle. Crackle...

Fire! The distinct sounds of fire. Lightning flashed across the window.

Maybe that's all it is. Just the sounds of a forthcoming August thunderstorm. But why that smell? It began to permeate the house.

"Anna!" Adolph rushed inside, searching for them both. No sounds. "Anna, where are you?"

"Here, Adolph, feeding Phyl."

Adolph's eyes were filled with panic.

"Grab her baby clothes and something for yourself. Dress quickly, Anna. We haven't much time. I'll get some cash and food. Hurry!"

"What's wrong, Adolph?" Anna laid the baby down on the bed and dressed quickly.

"Anna, Mullan is under siege—the siege of a forest fire gone wrong. Come with me now, Anna. We must act quickly."

Anna grabbed all she could and stuffed clothing and personal items into a bag.

"Oh, my God, Adolph. Look! The neighbor's house is aflame."

Adolph grabbed her hand and began to run.

"Where are we headed, Adolph?" Anna held the baby so tightly, she awakened screaming. "Oh, Baby. Sorry. Tell me where we're going, Adolph."

"To the train, Anna. You two are going on the train to Spokane. Right now! Anna. Don't be dumb! I will join you when I can. I am staying. You're going."

They listened to its distinct sounds and saw the steam puffing out of the train coming toward them down the trestle.

"No, Adolph. I will not leave you."

"You *will* leave, Anna."

The train pulled to a stop. Adolph had purchased two tickets to Spokane before he had gone home to get Anna.

"Step aboard."

Adolph helped Anna step inside the train. He laid the baby in her waiting arms. She again looked back. Her stomach cramped with fear.

"I'll see you two soon, Anna. In Spokane. You have cash, food, and clothing. You'll be all right." Adolph turned and walked away.

Would Anna and Phyl ever see him again? Mullan was burning. People were screaming and running for the train. Adolph was out of sight. Forever? How had this horror begun? Why?

It began with a lightning strike to the tinder-dry forest near Wallace, Idaho. Fierce winds had whipped the flames westward.

Then it had reached Anna's town of Mullan.

Screaming, burning, and bleeding were the sights and sounds Anna remembered. She and Adolph were nearly newlyweds. Adolph worked as a miner in the Federal Mining and Smelting Company's Morning Mine in Mullan, Idaho. Her first baby girl, Phyl, had been birthed in January. Phyl competed with the wailing voices. Thank God they were safe. Almost.

The entire village was ablaze. Before it completed its destructive path, the fire of the century had burned three million acres and sent ashes around the world. In the late afternoon, the sky darkened, the air became hot and oppressive. The wind was hurricane strength. The combination was like the roar of a train thundering down upon the town. Some members of the crew were held at gunpoint. They were too desperately needed to fight the fire. They could not be allowed to flee. The water from the stream became alkaline, polluted from the dead fish. Some who jumped into the stream caught pneumonia. One crew member was annihilated. One described the intensity of the fire like touching a candle to a mosquito.

The stench of burnt flesh slapped Anna in the face as she moved farther into the train. The sickening odor permeated the passenger car. Yet, Anna decided that it was and would be for the entire journey and that she must determine to accept it. Beyond her personal, inward feelings and offense, she knew she must use those feelings to face what was real and reach out to others in need. For the moment, she dealt with her fear, fatigue, and duties to her baby. *How wonderful to find one vacant seat,* she thought. The baby was just fine in her lap. Anna leaned far back in her seat and relaxed while Phyl fed hungrily at her breast. When the baby finished feeding, she slept in Anna's arms. So did Anna sleep, exhausted.

Agonizing sounds of pain aroused her to consciousness. Many screamed in pain. Others passed out. There was no medicine aboard. People did what they could to comfort the sick and dying. Anna arose from her seat holding her baby. She placed some personal items to hold the seat, hoping no one would occupy it. She had to do what she could to comfort or heal the wounded.

A man sat in the far back corner, screaming in pain. Anna found a salve in her satchel—a healing balm for burns. She approached the wounded man and gently spoke words of comfort in a whisper so as not to frighten him. She told him she had lotion for a burn, and she was going to touch him to apply it. She scrubbed her hands with soap and water in the toilet area of the train. Then she returned to the young gentleman.

"I am ready now. It may hurt for me to touch you. I will be very gentle. What is your name?" Anna wanted to bond with the hurting man to heal him physically and emotionally.

"Arthur. And yours?" He spoke with a raspy voice. His clothes were torn and sooty.

"Anna. My husband is Adolph. He stayed behind to help in Mullan. This is my baby daughter, Phyl."

Arthur's tears streamed down his dirty, sooty cheeks. He did not complain. She could tell he was hurting and holding back.

Anna cried also. As she looked at Arthur, her tears seemed to be for all of Mullan. Anna first washed the wound to eke out as much dirt as possible.

"I hope and pray that this will be soothing to you, Arthur. I hope it might begin to heal your wounds and your pain. Perhaps you will be able to rest."

"Thank you, Anna. God bless you. When I get to Wallace or Spokane, I will find a doctor to help me. Yet I guess most everyone on this train will be doing the same thing."

Phyl was ready to feed again. Anna placed a small blanket over her torso to cover the baby and herself. *It is so nice of God to provide instant meals for babies right from their mothers,* Anna thought to herself. She glanced around again at Arthur. He was sound asleep. The only noise he emitted now was snoring. Anna thanked God silently.

After a long journey and a little snack she had managed to gather in her satchel, the train finally arrived in Wallace.

"Now, dear Phyl, we will find some lodging and a good meal. We'll even have a refreshing bath and a long, sound sleep before we board the train for Spokane—*if the Lord wills.*" Phyl cooed an echo of agreement.

Anna watched as men and women were carried off the train with traumatic injuries and burns. *Some may never make it,* she thought. *God help them. And Adolph, God, please keep Adolph safe and bring him to us in Spokane. Death,* thought Anna, *why must death follow me?*

For the moment, Anna felt safe for herself and her baby. What about Adolph, though? She pondered what he might be dealing with in the midst of Mullan's turmoil.

Adolph's thoughts were much divided. He wondered how Anna and baby Phyl were doing, where they were, what they encountered along the journey, and their pending reunion in Spokane.

Some of the men who died, Adolph had known well. The list was long. Adolph read on.

August 15, 1910, Otto Nelson died. He had been a timber helper who was only thirty years old. He had also worked for the Federal Mining and Smelting Company, Morning Mine, Mullan, Idaho,

Shoshone County. Nelson had been crushed when large rocks had fallen from the back of his stope. His head was so badly crushed that he could not even be recognized early into the accident. He had lived around the Mullan area for eight years. He had left behind a cousin in Troy, Montana.

Adolph remembered Bert Roy Thrasher, who had also worked with him in the Morning Mine. He had died March 10, 1911, and was only twenty-five years old. He had been single when he died. He had been carrying a drill steel hung over his shoulder and was at the 800-level station in the Morning Mine. He had accidentally hit the high-voltage line with the steel on his shoulder and had been instantly electrocuted. They could hear him whistling as he was walking, then he had suddenly sunk to the floor. He never uttered another sound. He was not that well-known because he was fairly new, but Adolph remembered him. Nice guy. He had been born in Umatilla County, Oregon. It was thought by many that he had a wife. He had lived in another town nearby. Some had determined he was single.

Another miner Adolph remembered was John Bowman. He was a hoistman, middle-aged, about forty-three, and had died July 12, 1911, about midnight just as he was going off shift. He was riding the trolley motor to the portal tunnel. The trolley motor was traveling at excessive speed and lost a wheel. It jumped the track. Pieces of the metal struck Bowman and fractured his skull. They rushed him to Providence Hospital in Wallace, Idaho. He died on the operating table early the next morning.

Then Adolph stood in horror as he watched a man stumble out of the mine.

Oh, my God in heaven, Adolph grieved deeply in his spirit. *That man looks to be nearly burned alive. I must reach him.*

Adolph moved frantically through the erratic crowd of people, burning buildings, and chaos to reach the man. Why *this* man out of all the others stood out to him, he did not know. *Perhaps it was because of the mines.* Adolph had spent his whole working time in those silver mines. Therefore, he determined they were comrades. He must help a *brother.*

Adolph held the badly burned man in his arms.

"I'm going to die, Adolph, aren't I? I'm in so much pain. Even the morphine doesn't help. Please say goodbye to my family—if you see them. Please help them, too, if you can."

"You know my name! Do I know you?" Adolph inquired, though he wondered if he should ask questions now when the man was in such obvious pain. It was just that he wanted to bond by remembering.

"Am I *that* bad, Adolph?" the man asked.

"Remind me who you are?" Adolph asked.

"I'm Paul. Paul Pendergast. We have worked together in the Morning Mine. My wife is Patricia."

"Oh, yes, Paul. I remember you. You are a good man, a good worker, and friend." Adolph turned his head aside to deal with his inability to recognize one who had once been such an obvious and excellent coworker.

"Adolph, stay with me and find my family."

Adolph nodded and prayed with the man. He could help a few. There were thousands. Now, he must also think of his fleeing family and their needs. Every need had value beyond his own. The tent city for the miners burned to the ground. Sobbing—deep guttural sobbing—could be heard around him. The fire continued to consume. Adolph looked down again at the now silent man in his arms. He was asleep—deep sleep. He was dead.

"Adolph, Adolph!" the man cried to him from afar. "The train is leaving! Grab what you can and come quickly."

Adolph ran and never looked back. *If I look behind me, I will never leave here. God must help Paul's family now.*

Adolph caught the last train out of Mullan. The trestle burned behind it, and there would be no escape for the remaining victims.

It was the final run to Wallace. He coughed and coughed during the whole trip. *Just all that smoke and burn,* Adolph told himself. If it worsened or continued, he would visit a doctor in Spokane.

"Adolph." Adolph thought he heard a soft voice. Maybe he was delusional from all he had seen and heard. He sat back quietly, fatigued.

"Adolph." There was no mistake now. He turned his head to the left and looked behind him. No one he knew. He turned to the right and looked across the aisle. A woman stared at him.

"Do you remember me, Adolph? I'm Patty. I thought Paul might be on the train. It was my last hope."

Adolph looked away, out the window, down at his feet. "I'm sorry, Patty. I saw him just a short while ago. He didn't make it, Patty. I'm so sorry." Her weeping silenced him again.

"Are you headed to Spokane?" he asked her after a while.

"I don't know where I'm headed, Adolph. Wherever the train ends, that's my destination."

"Let me know if we can help." Adolph laid back his head to rest.

"Where is the rest of 'we,' Adolph? Did Anna and the baby survive the fire, or are you alone now?"

Adolph took a long time to ponder that statement. He wasn't sure if he should respond. He decided he would not.

"I could use your help when you arrive wherever you're going. Perhaps we could find a place to stay together." She smiled warmly at Adolph—even winked.

Adolph's friend sat beside him and looked at Adolph. "What kind of an offer was that, Adolph? Didn't you say she just lost her husband?"

"In my arms."

The mixed smell of burnt cinders, smoke, and flesh from those he had held in his arms covered his aching body. Exhaustion filled his very being. He leaned back and made an attempt to rest, but rest would not come. He began to cough until blood spit from his lungs.

Adolph's friend opened his thermos of water and offered Adolph a drink.

"Better take care of that cough when we get into town," his friend said.

"It's just a little left over from the fire," Adolph replied.

"Not with blood in it," his friend responded.

"If it persists, I'll have the doc take a look at it. We survived. Many did not make it. A cough is the least of my concerns right now." Adolph took another swig of water and coughed up more phlegm and blood.

"Nevertheless, Adolph, your point has been made. We do not need another death. Take care." His friend tried to convince the stubborn Swede.

Pain now encompassed his chest. Someone on board offered Adolph a teaspoon of medicine. It calmed the cough. Adolph lay back on the seat, reflecting.

He thought about Anna. He valued her more than ever right now.

What were Anna and Phyl doing right now? Had they arrived safely in Spokane? Did Mary take them in?

It would be another day before he would have answers.

Anna took Phyl in her arms while she found lodging. Approaching the only hotel in sight, Anna stepped inside.

"I need a room for me and my baby daughter," Anna said to the clerk.

"You and a hundred other people. I think we're filled up already." The clerk did not even bother to look up into Anna's desperate eyes.

"Please," Anna said. "We need food and lodging and a nice clean bath." Anna stood her ground, determined to have a room.

"We got a room near the pantry. You will have to share it with one of the cooks. Female, of course. It will be two dollars a night, meals extra." The clerk continued to look down at her books as if Anna and Phyl were not human.

"We'll take it. Here is the two dollars. When is the next train out of Wallace to Spokane?" Anna begged.

"You'll have to check that out with the train station," the man said.

"Could you call them for us? We are so tired, dirty, and hungry."

"I cannot play nursemaid to everyone who comes here. I've got work to do." He paused and, looking at Anna and down at Phyl, spoke again. "Wait here a minute. I will see what I can do."

The clerk returned. "Train leaves tomorrow morning at 9:00 a.m."

"What time does it arrive in Spokane?" Anna inquired.

"Look, lady, I am not *both* the hotel clerk and the train depot. You will have to get that information for yourself. Two dollars. Here is your receipt. One night only?" The clerk placed the receipt in Anna's hand.

"Someone will show you to your room."

The attendant arrived and led Anna into the tiny room. Anna found the bathroom. She began to undress herself and remove Phyl's shoes and socks.

"We are going to have a nice warm bath, baby girl."

"Who is in there? Get out of my bathroom right now!" Fists were pounding on the bathroom door; yelling and screaming came from the bedroom.

Anna walked into the small bedroom with Phyl.

"Who are you! What are you doing in my room?" The red-faced cook was obviously furious.

Anna looked at the flushed cook. "I'm sorry. Did the clerk not tell you that this was the only room available for me and my little girl? We are just here overnight and leave tomorrow for Spokane. He said there was an extra bedroom and brought us here. I am so sorry he did not tell you. How awful for you." Anna felt embarrassed and compassionate for the bewildered cook.

"But who are you?" the cook insisted.

"We just arrived from Mullan, Idaho. My husband is back there still. He is doing whatever he can for the people. He will meet us in Spokane tomorrow. Everything burned—our home, our town, even the people."

The cook stood and stared at Anna and Phyl for what seemed like an eternity. "I'll be right back. Don't touch anything!" She stormed out of the room. When she returned, she was much calmer.

"I had no idea what happened. No one told me. You and your daughter may have this bedroom and share my bath. You will just be here overnight, correct?"

"Yes," Anna said. "We leave in the morning for Spokane. We will be eating all our meals in the dining area. We just needed a room to sleep. Now, we will dress and go to the dining room."

"I hope you like the food." The young woman left to prepare for the next meal.

Anna dressed Phyl and sat her quietly in the chair while she readied herself for dinner.

"What would you like to eat, Missy Phyl?" Anna gently pinched Phyl's fat little cheek. "I will see what I can do. Would you mind sharing a meal with your mommy?" Anna smiled at Phyl as her excited eyes canvassed the room. "I will order something we both like." Anna searched the menu.

When the order came, there was a note beside it that read: "Compliments of the chef. Enjoy!"

Anna was so grateful. She had very little money with her. It was a generous act of kindness. They needed kindness right now—and sleep.

They both slept soundly. Phyl cuddled up to her mommy.

The morning sun was unusual in its color. It was a very dark red—like the fire from the lightning strike. They cleaned up, enjoyed a quick breakfast, thanked the cook profusely, and climbed aboard the train for Spokane.

"We are going to see Papa." Anna smiled at Phyl.

"Pa-pa." Phyl tried out one of her few words.

She wondered what Adolph might be doing and prayed for his safety and health.

En route to Spokane, there was plenty of time to remember. Anna took her thoughts back to childhood and dreamed.

Anna
Death Defined Her

Anna recalled her life before Mullan, before tragedy struck her life, when she had been young and everything about living was before her. Her hopes and dreams had been pure then. They had not yet been polluted by life. That was 1901. Anna was just thirteen years old.

"Wilhelmina! Oh, my God, no!"

Anna could hear Papa yelling. Had she given birth yet? What was wrong with Papa? She listened for the sounds of new life. A baby's cry. Anna sat in the kitchen waiting for Papa's permission to enter. Another sibling! How many more?

"Anna! *Anna!*" Papa sounded distressed. Was this not a day for joy—at least for him? "*Anna!*"

Anna bounded up the stairs, nearly tripping on the long new dress Wilhelmina had taught her to sew. They had just finished yesterday. Such fun and giggles they had shared together. Reaching the top, Anna joyously went bounding into the room.

"Take the baby, Anna! *Take the baby, Anna!* Wash him!" Anna stood frozen, hearing her beloved papa's harsh words to her. She gazed across the room. The baby was screaming. She had never seen Papa so distraught. Wilhelmina was not moving.

"Anna! Take the baby!" Anna reached down and cupped the tiny bundle of reddened, screaming, messy flesh into her arms.

"What's wrong with Momma? Why isn't she moving, Papa? Why doesn't she nurse the baby? Doesn't she want it? Momma?"

"She's dead, Anna. It was a long and difficult birth for her."

Anna felt nausea creeping from her stomach into her mouth. She threw up all over the baby—and hated him.

Anna walked over to her papa and put her arms around him. They clung to each other and cried together. The deep grief overwhelmed them both. Yet Papa knew there were things he must do despite how he—or anyone else—felt. Time was of the essence. Wisely, even in his deepest sorrow, he held Anna at length and spoke.

"Anna, get ahold of yourself. The baby needs attention, cleaning, and feeding. He is now your responsibility. While your mother is still warm, I want you to extract the milk from her breasts and place it in the containers in the icebox. Clean and wrap the baby. Feed him some of her milk. We must work quickly, Anna, even in our grief. Time is not on our side. Call Albert, Jr. to come and help me take your mother. I will call the morgue and the church. I pray that they will have a nursing mother who can help."

"No, Papa. I am only a child, too. I can't do this!"

"Anna, you can, and you will. Obey me, Anna. I am in no mood for your childish pouting. I have just lost a wife. You and the children have just lost your mother. It is a very sad day for the Lindquist family. You will take care of this baby, Anna, and raise it. I will take care of you. Now, leave me alone. Go do your job."

Papa's harsh demands cut deeply into her spirit. It did not make the suffering she felt any easier.

Anna looked at the baby in her arms with disgust. She looked at her dead mother, still warm. She lay the infant down on the clean sheets—bloody mess that he still was. She opened up her mother's nightgown. She had never seen a woman's breasts before—not even her mother's. Her hands tightened around them as the tears fell. She grasped the clean jar and slowly squeezed her mother's milk into the jar. When she finished, she closed up Momma's gown and stroked her mother's cheeks gently, blending her tears into her mother's skin. Blueness began to set into her mother's lips.

"Oh, Momma. Yesterday we had such fun. We sewed and giggled and dined together." Anna looked over at the child. She hated him with every ounce of her being. His tiny arms and legs were kicking while he screamed for attention. She took the little boy and washed him with warm soapy water. Placing some of the milk in a small bottle, she placed on it a top with a nipple and closed it. She placed the bottle into the baby's mouth. He drank heartily.

"I'll give you attention, that's all. My God in heaven, how I resent your very being. You killed my mother. She didn't need another hungry mouth to feed, another child to raise." It would not be Momma's burden. It would be Anna's. "How dare you!" Anna cried. "I am a child caring for a child. What a pair!"

She changed the baby and placed him to sleep in his little bed. Then, she sat beside him and cried until she fell asleep herself.

Anna's responsibilities seemed now more numerous because of her age.

What determines life and death? Who decides? Why do some babies live and some die? Where do they go? How does a woman get pregnant? What does it feel like? Anna had more questions than answers. There were other things to think about now.

Anna awoke abruptly with the baby's cries. She placed her arms under the tiny infant and supported his head. She had no idea how tense she was until the baby screamed.

Papa came rushing up the stairway and into the room.

"Anna, what are you doing to that child? Why is he screaming?" Papa's face was a mixture of fear, anger, and compassion.

"He's just hungry, Papa. He will be fine once his tummy is full again. Do we have some blankets I can tear into diapers?" The care of a baby was nothing new to Anna. She had always observed her mother and assisted when asked. Now, she was in charge.

"Anna, are you angry with the baby?" Papa's direct words hit home to her breaking heart.

"I suppose that I am, Papa. After all, he took my mother's life and left his own as a replacement. Yes, I resent him bitterly." There, it had been said. *How would Papa respond to such honesty?*

"Anna, I forbid you to take your feelings out on that helpless infant. He needs love, Anna—your love. He needs all the love you can give him. It is *not* his fault. Are you blaming him, or are you blaming God?" Papa's wise words cut like a sword.

"I have not sorted that out in my mind, Papa. I suppose that I am angry with *both*. Why aren't you?"

"Because it is not the baby's fault. And I do not blame God. If he needed Wilhelmina with him in heaven, it is his decision, not mine. I do not tell God what he can do. Neither can you, dear daughter. You need to go before God and talk to him about how you feel. He will listen and he will understand. Now, make the baby comfortable, and we will see about blankets when you are through." Papa walked out of the room. Like God, Papa's word was law!

Anna changed the baby and placed his sleepy body back into his bassinet.

She sat back in the rocker and bowed her head. No words would come. She knew she must wait until she could be honest about her feelings before she could bring them before God.

Her siblings waited downstairs. Papa walked heavily down the stairway to the bottom floor. They all stared at Papa in wonder. Papa spoke first.

"Sit down with me, children. I have something to tell you." Papa dropped into his big chair.

"What is it, Papa? How is Momma? The baby? Is it a boy or girl? Can we see it?" It was Albert who sensed something very wrong. He walked over to Papa and placed his arm on his shoulder.

"Something has happened, hasn't it, Papa? Something tragic. Is it the baby? Did the baby die? Was it a boy or girl?" Albert waited for Papa's response.

"Albert, children, it is your mother who has died." Papa tried to be strong. The tears trickled down his cheeks and onto his trousers.

"Oh, my God in heaven, no! Not Momma!" The wailing sounds resounded throughout the house. Anna heard them from upstairs.

Pastor N.J.W. Nelson knocked on the front door. Albert opened it and greeted him.

"Come in, Pastor."

Pastor Nelson took one look at Albert and the family and reset his agenda.

"It is a very sad day for the Lindquist family, Pastor. I have just lost a wife. The children have lost their mother." Papa hung his head. He did not feel like shaking anyone's hand.

"Johnn Albert, I am so sorry. I came to give congratulations, not regrets. And the baby?"

"The baby is a boy. Anna is upstairs caring for him right now. It is good that you are here, Pastor. We need to make arrangements for Wilhelmina's funeral." Papa did not really want to think of such things. His heart was too heavy to plan.

"I will take care of everything, Johnn Albert. You have already paid for a plot. Do you want me to state the obituary and have it placed in the paper? I can also take your phone calls, so you do not have that added burden." Pastor looked to Papa for answers.

"Anything you might take care of would be a burden lifted from my heart and this home. Perhaps Albert could help you." Papa looked up at his eldest son.

"Anything I can do to help you, Pastor, I will." Albert shook Pastor's hand.

"If I need someone to help, Albert, I will call upon you. Thank you. I will return to the parish and call the mortuary to pick up Wilhelmina." Pastor Nelson hugged each sibling and gave Papa a big hug, too, before he headed for the door.

Anna listened as Pastor Nelson walked outside. She came downstairs. She remembered when Pastor Nelson had performed her Confirmation. That had been such a joyous and special time for her. He had baptized her. Precious memories.

Now, Anna remembered the events that were coming upon her this very week. She smiled at the fact of advancing two grades during her eight years of school. For that, she needed to prepare. Graduation. Commencement. To Anna, it was not the beginning. It was the end. She must tell Papa. There were many things to do. The event should have been a time of great rejoicing. Her friends were calling and expressing their excitement. Anna pretended to be eager and anticipate her future as they prepared for their own. She tiptoed down the stairway and knocked on the door of Papa's den.

"Come in," Papa yelled from inside. "Anna, come sit down beside me. What do you have on your mind?"

"Papa, my graduation is this Friday. Will you and the children be able to attend?

"Yes, Anna. Here is five dollars. It's all I can afford right now. Go buy yourself a dress. I want you to look pretty for your Momma and me."

That Friday, Anna took care of her household duties and skipped down the street to the clothing store.

"That one! I'll take it! How much?"

"Three dollars and ninety-nine cents, Anna." The clerk held up the dress so Anna could take another look. She handed the clerk the five dollars and took her change to the shoe store.

"How much?" Anna handed the clerk one dollar.

"Not enough, Anna. I need another dollar." Anna looked down. Then she remembered Momma's shoes still in the closet. "That's all right. I won't be needing any just now. Thank you."

When she got back home, Anna ran upstairs and tried on her momma's shoes. They fit beautifully, and there was a pair that matched her dress. "Thank you, Momma. You will be with me tonight, everywhere I go."

"Are you ready, Anna?" They had finished the evening supper. The siblings had done the dishes. The sitter arrived to be with the baby.

"Anna, I know you have many questions regarding your mother's whereabouts. She is in a place called heaven. That is where people go when they die and have given their life to the Lord. It will now become your responsibility to take her place in this home. After tonight, Anna, you must drop out of school. There is much work to do. Your mother instructed you well. I believe you are capable of taking over the needs of the family. Today you are an adult."

"I don't *want* to be an adult, Papa! I want to finish my childhood—and my schooling!"

Anna's heart ached inside.

Anna walked down the aisle to receive her diploma. She felt such a sense of self-worth and accomplishments.

"Anna! We did it! Next fall we will enter high school. I can hardly wait! How about you, Anna? Are you excited?"

"Sure." That was all Anna could say.

Papa beamed with proud joy at his daughter. He looked forward to having her home.

"Papa, some of my friends have invited me to a party to celebrate. May I go, Papa?"

"For a little while, Anna. We need you at home to care for the baby soon."

"What courses will you take next year, Anna? What do you want to be and do when you graduate?" her friends asked her, eager with excitement and the joy of maturity.

"I think I am already experiencing maturity," she answered them stoically. They looked at Anna with puzzlement.

Summer was in full swing. Classmates came by for a time.

"Come, Anna, grab your swimsuit and bring a picnic lunch," they yelled.

Summer ended, and so did their contact with Anna.

Anna's heart ached inside. When she arose in the early morning, she went to a quiet secluded place in the house to be alone with her thoughts. In anger she cried out, "God, I thought you were omnipotent, omniscient, and omnipresent! Well, not today, God! You're not here today. This would never have happened to my mother if you had been here. You let me down, God! You let my mother die! Why, God? Why?"

The Swedish Lutheran Church of Moscow, Idaho, opened its doors to the family and friends of Wilhelmina Lindquist. Anna took Papa's arm on one side. Albert took the other. The weight of Papa's loss weighed heavily on him, especially today. They walked by the casket and viewed her body. She looked beautiful, almost alive. Papa leaned over to kiss her cheek.

Pastor Nelson gave a beautiful message praising Wilhelmina for all her attributes and contributions to the church. He praised Johnn Albert for his hard work as the church janitor. He reflected upon how these loving and compassionate skills were shown in their family. He explained to the congregation the role of Anna's going from a young child who was just beginning to blossom into adulthood to someone who was now in the role of a teenage mother.

He begged the congregation to reach out to Anna, to Papa, and to the entire family, not only in their time of grief, but in the days and years ahead. They occupied a difficult and unusual role.

The townspeople grieved, too. Offers poured in from the

Moscow, Idaho community to take the children into various loving and caring homes. The church responded with many offers. Moscow's upstanding doctor and his wife offered to take Anna.

"I will *not* divide my family!" Papa roared. "We are one and we will remain one!" That was the last word on it.

For the next five years, Anna relinquished her own life to fulfill the roles and responsibilities of her beloved mother for whom she desperately grieved. She never complained about the daily routine of caring for a new baby, cooking, cleaning, getting her brothers and sisters ready for school—even intervening in their frequent spats.

"Selma," Anna said as she sat beside her eldest sister, "look at this hat. The city women wear these. I wonder if they will ever catch on in Moscow. I think I would like to make hats someday."

"Why are you waiting for 'someday,' Anna? Why don't you start today?" Selma was the great encourager. She felt great empathy for Anna, who had to carry most of the household burden.

"Will you go shopping with me, Selma? I have saved up a little money. We can buy some fabric and—maybe—a book. Momma has certainly taught us how to sew." Anna welcomed Selma's support.

"Let's go!" Selma grabbed her coat and hat and helped Anna into her own.

Down in the middle of Moscow was a little fabric shop. Anna and Selma looked for an hour over the many choices.

"Anna," Selma began, "here is a book on millinery: *Everything You Want to Know about Making Hats.*"

The girls found fabric and ribbon. Next, they scouted around an old secondhand shop and found old hats. They bought all of them.

"Selma, my money is completely spent. Let's head home. I have a baby to feed and a meal to cook." Anna reached into her satchel and pulled out the little bit of change she had remaining.

"What on earth do you have there? It looks like you bought out Moscow!" Papa said.

"We're going to make hats!" Selma put her arm around Anna and grinned.

"When are you going to make dinner?" Papa asked.

"After the baby is fed, diapered, and put back to sleep," Anna said.

"I'll start dinner, Anna. Get the twins to help. They need to learn responsibility." Selma left for the kitchen.

They all sat down to dinner. Anna had fixed stuffed pork chops. Selma put a big bowl of applesauce on the table. Brussels sprouts had just ripened in the garden. First, Selma crisped them by placing them in some ice water. Then she transferred the little cabbages to the pan of boiling water. She removed the pan and let them simmer until they were just tender.

"Next week I want you boys to bring in the corn, husk it, and get it ready for the girls to can." Papa looked over to the young men at his table. "Albert, I want you to kill some of the chickens. The boys can help pluck them. The girls can be canning those, too, for winter."

Thank the Lord, Papa always planned ahead.

"Papa," Anna began, "what do you think about the idea of my opening up a millinery shop—with Selma's help, of course."

"Just *where* do you suppose we can get the money for such an extravagant adventure?" Papa wanted to know.

"We could always do it from home. Selma and I could advertise and place posters around town."

"Do you think that Moscow women are ready for high society living?" Papa was trying to picture some of these country women wearing hats. "Maybe for church on Sunday."

"That would be enough incentive, wouldn't it, Papa?" Anna was determined for Moscow women to become modern.

"Not being a woman—" Papa was cut off by the boys' giggles.

"Oh, Papa!" the girls exclaimed.

Selma cut out the patterns Anna selected. Anna chose the fabric and design. Selma helped put it all together. Their first hat was complete. They were ready to sell.

"What if we get so many orders we cannot fulfill them all?" Selma looked over at Anna with deep concern.

"Sister! We need to sell *one* first! Let's get started on making our advertising posters." We can start with our uncle's laundry. The pharmacy where Albert works part-time would probably take one. The fabric store definitely should take one. After all, we spent most of our money there." Anna felt like quite the young entrepreneur.

"What about church, Anna?" Selma said.

"No, Selma. The Lord does not want us to *sell* anything at church." Anna remembered reading in the Bible about the money changers in the temple.

Posters were placed all over town. Owners thought it was a cute idea the girls had—nothing serious.

Anna received her first phone call. "Selma, she is a very high society lady in Moscow. She wants us to show our hat at their next meeting. We're on our way!"

The day arrived. Anna and Selma attended the luncheon and listened to the singer. It was now Anna's turn. She brought up the hat and spoke to the ladies, passing the hat around to the ladies. They applauded. At the door, one lady said, "I'd like to buy the hat. How much?"

Anna had not thought about a price. She quickly said, "It's five dollars."

"Here is five dollars. Thank you."

Anna was thrilled. She and Selma ran home to tell Papa and the siblings.

"Anna, did you see this in the newspaper? Look at this ad. A millinery store has opened up in Moscow—downtown. Look at that hat for sale. Isn't that the one we made?" Selma shoved the paper over to her sister.

Anna was devastated. "That lady stole my dream, Selma!"

"She cannot do that, Anna! Let's go down there right now!" Selma was furious.

"No, Selma. No. I have my book and my ideas. Someday, in God's timing, not mine. This was not meant to be. Let it go. We have plenty to do right here."

Anna went up to her room and cried. Then she picked up the baby boy and began her duties as a teenage mom once again.

God, I am sorry I did not ask your permission or even seek your advice. Forgive me. Maybe making hats is not to be my ultimate calling. Maybe you have something else for me to do, Lord. What will it be—and when?

From Sweden to Spokane

"Anna, I wish to speak to you about some news that I believe will be very well received. I hope you will be as excited as I am in telling you. I have written to your mother's sister, Mrs. Olson, in Spokane, Washington, about your desires and your personal history that has taken you to this need for change. She and her husband have a lovely home in which they house boarders. She also cooks for them. They have agreed that you may live there with them. Mary—Mrs. Olson—will help you find employment in the city. What do you say to all of this, Anna?"

Anna's emotions were divided. More than anything, she desired to experience the world of opportunities awaiting her. Yet the thought of severing herself from everyone and everything familiar to her tore at her heart.

"Anna? Did you hear me? What do you think about moving to Spokane? I need an answer from you. Are you not grateful for the opportunity? I thought you wanted to be on your own now."

Anna gave it a few moments' pondering and responded with an excited, "Yes! Yes, Papa, thank you!" She hugged him and gave him a big kiss on the cheek. Papa smiled appreciatively.

It was not an era for a young woman to venture out alone in the world. It was very much a man's world. Women were to live properly and be escorted. Anna secretly bore little butterflies inside her. She packed. Her siblings also packed remembrances of their world just for her.

What does a young town girl take to a big city? Am I a woman now or still a young girl? What defines womanhood? Do I take mementos or should I start anew? What is *my identity? What defines* me? *Will the city accept a woman my age without education or training?* Anna's image, her presence, would always be a part of her. *I wonder, what are the styles for a young working woman in the big city? I want to look the part. To whom do I answer? Am I under anyone's authority now, or am I an emancipated woman?*

"When must I leave, Papa?"

"Mary expects you there just as soon as you can pack and travel." Papa felt mixed emotions too, but having been trained not to show them, he held back.

All of her siblings helped her pack. Anna laughed as she kept pulling out little mementos each had put in.

"Give me a photo of each of you. I will decorate my room with your faces!"

Everything was ready. Papa carried the trunk down the stairs with young Albert's assistance. He stood by the doorway waiting for Anna.

One by one, she hugged and embraced each sibling, giving each an assignment to help Papa bear the load. She turned to Papa and Albert.

"I'm ready! Papa, I have a favor to ask of you. May I send for the piano someday? Is it really mine, or is it part of the house?"

"It's yours, Anna. Of course you may have it anytime you want."

"Thank you, Papa. When I marry someday, I want to teach my children and allow them to learn through their mistakes. I will sit them down and talk to them about how mistakes help us and give us the motivation to do it right the next time."

No words needed to be spoken. The lesson was understood by both.

"I want Albert to accompany you on your journey to Spokane, Anna. This is your first journey alone, and I want you to be safe."

"Oh, Papa, all that expense for two people? He would have to come right home, wouldn't he? I will be just fine. After all, I'll be riding with other people. I won't be all alone. And Papa, God is always with me!" *If I am to be an independent woman, I must act alone. I* can *do this!*

"It would be a last-minute change for Albert. He has his schooling and work. All right, Anna. Be careful. Remember, don't be too cozy with strangers."

"Oh, Papa, I promise!" Anna felt much more mature riding on her own. After all, it was just a stagecoach ride. What could possibly happen?

"You are right about this trunk, Anna! It is heavier than it has ever felt."

The stagecoach was right on time.

"Step inside the coach carefully, Anna. The coach will take you to Spokane. It is a long journey. It will be more than a day's ride—several days, in fact. Here is money for lodging and food along the way. You are young. You'll do just fine. Do not be too trusting of strangers. Be alert. Watch over your things. Mary—Mrs. Olson—will be there to greet you and take you to your new home."

Parting was difficult. As if to make up for all the previous lack of conversation, Papa spoke first.

"Anna, you are now the youngster all grown up and ready to meet the world. Serve your aunt and your new employer. Mostly, Anna, serve God. Serve them well. I can only give you a foundation. The rest is up to you. And remember, you have good job skills and training. Think on these things on your journey. Focus on the assets God has given you to take to any position you pursue in life."

They hugged goodbye. Papa wept all the way back home. Anna wept, rejoiced, and reflected. She was not giving up the old. She was anticipating the new.

Anna found the journey to Spokane long, yet she enjoyed meeting new people, reading, and viewing the countryside.

Many past and future thoughts ran through her mind of a life that had been and the life that was yet to be. She smiled in anticipation and hope.

After a long and tiring journey, the coach pulled into Spokane. Anna peeked out to see any kind of familiarity on the part of the bystanders. Each of them had only a photo.

That must *be my aunt! She is beautiful and beautifully dressed. Just a little plump! She resembles Momma.*

"Oh, Anna!" Mrs. Olson said. "What a delightful surprise to learn that I could share my home with my sister's daughter. I knew you immediately from your photograph. You are lovely, Anna! You will bring into my home fond memories from my sister's sweet spirit. I miss her, too, Anna. You are so grown up! Come, let me show you your new home. I take in boarders. Your papa probably told you. Please call me Mary. Aunt Mary, if you prefer."

Anna felt at home immediately and at peace. They hugged, chatted, and enjoyed afternoon refreshments. Anna was tired from the trip. However, she offered to be of help. When Mary declined, Anna requested permission to rest awhile before assisting with dinner. She was exhausted and slept soundly.

When she arose, she inquired, "Tell me about the boardinghouse, Aunt Mary, how you got started, and just how boardinghouses began as a business."

"The American boardinghouse is one of the first stages of the growth of large cities. A young man might be coming off the farm and looking for a job in the city, needing some kind of shelter, and the boardinghouse family offers that. For a reasonable sum, one can find a room (though not always private), meals (hopefully good), and sometimes laundry. The man might be taught manners and city life and be introduced to church. In that way, he might exert a strong moral or political influence on the community." Mary was delighted to instruct her niece.

"This is a home away from home for him. The boardinghouse keeper is often a married, middle-class woman, as I became, Anna. The role often contradicts the ways of society, which traditionally places women in a more subservient role. I had a difficult time at first, before I married. Even after I married, some people thought it should be that only my husband change to should run ran the boardinghouse. For me, we were a partnership. It worked for us, and we let others know we were comfortable with our decision. Then, eventually, they left us alone.

"Anna, when I emigrated from Sweden, I wanted to find work in America. My mother had taught me well how to cook, sew, take care of my brothers and sisters, and do laundry. Since I learned the other skills as well, when I came here, my first thought was to use them to my advantage. I knew it was a man's world. I understood that it was the man who made the living and the women stayed at home and had babies and did all the other things I learned. I had no children of my own. The city life offered the best opportunities. Now I am married, and we do this together. I experienced some feelings of humiliation, Anna, in trying to be accepted as a woman who sought her independence and freedom. I wanted my own identity, yet the people in this town were not accepting of a single woman entrepreneur. At first they treated me shamefully. It was as if I were opening a house of ill repute to have strangers board here and to make money off of them for a living. Men can get away with that—almost anything. A woman must fight her way, build her integrity, and never give up hope, Anna. Is that what you are seeking for yourself?"

Anna looked at Mary and felt joy. She had found in her someone with whom she could identify her own needs and hope for a future alone.

"I came here for that purpose, Mary. I'm terrified of stepping out and finding my way. I am a country girl with no education or experience. I have never felt so alone."

"That's why you're here, Anna. A woman does not have to be educated in the matters of schooling. That's for the man so he can support the woman. You have experience. Wilhelmina must have taught you everything you know—since birth! You have the experience and the skills to begin, to be independent. You are a woman now—a woman of great worth. All you need to do is apply what you have to the right position. Together, we will find that connection. Let me tell you about Spokane." Mary knew she needed to be a mother to Anna—and a friend. She understood what Anna was going through. She had been there.

Mary continued. "Spokane is a rapidly growing community. People are migrating here for various reasons, and they need work *and a place to stay.* I searched until I found the right-sized building. Actually, this is someone's former home with many bedrooms, a huge living room, and kitchen. It was perfect. I had the money I had saved and put it down for a down payment. I brought many of the recipes from home that had been handed down from generation to generation. All I had to do was multiply them by the number of residents, and I had meals.

"It was also important that I made enough from each resident that we could pay all our expenses. Yet I knew I must be reasonable in what I charged. I placed an ad in the newspaper for boarders. I screened each boarder, Anna. I lived alone then, and I knew I must be very careful. Pretty soon, I had a house full of men and women…mostly men. I began first with a woman boarder, then a man. I asked them what they liked to eat. I let them know I would cook what they like, but that I am the one who makes those decisions for each meal.

"The boarders have been so interesting and helpful. I love their stories. Very few leave. They have become my friends and extra family.

"That's my story, Anna, and that is the story of boardinghouses. I hope I haven't bored you!"

"Oh, not at all. I am very grateful I could be one of them, Aunt Mary. Anything I can do to help while I seek employment, I will be happy and blessed." *I especially like your independent spirit. You never felt limited,* Anna thought.

"There is something you can do to help, Anna. I will pay you while you help me with laundry, in the kitchen, setting the table, and other chores for the boarders and ourselves and assistance in the cleaning of the rooms. That should carry you over until you locate the position you want elsewhere." Mary studied Anna just as she did her boarders who applied. Anna loved her room and its view of Spokane. In the distance, a magnificent structure rose, still under construction.

"What is that, Aunt Mary?" Anna inquired.

"That is a new building owned by the Davenport family. It is a restaurant. They are expanding to include a ballroom atop the restaurant. There are rumors of a big hotel," Mary replied.

"Tell me about Mr. Davenport, Mary. I want to know about Spokane and its history and development."

"Anna, the Davenport family originated from England, as I recall hearing. Some immigrated to New York, then to Nebraska, and took up farming. A child was born to one of the sons and was named Llewellyn Marks 'Louis' Davenport. Louis and Elijah (Louis's uncle) operated a business together, disagreed, and parted. Elijah left Spokane. Louis became vice president of a wholesale produce company. By 1891, Louis was living above his restaurant. The restaurant is famous nationally. Washington State was admitted to the union in 1889, signed in by President Grover Cleveland.

Louis had worked as a clerk who had restaurant experience before he came to Spokane. There was a great fire on August 4, 1889, which destroyed most of the businesses, including his restaurant. He then gathered up equipment and supplies and re-opened for business.

"Now, Anna, that's what I call real determination and perseverance. He was a true entrepreneur in every sense of the word. He constantly, continually improved his business. Each improvement brought the curious to look it over. I enjoyed a delicious meal there. Let's see if I can still recall it and the prices. Yes, I had clam chowder, stuffed chicken for thirty-five cents; California grapes—very delicious—for only ten cents; a shrimp salad for ten cents; baked sweet potatoes for ten cents; Schnittbohnen string beans for ten cents; a cream tart for five cents; and for dessert I had brandied peaches for fifteen cents. I placed the brandied peaches atop the cream tart—delicious! I thought I had a fabulous meal that fit into my monthly expenditures. It didn't hurt to splurge a little once in a while. Anyway, my tummy was full, and I enjoyed every moment.

"A write-up in 1896 said the restaurant had ten thousand square feet and was decorated in white and gold. It is a beauty. It had a public dining room and seventeen private dining rooms, plus a banquet hall.

"In 1904, Louis Davenport announced plans to build a ballroom for use in weddings and social functions. It was to have a medieval theme: Hall of Doges. Mr. Davenport spent thirty thousand dollars on this new project established over the restaurant. The ballroom is to be about thirty by sixty feet and topped by a dome—Byzantine in its style. The ballroom will be surrounded by a twenty-foot wide promenade.

"Many, many famous people have visited Spokane, Anna, just to see his restaurant.

"Anna, why are we just *talking* about it? Get dressed up in your finest. Let's go eat! I will treat you to lunch, my dear! We'll take the streetcar. Later, we will shop. That's what women do, you know—shop until they drop!

"Anna, when I was younger, I used to go downtown and eat at Louis Davenport's Waffle Factory. There was every kind of waffle and topping imaginable. The great fire of 1889 began, I believe, in a tent. It was located on Sprague Street, where the famous restaurant is now. It was on the north side. In fact, it used to be a coffee shop before it was a waffle foundry. Oh, what fun we had. Life was simple then."

What attracted Anna's attention as they made their way downtown were the hats women wore. Every single hat was unique and different. She became distracted from Mary's conversation. She focused on the detail that went into making each hat. *I can do that,* Anna thought to herself. It brought back memories of a more difficult time when Anna and Selma had tried as kids to establish a hat business and been betrayed by a lady from the city.

"Mary, where do women buy these hats? Who makes them? Are they expensive? They're absolutely beautiful!"

Laughing, Mary looked at Anna.

"I didn't think I had your attention! They buy them at one of the finest stores in town. There are a few specialty shops. There is one lady who makes them from home. Shall we go look at hats today, Anna? I want to buy you your first one. You find what you like. Just let me know. That would please me so much. I can tell you are already becoming a woman of the times!"

Anna gave Mary a huge smile and a big hug. Hats! She could do hats!

They went from store to store until Anna found what she most desired. She also purchased a new dress, a suit, and some good shoes, stockings, and undergarments, including a corset that Mary would have to lace up.

They were now ready for lunch. They walked to the Davenport Restaurant with their purchases. Exhausted, they were escorted to their table and sat, tired and hungry, by the window.

Louis Davenport's restaurant was huge and becoming quite famous. A ballroom was planned to be built above it. A hotel was in the planning stages as well. Louis had met and married Versus. When their first son, Llewellyn Marks "Louis" Davenport was born, they placed an ad for a nanny.

"Aunt Mary, look at this ad. That famous restaurant man you told me about, the one whose restaurant we can see from here, is looking for a nanny for their baby boy. That is what I have done all my life, Aunt Mary. I have been a nanny since I was a teenager."

"By all means, dear Anna. You are ready-made for that position! Apply!"

"I will!" exclaimed Anna.

Within a few weeks, Anna and her aunt Mary had toured the many fascinating places of Spokane. The appeal of the city created tingles of childish joy inside of her. Anna desired employment and independence. Mary pursued her connections and soon found Anna a place working for a young doctor at his office. She needed a job right then, though she wanted to be a nanny. If that opportunity did come, she would take it.

In Moscow, there was excitement and change inside the Lindquist home. It would be yet

another change for Anna.

Replacements and Roots

"A letter from Papa, Mary!" Anna ripped open the letter. She had not heard from home since her arrival in Spokane.

Anna placed the letter in her lap and sat in silence.

"Anna, what is it? Is Johnn Albert well? How are the children? Anna, what's wrong?"

Anna handed the letter to Mary while she dealt with her feelings of frustration.

"What a joy! Your papa has finally met someone to love! Anna, what's wrong? Why does this news bother you?"

"My mother has been replaced!" Anna felt her first real surge of anger rising up within her. "No one. *No one* will *ever* replace my mother!"

"Anna, no one is replacing Wilhelmina. Your

father has the right to love again. He is lonely. He wants to love again. Shame on you, Anna. Shame on you! That is a very childish, selfish attitude toward your papa!" Mary felt the motherly instinct rising inside her toward her niece.

"I don't know what it is to love, Mary. I only know that Papa loved my mother. Now, he has sent to Sweden for a housekeeper and is making her his wife. He had a wife. That was my mother. He is replacing my mother's love with love toward this other woman. How could he!"

"Anna! Someday you will know the love of a man and you will understand. He loved your mother. He wants to love again. Grow up, Anna. You will never amount to anything if you do not see outside of your own world! Here, take the letter. Think about it long and hard before you write your papa. You had better get it all worked out in your childish mind before you respond to him, because the way you are thinking now, you could sever your feelings toward each other forever. Right now you are being very selfish and immature!" Mary stomped out of the room in disgust and left Anna to her thoughts.

Anna folded the letter and placed it back in its envelope. She walked up the stairs to her room, sat down at her desk, and began to write. Tears spotted the ink.

"Papa, I have missed you and the children. Children. They are growing up now, too, and I'm sure are a great help and joy to you. How are they doing in their schooling?" Anna felt a stab of pain in her heart. Schooling. How she missed what she could never have. There would be no replacement for that education she had relinquished. "Has Albert found a job yet, or is he pursuing a vocation? How are you, Papa? All of you? Thank you for sharing your news about Ida. She sounds like a very lovely person. I'm sure you are very happy." Anna could not say she was happy for him. She was not. Why? "Write again soon. Your loving daughter, Anna."

Was she really *a loving daughter? Or was she an immature, selfish child? What was holding her back?*

"I am going down to the post office, Mary. Do you want anything?"

"Anna, are you jealous of Ida?" Mary looked Anna in the eyes and did not look away. She wanted an answer. She thought she already knew it.

"Of course not! Why would I be jealous? I don't even know Ida!" Anna turned to walk away.

"Because, Anna, Ida has *replaced* you and your mother in that home. At least, that is what you are feeling. Right?"

"She will *never* replace my mother! I only had one mother. That was Wilhelmina. Not Ida! I will never love this Ida. She is not my mother!"

"When you return home, Anna, I would like to tell you the story about your birth. You were a miracle baby. You should have died. You were so tiny. Your mother is a very special person who was determined you would live."

"I'll be right back, Mary."

Anna kicked the stones along the road. The road to maturity seemed long. The journey was difficult. Was Mary right? Was she a jealous child? Why could she not be happy for Papa if he was full of joy and love?

Perhaps she needed love in her own life. First, she determined, she needed employment.

Her birth. She had never heard the story about her own childhood. Perhaps her mother had planned to tell her one day and just could not find the time. She had been so busy giving birth to so many!

Anna stepped back inside the Olson boardinghouse after returning from the post office. The guests were sitting down for lunch. Anna assisted Mary with the serving and cleanup. It was time to do the dishes. This was a great opportunity to visit. *What had she to learn about her unusual birth? Why was she a miracle baby?*

"It was 1888," Mary began. "It was winter. I am telling this as best I can remember from your mother's story. Wilhelmina was reading from her Bible, Deuteronomy 6:7 in fact, about teaching the children from generation to generation, remembering the stories about her own heritage, the struggles and emigration from the old country to a new life. The birth pangs began to become closer and closer. You were not due for another month. She had turned to your papa. 'Johnn Albert, it's time! The baby is coming!' She lay in bed, wavering between fear and excitement.

"Johnn Albert walked the slippery path on that cold January morning to the carriage, hooked up the horses, and headed to the midwife's home. Knocking frantically at her door, he finally heard her say, 'Just a minute! Who is there, please?'

"'Helga, hurry! It is Johnn Albert. Wilhelmina is having birth pangs!'

"Helga—stocky and determined—stepped into the carriage. Johnn Albert gave the horses a tug and away they went down the snowy, somewhat treacherous streets. When they arrived at the Lindquist home, Helga exited the carriage and went as fast as her fat feet could carry her to the door.

"Johnn Albert opened the front door. He could hear your mother yelling, 'Johnn Albert, the baby is coming!'

"Helga busied Johnn Albert with pans of water and towels. She wanted him out of her way. She entered the bedroom, greeted Wilhelmina with a loving smile and a comfortable assurance, 'I'm here now. Everything will be just fine.' Just in time was right! Your tiny head was protruding. She gently guided you out with her freshly scrubbed hands down into the clean towel. She thanked your momma and papa for a job well done in each part of the delivery. Then, she looked at you. You were so tiny. And you were quite blue.

"'Go for the doctor, Johnn Albert. This baby has been born too early. She is fighting for her life!'

"The doctor arrived, took one look at you, Anna, and placed you in the hospital. It was said that your head could fit into a teacup and your entire body into a matchbox. You began to thrive under the hospital's care. It was so difficult for your mother to have given birth and not be able to be with you. Soon you came home to your papa, momma, and your older brother, Albert. Your mother gave you every bit of love, attention, and nurturing she could possibly do to assist you in your growth.

"When you were just two years old, Johnn Albert decided he had had enough of Massachusetts winters. He had heard about opportunities out West and persuaded your mother to pull up roots and travel across the United States. That is how you got to Moscow, Idaho, Anna. Now, would you like to hear about how your mother met your father?

"It was said that your papa accompanied his father into Stockholm one day from Laholm. Your grandfather had business in town. When they knocked on the door, 'the most beautiful woman he had ever seen' answered the door. He desperately wanted to court her. However, she was a woman from a very wealthy, cultured family. He was but a farmer. He knew the two were too distant in their money and education to ever be together.

"Johnn Albert booked passage for the United States when he reached his manhood. One day on board, he looked across the room and spotted the lady from Stockholm. He was nearly struck dumb! When she turned and saw him staring, she smiled and said hello. That was all it took for him to strike up a conversation. They had plenty of time for courtship aboard their long voyage. By the time they reached the United States, they knew they were in love. They settled in Worcester, Massachusetts. The rest is history."

"Thank you, Mary. I had never heard the story. Now, the pieces of my identity are coming together. How precious I must have been to my mother. She nearly lost me." Anna began to understand that others, besides herself, had experienced tragedy—or nearly so. She understood now the grief her papa had known in his loss of her mother. And her siblings had also suffered the loss of their mother. Anna began to think outside of herself. For Mary, the change was refreshing and timely.

When Papa wrote again, he had wedding plans.

Moscow Wedding #1

"Ida, I would like you and I to meet with Pastor Nordgren at the Swedish Lutheran Church. Wilhelmina and I attended there ever since moving from Massachusetts. All the details and planning I will leave to you. The children can serve also. We have a wonderful group of women who will decorate and prepare a meal, if you like. Would you like Anna to be your maid of honor?" Johnn Albert translated many of the words from English to Swedish and back again. Ida was progressing well with her tutoring. *Would she understand the vows?*

"Yes. Please write to Anna, will you?"

Johnn Albert and Ida walked together down to the jewelers.

"Oh, Johnn Albert, this one is spectacular! Can we afford it?" Ida had found the perfect wedding ring.

"Yes, Ida, if that is what you want, it will be yours. It is for a lifetime, after all." *My goodness, this girl does have expensive tastes. I want to make her happy!* Johnn Albert took out his wallet and looked in his cash supply. It took every penny he had brought with him.

The church's wedding planner, Sophie, implemented all of Ida's desires. She understood both Swedish and English. It was going to be the highlight of Moscow. The plans were to keep it in the context of Sweden. Yellow daisies and red poppies with white baby's breath dominated the floral arrangements. Ida, of course, chose a white wedding gown, Johnn Albert selected a navy blue suit, and the wedding attendants wore yellow.

Anna arrived the night before the wedding and helped Ida and Papa with last-minute details. *How good it is to be home.* A flood of memories streamed through her being as she saw each member of the family, the home, and her beloved Moscow.

She arose early the next morning. The weather was already warm. She bathed and dressed. She walked outside and strolled around the home, remembering. Seating herself on the porch swing, she gently rocked as she sipped a cup of freshly brewed coffee. The birds were chirping their welcome home to her.

Ida looked beautiful in her gown of satin and lace. Anna looked at Ida. How could she continue to resent this woman? After all, Papa loved her. He would never think of hurting Anna. Not for a moment. So, who was being childish and selfish? It certainly wasn't them. It was her.

"Ida. How may I be of help to you?" Anna began to accept this stranger in her world.

"Just accept me, Anna. I do not expect you to love me. If you ever do, that will be a blessing. For now, I just want to know you even like me. That is all."

Anna felt so ashamed. "Yes, Ida. I like you. Papa loves you. That is enough for me, too."

Pastor Nordgren performed a meaningful wedding service. Johnn Albert and Ida were now husband and wife. Retreating to the basement, the townspeople had supplied enough food for the church to feed the entire community! It was so cool and refreshing downstairs. The wedded couple thanked their guests and servers and returned home. Anna would leave early tomorrow morning for Spokane.

"Someday you will find love, too, Anna," Ida told her. "Take your time. It is a lifetime commitment. You must know yourself well before you know a man. He will be your provider. You will be the shining light in your home—the one who keeps the home together no matter what happens."

For Anna, that established a bond between them. She realized Ida was like Mary. Wise.

"What a joy to have you home again," Anna's papa said. "How can I pray for you?"

"For a job, Papa. Mary has been so dear to me. She is very wise. I have enjoyed working in the boardinghouse. Now, I need a position of my own. Thank you for your prayers."

Anna drew together each of her siblings. Albert was studying at the university to be a pharmacist. Elfin was now playing three musical instruments and seeking a position with a band. Selma was studying nursing. Lilly was content to stay home and be a homemaker's helper with Ida. Pete was still in high school, as were the twins, Hilda and Hilma. Anna prayed with them and for each of them. She loved each of them dearly and missed them. The stepbrothers and sisters were still somewhat strangers to her. Yet they were "kin."

Anna gave Papa a hug. "Thank you for your prayers for me."

"You have them. Be careful on your journey home, Anna."

"Papa, what can possibly happen on a short ride by coach between here and Spokane?"

Stages, Outlaws, & Cowboys

The coach felt comfortable and cool, but it was early in the morning. A two-day journey with one overnight stay was a long ride in a coach as it experienced every bump in the road, tossing passengers around like a rider on horseback.

Anna settled back in her seat, waving goodbye to Papa. Beside her were a mother and young daughter. Across from her sat a classy older gentleman and what appeared to be a cowboy. It should be an interesting ride.

She remembered Papa's words of caution about strangers. She was a mature woman now. She could handle anything. They would be in Spokane shortly.

A few miles out of Moscow, she fell asleep, tightly clutching her satchel. Her shipping trunk was snug on top with all the others—a little noisy when they slid back and forth above them.

She awoke abruptly when she heard screams from inside and shouting outside. She looked up to see frightened stares. Then she saw the two men on horseback coming alongside the coach and shouting for the drivers to halt the horses. Another man was in the distance with a rifle by his side. Quickly, she buried her satchel inside her clothing, attempting to blend the bulges with her own. The horses halted. The drivers descended. The passengers were ordered to step out. They were somewhere in a vast, empty area.

"Throw your wallets and purses to the ground. *Now!*" shouted one of the men. The passengers did not hesitate to comply—not with guns pointed toward them.

"Put up your hands," shouted the other. The child wailed in fear. Trembling, she ran to her mother's arms.

"Shut the child up!" Her mother bent to hug her daughter to her and gently whispered to keep her calm.

Anna prayed silently, "Lord, you know our dilemma. Let me see your power and your presence. Help us now."

"Hand over your cash. Don't try to go for a weapon. We'll kill you if you try."

One cowboy looked at Anna.

"What's the matter, sweetheart? No money?"

"No money," Anna said. She did not bother to explain.

"Just how is it that a young woman traveling alone has no money?"

"I don't need any," Anna replied. "I have food and books. Everything else is at my destination."

"Maybe you have something else to offer us, honey." The men laughed and stared at Anna.

Don't be frightened, she could hear her spirit say.

"I can offer you food. I don't think you like poetry." It was Anna's turn to smile.

"We'll take the food."

Anna handed over her sandwich to the outstretched hand. She would rather starve, anyway, than be mixed up with these outlaws.

"Mighty appreciative, Ma'am!"

Seeming to be satisfied with their monetary return, they calmed down.

One cowboy began munching on big chunks of the sandwich.

"Delicious! Thank you!" The outlaw cowboy gave her a big grin.

Anna turned to look away, nearly drooling from hunger.

"Get inside the coach, all of you, including your drivers. Stay there until we are out of your sight. If you do, we will let you live. If you attempt to move before, we will return and take your lives. Your choice." With everyone inside, they straddled their horses, gave them a nudge, and rode off toward the hills.

When the riders were completely out of sight of all the passengers and riders, the drivers exited the coach, climbed atop to their seats and, shaking, took hold of the reins, ordering the horses to move forward.

Some of the passengers were kind enough to offer portions of their lunches to Anna.

She graciously accepted a little fruit and two cookies.

It was dark when they moved into Colfax, Washington. There was a nice hotel there. Everyone stepped out of the coach, relieved to be alive. They were tired and starving.

Thank God there were enough rooms available for everyone, and the dining room would still be open for another half an hour. When the hotel owner learned about the robbery, he graciously gave them free room and board and meals for one evening.

The drivers brought in the shipping trunks. They preferred to leave them atop the stagecoach. However, caution and reason prompted them not to.

Anna headed to the restroom to wash her hands in the bowl

provided. She grabbed one of the lovely hotel hand towels and rubbed them dry.

The dining room menu offered a lovely dinner for a dollar and fifty cents. Roast beef au jus came to her plate as a nice slice of prime rib. That was a wonderful surprise! Fresh green beans, corn on the cob, new potatoes, and a delicious fruit plate accompanied the meat. She ordered a tall glass of milk to calm her nerves.

"Dessert, Ma'am?" the waiter inquired.

"Yes!" she quickly responded. *I deserve it,* she decided.

Her room had a view of the town and the coach. The bed was huge. There was a large white bowl and a pitcher of water and some hand towels on the stand. She decided to take a nice, long sponge bath. When she finished, she crawled into her lacy long gown, curled up into the bed, and slept ever so soundly until the morning light. There was time to wash up, get into some fresh, comfortable traveling clothes, and enjoy a leisurely breakfast before boarding the stagecoach again. "I hope there are no more incidents," she whispered to herself.

In the dining room, she selected a table by the window and ordered some hot coffee, porridge, toast, and juice for fifty cents. She had brought along her book of poems and leaned back to enjoy her meal.

"Mornin,'" someone politely drawled.

Anna quickly looked up from her reading. "Oh! You startled me! You're the cowboy from the stagecoach." Anna smiled politely.

"Yup! Ya looked like you might like some company. May I join you? Or would you rather have peace, quiet, and readin' t'ame?" the cowboy drawled again.

"Please do join me. I can always read poetry. I would rather have a conversation and get to know someone new." She remembered her papa's warnings. "You have a drawl; where are you from, Cowboy? Or *are* you a cowboy?" Anna felt embarrassed with herself for having made such an assumption.

"Texas. I'm headed to Spokane to meet a friend and head up to Montana to herd cattle. My name is Artie. Yours?"

"Anna." The next thirty minutes were filled with a fervent exchange of their personal histories.

"Time to go, Anna. Time to board the coach for the last leg of the journey." He helped her into the stagecoach and sat across from her, continuing their conversation.

They stopped again at a little restaurant near Spokane and enjoyed another meal. Again, Artie joined Anna and they conversed. This time, he told her all about cattle drives.

"We'll be driving a herd from the north down to New Mexico. There will be about five or six of us moving the herd. We move about fifteen miles per day. It used to be twenty-five. As ya might guess, the cattle were losin' weight by the t'ame we reached our destination. So we cut back. It takes us longer. We have a great t'ame, Miss Anna. It takes us about two months in all." Artie gave her a big cowboy grin and tipped his hat.

"Where on earth do you sleep?" Anna could not picture sleeping out in the dirt and dust.

"Oh, we just throw some bedding and a pillow out on the open spaces." That seemed quite normal to Artie.

"Where do you bathe?" Anna was getting the bigger picture.

"Wherever we can find a crick!" *What a funny question,* Artie thought.

"Naked?" Anna blushed, embarrassed by her question.

"Well, we sure don't bathe with clothes on, Ma'am!" Artie gave a hearty laugh.

"Oh, dear!" Anna was trying to picture this, then looked aside again, embarrassed.

"What about cooking, Artie? Are there any restaurants?" Anna could not imagine eating out on the ground—unless, of course, it was a picnic with a nice clean blanket and covered food in a wicker basket, with napkins and washcloths.

"We take turns cooking. It's pretty simple. One of us builds a fire, places some food in the cooking pot, and we eat." Artie was enjoying her questions. He was enjoying *her.*

"What do you use for fuel?" Anna realized she was totally ignorant in such endeavors.

"Cow chips or buffalo chips." Artie knew this would provoke further discussion.

"Cow or buffalo *what?*" To Anna, chips were what you ate with fish.

"We look for droppings from cows or buffalos. They make great fuel," Artie said.

"Don't they stink?" Anna could already smell them. How could he enjoy eating, smelling that?

"Naw. They don't bother us. You get used to it." *Strange questions,* Artie thought.

"Where do you get your food?" Anna knew she needed to stop asking so many questions.

"We slaughter a calf or some kind of meat. We take supplies from the beginning of our trip or we send someone into town for supplies—like more beans. We could sure use a pretty girl like you, Anna, to come along and do our cooking!" Artie gave Anna gave another big smile and a wink.

"And bathe naked!" Anna joked, then immediately flushed from embarrassment and surprise at her own boldness.

"Sure!" Artie laughed. "We would turn our heads. Want to come along? We'll teach ya how to be a cowgirl." Artie was serious.

"You are such an interesting man, Artie. I'm afraid I am a city girl with high hopes and dreams for my future in Spokane. Riding herd! Hmmm…" Anna pondered for only a moment. She didn't think that would ever appeal to her.

By evening, the stage was back in Spokane. Mary and her husband had walked down to meet Anna. Anna introduced Artie to Mary. They exchanged polite hellos. Artie then turned and said goodbye to Anna.

"Maybe we will meet again someday, Anna. Take care. Pursue your dreams."

She said she would. *What were her dreams? What did she really want to do?*

"Well, Anna. Who is this fine young gentleman? Is there a romance in your life?" Mary was delighted to have Anna return.

Anna laughed. "No, Mary. Not a cowboy. I don't think I would enjoy cattle drives from Montana to Texas. He was just an interesting passenger."

Anna took Mary's and her husband's arms as she told them about the wedding.

"Now, Mary, I want to 'pursue my dreams.' I need to find work in Spokane. Perhaps the two of you could help steer me in the right direction."

"I already have you lined up for an appointment with a doctor, Anna," Mary said.

"I don't need a doctor, Mary. I need a job!" Anna winked at Mary.

"No, no, dear. A job with a doctor. A very nice man. You would be working in his office."

"But, Mary, I know nothing about office work." Anna felt some resentment that Mary had stepped out ahead of her. This was *her* life.

"Do you mind meeting him, Anna? The decision will be yours, of course. He is willing to train you. It is a wonderful way of meeting people—and helping. You are trained to help, Anna."

"When?"

"Tomorrow morning."

This is not *the way I had planned on pursuing my independence.* Anna felt upset with Mary. *Perhaps,* she thought, *I am just acting childish again.*

Anna dressed the next morning in a new suit, heels, and hat. Mr.

Olson drove her to the doctor's office. The job was already waiting for her. She should feel grateful. The doctor was a very kind and gentle man. Why was she so unhappy? She wanted to make her own choices. She wanted her own identity—that feeling of self-worth she did not yet have. *Time,* Anna thought. *I will wait and look.*

Davenport Nanny

"Aunt Mary, I would like to take another look at that ad for a nanny with the Davenport family. I read that it is still available. Working for the medical doctor has been so rewarding, Mary. I thank you for helping me get that position. Now, I believe I would like to move forward." Anna hoped and prayed that Mary would not be offended. She had worked so diligently to provide Anna the dignity of having her own position and income, even getting her started by letting her assist in the boardinghouse Mary and her husband ran so well.

"By all means, Anna dear. Your work with the doctor was only a stepping stone to bigger and better things!" Mary smiled at Anna's youth and innocence.

Anna contacted the Davenports' secretary to apply.

The wait seemed eternal. Eventually a letter came addressed to Anna. She was scheduled for an interview next week. *What to wear? What to say?* Anna pondered her childhood of wearing hand-made clothing and never having schooling beyond the eighth grade or any formal education or speech. Then she remembered the clothes she had purchased when she and Mary had dined at the Davenport for lunch. She knew she would look her very best. Even the hat would make her look sophisticated and mature!

Versus Davenport was introduced to Anna by her secretary. The two privately chatted. Change to VersusVirus was personable and warm, yet she was also very businesslike.

Anna was nervous yet confident. She *knew* she was qualified with all those brothers and sisters! No education on earth could better qualify her for the position of taking care of a child than the years she had spent helping to raise her siblings. *What could the Davenport baby do that has not already happened in my own family?* she thought.

A letter arrived for Anna with the letterhead of the Davenport Restaurant etched at the top left. She nearly ripped it open.

"Mary! Aunt Mary! I got the job!" Anna squealed with delight.

Anna was to be the first nanny to the Davenport son.

"Mary, would you have time to walk down with me to the doctor's office while I prepare to tell them about my new position? I would just like the comfort and companionship as I prepare to tell them I will be quitting."

"Anna, I would be very happy to do that for you. However, I have responsibilities here today. You are now a young adult woman and very capable of presenting yourself and making mature decisions—including this one. I hope you do not find my words to be harsh. It is time you stepped forward on your own."

Anna was surprised. She had always had the full support of

anyone whom she'd engaged—especially family. Why would they not support her now in her time of need? She thanked Mary, then excused herself to get dressed. What she really wanted was time to think.

How will I tell the doctor I am leaving? What will I say? I am so inadequate in speech and decisions. Anna dressed for the interview, called the doctor's office to see if the doctor was in, and asked if she could have a few moments of conversation with the doctor. It was set.

Anna thanked Mary for her comments, though she really did not agree. She took the streetcar down to the doctor's office and stepped inside for her appointment.

"Good morning, Doctor," Anna began.

"Good morning, Anna. What a nice surprise to have you come in for a visit. How can I be of help today?"

"I have responded to an ad for a nanny to the Davenport family to care for their infant son. They have hired me for the position. I apologize for not telling you I was going to do this, Doctor. It all happened so fast." Anna started to go on, but the doctor interrupted.

"Anna, you are much too qualified to remain here. I am delighted for you. When do you begin? You can count on me to give you an excellent reference."

"Oh, thank you, Doctor. Thank you! I just received word that I am hired. A date has not yet been set." Anna was beginning to sit back and relax.

"Anna, you have been here faithfully every single day. You have fulfilled your position here above and beyond what I would expect you to do. I am going to get a temporary person to take your spot and give you a little vacation time—with pay—before you begin your next job. Does that sound okay to you?"

"Oh, no, Doctor. I do not want to impose upon your good nature. I will fulfill my time with you until you can hire someone else." Anna really preferred the vacation.

"I insist, Anna. It is my way of saying thank you for a job well done." He got up from his chair, went out to the office assistant, and told her to write Anna a check for one hundred dollars. The doctor handed the envelope to Anna, told her not to open it until she arrived back home, and bade her farewell and good luck in her new adventure.

Anna climbed aboard the streetcar and could hardly wait to arrive back at her Aunt Mary's boardinghouse.

"How did it go, Anna?" Mary inquired.

"He was so kind, understanding, and generous, Mary." Anna was already ripping open the envelope.

"What do you have there?" Mary asked.

"Oh, Mary! He gave me a hundred dollars and a vacation before I begin as a nanny." Anna felt a wide mixture of emotions. "I'm going to use it to buy new clothes."

"And a hat, I suppose." Mary laughed as she hugged Anna. "Anna, be wise enough to begin to save. Why not use fifty percent and save fifty percent? You never know what is ahead of you in life. Be prepared for it."

"Wise words. I will begin my own account tomorrow," Anna said.

"Today, Anna. What is wrong with today?" Mary advised her niece. "In fact, I *do* have a little time between lunch and dinner to go with you. We will go down to my bank and open an account in your name. We can shop and have lunch before I need to return here to begin dinner. Does that sound all right to you, Anna? That is a *lot* of money to carry around. You should not do so alone."

"I will be ready. Is there anything I can do to help you right now?" Anna was grateful.

"No. It is all done. I will let the others know I will be gone a few hours."

Anna felt so grown up. Her own wonderful new job. Her own

account in her own name. "Mary, I want to contact Versus to see when she wants to meet me to discuss arrangements."

"Excellent decision," Mary agreed.

Anna and Mary stopped by to see Versus's assistant. Versus came out and greeted Anna.

"Anna! What a delight to see you. Would right now be a good time for you? This will not take more than fifteen minutes, if you have time."

Anna sat down with Versus and discussed the position and saw the adorable little baby boy.

"Anna, I have things covered for the weekend. Could you begin next Monday? I will take you around and show you where everything is and what I expect."

"Monday it is. Thank you, Versus. It will be just like being home again when I took care of my brothers and sisters." Anna smiled.

"Anna, I would be pleased if you would live here. You will have your own room and board—that includes meals. Would you consider that, Anna? I really need you full-time. You will be paid well."

"May I let you know Monday, Versus? My aunt has depended on me to help her in the boardinghouse." Anna felt more in her heart than an upcoming decision to move. It would be a major emotional adjustment for her.

"That will be fine, Anna. Before, if you can." Versus shook hands with Anna and thanked her.

Anna and Mary lunched together, and Anna shared her conversation with Versus.

"Anna, you will be a much better nanny if you are living there. You are ready. After all, Anna, you moved from Moscow to Spokane!" Mary touched Anna's hand.

"But, Mary, you are my aunt. You are my flesh and blood." Anna needed reassurance and comfort.

"Anna, it is time to grow up. You are not a little girl anymore. You are a woman of worth. Life is full of decisions and responsibilities, Anna. Assume them. Challenge yourself."

The transition from the boardinghouse to the famous Davenport family quarters was another step up in Anna's life. Working for the doctor had been a blessing. It had taught her mature sensitivity, daily watching life and death pass her way. As she pondered her next step in life, she wondered, *How would her life matter? What would she contribute? What would be the next step in her life beyond caring for this little child?*

Anna and Mary returned home. She helped Mary prepare the meal, then excused herself to begin packing. At dinner, she shared her new venture with the boarders and prepared her heart to leave after the weekend.

Versus met Anna at the door on Monday morning. Louis, just an infant, was sleeping soundly in his bed.

"Welcome, Anna," Versus said. "Bring your things in, and we'll put them in your room. Then I will show you your schedule while we have tea and a small snack. I am so happy to have found you. You come with excellent credentials. The doctor for whom you were employed called to recommend you. You must tell me your story, Anna."

Anna felt so at home. "I was a child myself when my mother died," she began. "Just a teenager. I had to leave my education after the eighth grade. There were already many brothers and sisters in my home. I will take good care of your baby boy. My mother gave birth to a son just before she died."

"We're delighted to have you, Anna. We have such confidence in you. Welcome!"

Adolph

One of the travelers emigrating from Sweden to America was aboard the *City of Baltimore,* April 24, 1867. He came *only* to accompany his older sister to America. He had every intention of returning home to Sweden. He was listed as "A. Nelson" on the passenger ship.

Adolph came from Laholm, Sweden, a small village near Stockholm. His sister, Marleen, desired to see America. Even in Sweden, women of that era did not travel alone.

Adolph recalled his conversation with his father before he traveled to America. He had hoped his father would give him the permission he needed.

"Papa," Adolph interrupted his father's farm work, "may I speak with you, please?"

"Adolph, please tend the seed planting for me. We must plant our crop now for a timely late summer harvest. Hand me those seeds, Adolph. I am very busy. What is it you need?"

Adolph was certainly well beyond his age of emancipation. He had remained on the farm to help his father with the often back-breaking work of farming.

"Papa, Marleen has requested a voyage to America to live there. She desires that I accompany her aboard ship. Will you give us permission to leave for America?"

"Will you be returning, Adolph? I am very aware that you are old enough to make your own decisions—both you and Marleen. I need your help here and would be grateful for your

return to Sweden. What on earth does Marleen think she can do in America that she cannot do here?" Papa loved his homeland and had assumed his family would always remain there.

"We do have relatives there, Papa. I'm sure she will seek them out. I do not have any plans to remain there. I will return home as soon as I get her settled."

"Then you shall leave with my blessing. Is Marleen planning to say goodbye to her papa before she leaves?"

"Of course, Papa." Adolph looked forward to seeing America, but his loyalty was to his homeland of Sweden. He would return.

The voyage was long, crowded, hot, and stuffy. Many got sick as the vessel swayed to and fro across the ocean. They arrived safely ashore at Ellis Island, New York. Adolph inquired about passage home to Sweden, without much enthusiasm for returning. While he was a passenger across long days and nights, he had chatted with those who were immigrating to the land of opportunity. They had been very persuasive.

"I might never leave this place," he heard himself mutter softly. "It feels like a place where I want to be." His obligation to his father tugged at his heart and mind.

"We have relatives in North Dakota, Adolph. Why don't you find them and see if you can work there?" Marleen urged.

"Marleen, I promised Papa I would return. My heart feels divided right now. I have made a promise. I should keep that promise. Yet I have already fallen in love with America. There is such beauty and opportunity here. I do not want to leave."

"Write him, Adolph. I believe he will understand. He needs help with his crops and farming. He can hire someone. Surely, he must understand that you are also an adult and have a need to break free and find your own way."

Adolph contacted his relatives in North Dakota after getting Marleen settled into a New York apartment. He also waited until she had found employment. When a letter arrived from his distant cousin offering him a place to live and employment, he responded. He traveled by train to North Dakota, where his cousin picked him up.

The months on the farm offered shelter and an income. The long bitter months of winter cold challenged him once again. Then he and his cousin had a horrible disagreement, and Adolph decided to sever his ties with that part of his family. He would catch the next train and head north. Spokane looked like a place of opportunity.

As Adolph took his train trip, he wrote a letter to his papa, who must certainly be looking for his return by now. He mailed it at the next train stop. It was a difficult letter in many ways. He prayed that his papa would understand. Adolph had made up his mind to try American life to its fullest. If that did not work out, he could always return to his homeland.

Finally arriving in Spokane, he stepped off the train and walked to a place to eat, grabbing a newspaper as he did. His English was not perfect, but it was passable. He read over the ads for a place to stay and found an ad for residents in a boardinghouse. "Mrs. Olson! Sounds Swedish to me!" he heard himself say aloud. "I will check that out right now. In fact, I will walk there. Good exercise." He picked up a map of Spokane at the station, inquired about the location of the boardinghouse, and began his walk.

"Good morning!" Mary said when he arrived. "How may I help you?"

"Good morning. I saw your ad for a boarder, and I am looking for a place to stay."

"You have found the right place. Come in. You have an accent. Where are you from? Do you have time for a cup of coffee?"

"I'm Adolph Nelson, from Sweden. Laholm. And, yes, I would love a cup of coffee. Thank you." Adolph looked around the downstairs and liked what he saw. "You have a vacancy?"

"Yes, I do. I see you have your suitcase with you? Have you been traveling far today?"

"From North Dakota, Mrs. Olson. I worked for a cousin there. It did not work out. We disagreed. I decided to move west and heard about Spokane and its growth and opportunities."

"Before we go any further, my name is Mary."

"I have papers, if you would like to see them." Adolph pulled out his passport and photo.

Mary carefully examined them. "I have one room available." She named the price, which, she informed him, included room, meals, and laundry.

"Perfect. I can pay you a month's rent right now." Adolph handed her the money. Mary wrote out an agreement, shared the rules with him, and showed him around the house and to his room.

"We have lunch at noon, promptly. We have dinner at six p.m. Breakfast begins at six a.m. for those who need to get to work. It is open until eight a.m. for those who have the privilege of sleeping in." Mary signed her part of the agreement and waited for Adolph's signature. He signed and thanked her.

"I just baked some fresh cinnamon rolls. Would you like one with another cup of coffee?"

"Ya, sure!" Adolph felt as though Sweden had just come to America and landed in Spokane!

While Adolph was settling in his room, Mary made a phone call to Anna. "Would you have time to come for lunch, Anna? You can bring the baby. I have someone I want you to meet."

Anna fed and bathed the baby and placed him down for his morning nap. When he awakened, she called Versus to tell her about her lunch plans with Mary.

"By all means, Anna. Enjoy the lunch. We will see you for dinner." Versus was such a sweet lady. Anna loved her new position and adored the baby boy in her care.

"Anna," Aunt Mary began, once Anna arrived, "we have a new resident. He is from Sweden. Come and sit down, dear. Anna, this is Adolph Nelson. Adolph, I would like you to meet Anna Lindquist, my niece."

"My pleasure, Anna." Adolph stood and greeted Anna with a huge welcoming smile. Then, he looked at the baby, puzzled.

"Oh, forgive me, please," Anna said. "This is Louis Davenport. I am his nanny."

Adolph was visibly relieved!

"You are from Sweden, Adolph?" Anna inquired.

"Yes, from Laholm. What about you, Anna?"

"I am *of* Swedish origin, Adolph. I was born in Worcester, Massachusetts. I left there with my family and older brother when I was two. We moved to Moscow, Idaho, where I grew up. What brings *you* from Sweden to Spokane?" Anna was certain Adolph had never heard about Spokane in Laholm, Sweden.

"My sister desired to immigrate to America. I was to accompany her and return home to help my father on the farm. I did not realize I would fall in love with America, Anna."

"Was your father heartbroken when you decided not to return?" Anna understood about transition.

"He does not know. I intended to return. He should just now be receiving my letter. I feel that I am home here. I love the opportunity America holds and the beauty of its country."

When Anna was ready to return to the Davenport residence, she reached out her hand to Mary and to Adolph to say her goodbyes.

"May I call upon you, Anna? Perhaps we could go for a walk

together." Adolph was impressed with Anna's loveliness and her sweet spirit.

"Yes, that would be nice. Of course, I will have Louis with me." Anna wanted to make it clear that her work came first.

"You will be hearing from me soon, Anna." Adolph was ready for courtship. He hoped Anna might be, also.

The two of them were often seen walking the streets of Spokane with a beautiful baby carriage in tow. After all, as Anna had explained to Adolph, she was *still* a nanny. They were both amused when many people stopped to greet and congratulate them on their baby. Anna pondered what that might be like. Many thought the two were a loving young married couple. Gossip always followed. Mary curtailed that one!

It was odd. Aunt Mary had a strange, "very Western" kind of boarder for a short period of time. He was quiet, friendly, and struck Anna as someone she had seen before in a newspaper or photo somewhere. Adolph had commented about the Western-looking man who kept to himself and never talked about his past, present, or future. She checked Mary's records of all her boarders. The man's name was *William T. Phillips.* That name certainly did not ring a bell. He checked out before she had a chance to know if he had another identity. She overhead someone say he looked identical to a man they had seen pictures of named Wyatt Earp who may have come to Spokane under an assumed name.

Anna returned to her Davenport residence and the care of their baby boy. She had Adolph prominently fixed in her mind.

Within the compounds of the Davenport restaurant—upstairs—was an area designed and built for a ballroom. Anna daydreamed about its enchantment as the eyes of her imagination dazzled with the splendor of chandeliers and spectacular colors—furnishings unaffordable to most. The orchestra played and drew couples into each other's arms. Anna and Adolph loved to dance the night away.

The Davenports were throwing a big party with food for a hundred guests and a hired orchestra. Versus graciously invited Anna to join the celebration.

"Anna, I will hire someone to watch the baby that evening if you would like to participate in our party and bring a guest."

Anna's thoughts immediately turned to Adolph. It was not appropriate for a woman to ask a man for a date. She would ask Mary about protocol.

"Mary, it is to be such an elegant occasion. Most of Spokane and dignitaries from all over the country—some, from other areas of the world—will be there. There are even some movie stars scheduled to arrive. Versus has asked if I would like to participate in the event. Mary, I want to invite Adolph. What do you think I should do? Women just do not invite men."

"Come over for lunch today, Anna. Adolph will be here. I will initiate the conversation, and you can pick it up from there. We'll talk about the Davenport and dances. We will even talk about women not inviting men. Let's see where it goes!"

Anna giggled in delight.

She bathed and fed the baby. Then Adolph knocked on her door.

"Good morning, Anna. I thought perhaps you and the baby would like to walk with me this morning?" Adolph asked, and Anna eagerly nodded her assent.

"Let me help you dress him and get him into the buggy. Oh, what a healthy little guy you are! Okay, Anna, are you ready?" Adolph took charge of the buggy, gently guiding it down the stairs.

What a perfect opportunity this would be to tell him about the dance, Anna thought. "Adolph, the Davenports host many events and entertain dignitaries from all over the world. It is such a privilege to be in their employ."

"Do they have dances up there, Anna? I hear they just built a beautiful and very ornate ballroom." It was Adolph's way of leading Anna.

"They often have grandiose events which include dances. The ballroom is unlike anything I have ever laid eyes upon, Adolph."

"Anna, do the Davenports ever allow their employees to attend these events?"

"I would need to ask Versus, Adolph." Anna's heart was pounding. She smiled, turning her face aside.

It was time to return Louis for his naptime. Versus would be home shortly, so Adolph left Anna and Louis at the door and turned to walk home.

"Versus, Mary has asked me to dine with her for lunch," Anna said when Versus came home. "Would that be convenient for your schedule?"

"By all means, Anna. I will lunch here and keep an eye on Louis. Go, have fun. I will see you soon. By the way, Anna, have you thought about the dance invitation?"

"Oh, I *have,* Versus. I have!" Anna glowed as she smiled at Versus.

"And your decision, Anna?" Versus looked at Anna with warmth. She was reminded of her own innocence and love when she had first met Louis Davenport.

"I am going to discuss it with my aunt. I need to know if Adolph dances—or even wants to." Anna crossed her fingers under the table.

"Anna, come in and join us at the table," Mary said, when Anna arrived at the boardinghouse for lunch. She had the seating all arranged and placed Anna next to Adolph.

"Anna," Mary began as she placed her fork on her plate, "did I hear you mention that the Davenports are now entertaining for dances in their new ballroom?"

Anna grinned and blushed. "They are, Mary. Wonderful, elegant, and romantic settings with live music and decorations. It is worth it just to see!"

"Are you allowed to attend these dances, Anna?" Mary asked.

"Versus asked me if I would like to attend. They have a dance scheduled for this weekend, Mary."

"Are you going?" Mary's eyes looked first at Anna, then reverted to Adolph. Anna blushed again, looking down at her meal, fidgeting with her napkin.

"Anna," Adolph interrupted, "do you dance?"

"Yes, Adolph, Papa taught me to dance when I was a young girl. He thought that was an important part of our education."

"Now, it is my turn to continue your learning experience. Are you allowed to attend the dance, Anna? And may I invite you to the dance this weekend?" Adolph was now turned directly toward Anna.

Anna looked into his beautiful blue eyes. *He is so handsome,* she thought. Her heart was pounding as she struggled to find words. "Yes, Adolph, Versus has offered to hire another attendant for Louis that evening if I would like to go."

"What time may I pick you up, Anna? I would like to take you to dinner first. Would it be too dull to dine at the Davenport Restaurant first—to dine at the place of your employ?"

Anna looked over at Mary and smiled. Adolph looked quizzically at Anna.

"I would be honored, Adolph. Yes, I would love to dine at the restaurant. I believe seven p.m. would be an acceptable time for Versus. However, I will ask her and let you know."

When Anna reached for the doorknob to leave, Adolph had already gestured to open it for her. Mary squeezed her hand and gave her a hug.

"I'll walk you home, Anna." Adolph told her.

As they reached the Davenport residence, Adolph turned to Anna. *He is so handsome,* Anna thought again.

Adolph presented Anna with a gift from his heart. It was a cut-crystal jar about the size of a coffee cup. It glistened with a ruby-colored brim. On it was inscribed: *To Annie, From Adolph.* He was so proud to present it to her.

Anna was incensed. "Thank you for the gift, Adolph. That was very thoughtful of you. However, I am *not* 'Annie.' I am Anna. That is my name, my *only* name." Anna was visibly irritated with Adolph's choice of a nickname for her.

"I'm sorry, Anna. I meant no offense. I will not make that mistake again. You are Anna. From now on, I will call you that. Only now, for our next plan…I look forward to seeing you again soon and to preparing for the dance. I hope you do, also. Good day, Anna. I will see you tomorrow and we will discuss the arrangements."

"Yes!" Anna told Versus. "Adolph has asked me to the dance and to dine with him here at the restaurant."

Versus could see love in bloom. She knew it would not be long before Anna would be leaving her employ.

They danced. Their eyes met. The closeness of their bodies sent a tingle through Anna's whole being. She felt a stir within her that she had never known before.

Adolph looked at her beauty. Her figure was petite and sculptured perfectly. *That tiny waistline. How did she manage it?* Her eyes were large and a deep brown, matching her beautifully braided brown hair. He held her close as they waltzed around the ballroom.

"Adolph," Anna whispered to Adolph. That was all she could manage. She felt overwhelmed with emotion.

"Anna, I want you. I want to be with you," Adolph responded breathlessly.

Anna was young, lovely, petite, eligible.

Adolph was young, handsome, of a strong and slender build, and ready to meet the woman of his dreams.

"Anna, I cannot resist you, your warmth, and your touch. You are so lovely, so sweet, and so loving." He stopped, held her, and kissed her. "Oh, Anna, I want to be with you forever. I believe that I love you. I want to marry you. Will you marry me, Anna?"

Anna thought about her employ, her responsibilities, and stood momentarily silent. "There are many things to consider." She did not want to make a wrong decision—either way. Yet her heart led. "Yes, Adolph, I believe I love you. And, yes, I will marry you. Please be patient with me as I tell Versus—and my family in Moscow."

"Do you want me to write to or see your father?" Adolph wanted to do things properly.

"It is a long way from here to Moscow, Adolph. I will write Papa and let him know our intent, if that is acceptable to you."

"Yes, please tell him I am willing to meet with him if he so chooses." Adolph let out a sigh of relief. Now it was imperative that he find work as soon as possible.

Adolph began to pursue the newspaper employment ads. Nothing. He felt restless and useless. Thoughts of Sweden began to fill his mind. He missed home and longed to see it one more time. Besides, there was another reason for returning.

"Adolph, what a welcome sight!" Anna exclaimed upon finding Adolph at her door. "Did you stop by for another walk?" Anna's heart was so full of love for him.

"Yes, Anna. Let's walk. There is something I want to share with you."

They walked in silence for a while.

"What's on your mind, Adolph?" Anna could see he was troubled.

"Anna, I want to…I'm going to return to Sweden for a visit. I don't like the way I left so abruptly. I owe it to my father to return for a while. I hope you will understand." Adolph turned to look Anna in her beautiful big brown eyes. He *did* love her.

"Would you like me to go with you, Adolph? I'll see if I can arrange some time off. Will you be gone long? I would love to meet your family—and to see Sweden."

"No, Anna, this is something I must do alone. I'll return soon." His mind was made up.

What have I done? What have I said? Anna could feel Adolph slipping away.

Adolph felt he had to be certain. He had loved someone back home. He had had every intention of returning to Sweden when his sister had booked passage for America. He had pledged his love to another. Then, he had met Anna. He desired to explain. Under the circumstances, however, that would be foolish. His heart had to be settled. He knew it would be when he returned. Either he would return to Sweden permanently, or he would settle in America. Which woman?

Early the next morning, Adolph booked passage for Sweden. His head was spinning. His heart yearned for truth.

The Return

Svea was there to meet him at the dock. Adolph walked down the plank and looked into her deep blue eyes. Her blonde hair was waving in the ocean breeze. Her tiny body swayed as the wind blew her back and forth like a willow tree branch. She was breathtakingly beautiful.

"I wondered if you would get my message in time, Svea." Adolph was overwhelmed with the emotions he thought he had left behind.

Svea held up her arms to be swept into his own. Adolph did not return the invitation. He knew he had many decisions to make, and he must be wise.

"Where do we go from here, Adolph?"

"Home, Svea. I want to go see Papa." Adolph grabbed his luggage and placed them into her buggy.

Svea carried on the bulk of the conversation on the trip to the Nelson farm.

"How did you like America, Adolph?" Svea wanted answers.

"It is wonderful, Svea. Breathtakingly and indescribably beautiful. Full of opportunities. Beyond my expectations. A land of multiple opportunities."

"You didn't go there for that reason, Adolph. You went to accompany Marleen and planned to return to Sweden." Svea was probing and directed her questions toward the answers she longed to hear.

"Yes, Svea. I went to America with the *intent* to return to Sweden. Papa was expecting me home. I had promised him that much." Adolph did not like the direct questions. Yet he knew she and Papa both deserved answers. "I also promised you I would return."

"You betrayed his trust, Adolph. And, you betrayed mine. I thought you were returning to me. Now, I am confused." They had arrived at the farm.

Adolph stepped out of the car. Papa saw him from the field and ran to his son.

"Adolph! Adolph! *Välkommen,* Adolph!"

"Papa, oh Papa. I have missed you and Momma so very much. You look well, Papa. And, Momma. How is she?"

"Adolph, your momma is in the house. She is very ill and not expected to live much longer. It has been very difficult for us here. Now, you are home. We are happy for your return. There is much to do. Good to see you, Svea. Come in, please!"

The three of them stepped inside the farmhouse. Adolph loved the smells of home. He placed his luggage in his bedroom. *His* bedroom. Where *was* home?

Svea stayed and fixed supper. Before she left, she made sure Adolph's mother was comfortable and gave Adolph a hug.

"I'll see you soon, Adolph." Svea looked at him and smiled. Adolph had returned.

During his stay in Sweden, Adolph made no contact with anyone in America. Not even Anna. A week went by. Two weeks. His mother's health took a turn for the worse. Then, one night, she passed away quietly in her sleep. Adolph helped Papa make the arrangements and bury her.

"The farm, Adolph. Are you staying?" Papa looked deeply into his son's eyes for answers. Answers that would change *both* of their lives.

"Papa, I need to see Svea, and then I need to write home. I will let you know tomorrow, Papa." Adolph borrowed Papa's horse and buggy and rode into Laholm.

"Svea, I had to return. I wanted to see Laholm, Papa and Momma, and you."

"In that order, Adolph?" Svea sat across from Adolph as they shared a meal.

"Yes, Svea, in that order." Adolph knew their relationship was coming to an end.

"Is there someone in America, Adolph? I thought we were…in love." Svea was holding together as best she could.

"We were, Svea. We *were* in love. When I left Sweden, I had every intention of returning to my life here. I wanted to help Papa, to marry you, to have a home and family, and to carry on the family tradition here we have known all our lives. America has changed me, Svea. I will be returning as soon as I get Papa settled. I will not be coming back here again—unless it is to visit Papa and Sweden."

There was silence. A long, strained, silence.

"Do you love her, Adolph? You owe me an explanation."

"Yes, Svea. I love her. I did not mean to hurt anyone. Sometimes life has turns—unexpected twists and turns that change our lives forever. I do not *owe* anyone."

"You pledged your love and your life to me, Adolph."

"No, Svea. I will not be owned by anyone—not even you."

They parted without hugs or goodbyes. Adolph thought about Anna's sweet spirit that guided her life and her heart. He missed it.

Adolph wrote home to Anna about his mother's death and that he needed to make sure his papa was settled and able to carry on.

There were many family members and church family to help his papa through the years ahead.

He hugged and held his papa and said his goodbyes. They were not men of tears.

Adolph stepped off the ship in New York and caught the next train west. His decisions were formed. Home was waiting for him in Spokane, with a future and a wonderful woman who

had stolen his heart. He had answers to share with Anna. Anna. That name was sweet on his tongue.

"Adolph! It is so good to see you. I'm sure you have much to tell all of us. Mary has invited us for dinner. Is that all right?"

"Everything is all right now, Anna. I have much to tell. After dinner, I want us to have some time together alone. Can you arrange that, Anna?"

"I will call Versus. She knows you are returning."

"Yes, Anna. Of course you can have time off, Versus said, after Anna contacted her. "We will meet and talk tomorrow. Tell Adolph hello for me."

Anna put her arm through Adolph's. She loved his strength—not just physical strength. Anna also loved his strength of character.

"Anna, so much happened while I was in Sweden. Thank you for your thoughtfulness in letting me return home at such a delicate moment in our lives. I have returned to Spokane to marry you, Anna. I will be looking for work. We, together, will be looking for a home. Are you ready?"

"I have been ready, Adolph, since I met you!"

"Tomorrow, Anna, I will go job hunting. I must have work before the wedding. I want to take care of you—and our children."

"Goodnight, Adolph." Anna knew in her heart there had been someone back home. *Would she ever know the story? Did it matter?* This time death had been a blessing—death of a relationship that was never meant to be.

With her doubts put away, Anna laughed with joy and plans

began buzzing in her head. *Home,* she thought. *I am going to have a real home with roots and a foundation and friendships. I won't have to move anymore!*

A Letter from Papa

Anna received a return letter from Papa.

> *Dearest Anna, I am so proud of you and your forthcoming plans for marriage. I also am proud of your brother, Elfin, and at the same time, so concerned. His news to us about joining the Paul Whiteman Band brought great joy. Did you know that he is an accomplished musician in three—yes, three—instruments? No wonder he was accepted. He will be a great asset to their band. You have had a wonderful influence on this family, Anna. You have been their mentor. It is because of you that they have achieved. My concern for Elfin is his illness. You may not know that has wife from Montana left him. I have never forgiven her. He has suffered much emotionally and physically. Again, congratulations!*
>
> *Love, Papa*

Anna believed she had a better understanding of both Paul Whiteman and Elfin. Anna had also heard that her brother Albert had left Moscow and sold his pharmacy business there. Papa had said that people had taken advantage of his generosity. So many had not paid that he was going bankrupt.

Anna was proud of her family, just as Papa had said. Now in Spokane, Albert had opened up a chain of pharmacies and was doing very well. That was typical of many who had come home from the war. They were developing businesses and implementing new ideas.

Her sister Selma was now head nurse at Emmanuel Hospital in Portland. Anna recalled hearing about the scandal involving her dear sister. It had saddened Anna. Was it Selma's search for love that had caused her to have an affair with a doctor there? She had become pregnant. Selma never talked about her past. From that relationship, she bore a darling little girl and moved to Los Angeles to start over. How different was the faith of the two sisters. Anna had invited Christ into her life at a young age.

Anna hoped her family would be proud of her and her choices and could attend her wedding and meet Adolph.

Papa had been good about giving her the family news. Each of her siblings was doing well in their respective roles. The twins, Hilda and Hilma, were now married and having families of their own.

It touched her heart that Papa believed she had been a positive influence on her brothers' and sisters' lives. *Perhaps,* she thought, *she wasn't so dumb after all. Maybe life experiences are God's real training ground. Life really* is *an education.*

Anna's Dilemma

"Oh, Anna, how I missed you! When do you have some time to see me?" Adolph gushed.

"I get off at seven p.m. Versus will be home then to take care of the baby."

"I will pick you up, Anna. Wait for me. Where would you like to go? We'll start with dinner."

"There is a dance here tonight. Why don't we dine and dance right here?" Anna's heart was beating rapidly.

"At seven, Anna. Put on your dancing slippers and your loveliest gown." Adolph left for the boardinghouse.

When he came back later that evening to pick her up, he told her, "A weight has been lifted from me, Anna. Two weights. My timing could not have been more perfect to be back in Sweden. I buried my mother. I have received the forgiveness I needed from my father." He did not share any information about Svea. It would only hurt Anna. That, he never wanted to do.

Anna was grateful now that she had Adolph back. The loss she had felt was gone. Her world had not changed. Day to day it was the same. Yet she felt very blessed and fulfilled in the role she had as the nanny to the Davenports' son. She loved them dearly and felt so much a part of their family. They had been exceptionally good to her.

She spent time reading to Louis. "I know you cannot understand me, little one. I am going to continue reading to you every day from God's Word. God says that his Word will not return to us void. I am going to hold him to that promise for you. I will pray for you every day that he will use you and bless your life for him." She placed the Bible beside his crib.

There were many positive influences in her life. She saw Mary almost daily. Mary had been such a faithful friend to her.

Anna had selected a gown she had purchased several years ago when she and Mary had gone shopping. She put on her best hat, gloves, and dancing shoes.

"Let's dance!" Adolph swept Anna into his waiting arms. He held her tightly. *Too tightly,* Anna thought.

Adolph stood back and measured this Swedish icon, so new to his life. His eyes took in her thick brown hair wrapped up into a bun. Atop it, she wore a beautifully handcrafted hat. *Had she made this herself?* His eyes lowered to hers. They were wide and dark brown. He laughed. They reminded him of his heifer back home in Sweden. They were warm and sympathetic. And *inviting!* He slowly swept over her full bust and tiny waist, the bustle on her backside, and her tiny feet. He stood in awe of her.

Anna blushed. "Adolph! I feel like you are undressing me with your eyes!"

"I am, Anna. Is it strange to you that I find you inviting and desirable?"

Anna looked away. A surge of confused emotions filled her.

Adolph placed his right hand to her cheek. His left hand

surrounded her tiny waist, drawing her close. He kissed her, bringing her still closer to him.

"Adolph, we're too close. It isn't proper." Anna looked away from Adolph at the public.

Adolph laughed and held her. "Who is to determine what is proper! Do you love me, Anna? You are to be my wife!"

"Yes, Adolph. I gave my commitment and devotion to you before you left to return to Sweden. I said yes to you then. I still say yes. I know so little about being a wife. Adolph, no one has ever explained to me about intimacy with a man. My mother died when I was thirteen. Papa never addressed such issues."

"Let me teach you, Anna. That is the husband's role. Will you let me do that?" Adolph knew the role of persuasion. He was used to getting and keeping what he wanted. He wanted Anna.

"How, Adolph?"

"Come with me now, Anna. I will prove my love to you."

The music ended. The last dance had been danced in a silent closeness of understanding and anticipation.

Adolph drove Anna back to the boardinghouse. It was late at night. Everyone had gone to bed.

"Adolph, I'm not sure…" Anna began to pull away. She felt love and confusion, desire and hesitancy.

"Anna, no one will see us. Shh!" He grasped her hand and led her into his room. "Quiet, Anna," he whispered. "I'll have you home soon."

Anna struggled between her love for Adolph and her lifelong convictions. Love won over her common sense and training.

In the very early morning hours, Anna awoke. Confused, she looked around at her surroundings. Then she looked at Adolph lying beside her. She jumped out of bed and began to dress quickly.

Adolph awoke and grasped her hand.

"Adolph, I must go. Right now. Adolph, I must get back to the hotel. I am so ashamed of myself. What will Mary think? And Versus? How will I explain this to Versus?"

"Don't, Anna. You don't owe anyone an explanation. You stayed overnight at your Aunt Mary's."

Adolph took her to breakfast. She gulped her coffee and had another to keep herself awake.

Anna slowly unlocked and opened the door at the Davenports.' She tiptoed quietly into her room and lay down on the bed. She examined her thoughts. She never knew that love could be so beautiful, so desirable. Adolph loved her. *So this is what love is about?* What else could she possibly want?

Moscow Wedding #2

"Anna! Anna! Are you all right, Anna?" Versus lifted Anna up off the floor. "Anna, you fainted. You also threw up in the bathroom sink this morning. I am going to call the doctor. And of course, I cannot have you take care of the baby today. We need to find out what's wrong and get you well."

Anna crawled to her bed and lay down until she gained some strength.

"Too much dancing last night, Anna? I do hope you had a good time."

"Oh, Versus, I am so sorry. Is the baby all right? I wasn't holding him, was I?"

"The baby is fine, Anna. Who is your doctor?" Versus sat beside Anna as Anna lay down on the bed.

"I don't have a doctor. I worked for a doctor before I took the position here. He can be called. His number is in my satchel." Anna reached for her satchel and pulled out the slip of paper.

"Anna, I need to call your Aunt Mary and have her come and get you this morning. Do you have her number with you?"

Anna pulled out another sheet of paper and handed it to Versus.

"I'll be there just as soon as I finish serving breakfast here," Mary said after Versus told her of Anna's situation. "Will she be all right until then, do you think?" Mary was so concerned, not only for Anna, but for illness to the baby boy.

Next, Versus called Anna's old employer. "Doctor Svenson? I am calling on behalf of Anna Lindquist. She became very ill this morning. I have contacted her aunt Mary Olson who will be picking her up shortly. I wonder if she might make an appointment with you? She has fainted and is regurgitating." She paused while she listened for an answer. "Thank you, Doctor."

Mary took Anna to the doctor and waited, very concerned.

"Anna," Doctor Svenson began, "it is so good to see you again. I wish it were under different circumstances. I have examined you for influenza. You do not have the flu. I am now

going to ask you to lie down on the examination table for a full examination, which I do not believe you have ever had." Doctor Svenson gave Anna a thorough exam, including a temperature test. "Get dressed now, Anna, and meet me in my office. Do you think you can walk all right?"

"Yes, Doctor. I will be there shortly. Do you think it is serious?" Anna felt frightened.

"Anna, please sit down. I understand you have met someone very special in your life." Doctor Svenson looked directly into Anna's frightened eyes.

"Yes, Doctor. He is very special to me." Anna felt puzzled as to the questioning.

"How is your relationship to him right now, Anna?" the doctor continued his odd questioning, which to Anna, had nothing to do with medicine.

"He has asked me to marry him. We are very much in love." Anna wanted to find out what was wrong with her medically, even though it was nice of the doctor to be interested in her love life.

"I'm so glad to hear that, Anna. You are an absolutely lovely, capable, and bright young woman. You deserve the very best. Who is this lucky man?" Doc Svenson continued.

"He emigrated from Sweden and ended up in my aunt's boardinghouse here. We met and we fell in love. We plan to marry soon."

"Anna, you might want to move that wedding date up. I have what I believe is the correct diagnosis of your condition. You are pregnant. I am going to prescribe some medicine for your morning sickness and give you a healthy diet, and I want you to walk as much as possible for exercise."

Anna burst into tears. She sobbed uncontrollably. "No, Doctor. I will lose my job. I might even lose Adolph!"

Doc Svenson came around from his desk and wrapped his arms around Anna. "Anna, I am very proud of you. You have had a difficult childhood and have made great strides forward in your life and career. I realize that you had no one to tell you about such matters as you would have received if your mother had lived. I am concerned for your future. I am willing to talk to this young man, if you like."

Anna's head was still turned downward toward her lap. She thought long and hard. "Doctor, this is not your burden. I yielded myself foolishly. Adolph is very headstrong. I do not think he would talk to you." Anna rose up from her seat. "Is Mary still here?"

"Anna, let me at least try. Adolph. I would like to meet Adolph. Yes, Mary is in the waiting room. I will call her in. I value you, Anna. There is nothing wrong with you, except that you are vulnerable. You can come and talk to me anytime. Just call and make an appointment. In fact, I want to see you every month. I will be in charge of your health—for you and this baby. May God be with you, Anna."

Anna walked out to the waiting room. Doc was right behind her. He escorted Mary into his office.

Mary looked at Anna very puzzled. "Is she very ill, Doc?"

"Mary, please have a seat. I will explain about Anna's health and your part in her recovery." Mary thought it very odd that the atmosphere was so heavy.

After the doctor had given Mary the news, she walked out and took Anna's arm. She smiled and hugged her lovingly. They drove back home in silence.

When they got back to Mary's boardinghouse, Mary said, "Anna, sit down." Mary had much on her mind she must unload. "Doc Svenson told me about your condition. I already know about you and Adolph. Doc will speak with Adolph. You are very lucky to have such a wonderful support as this doctor, Anna. I, too, will stand behind you. This life inside of you belongs to me, too. First, we will see what Adolph's response will be. Then we will go from there. Right now, Anna, I want you to rest. You have had enough already for one day. While you rest, pray, ask God's forgiveness, and for his love and support and answers. He will show you the way."

Meanwhile, Doc called Adolph. "I saw Anna this morning. She is not feeling well. I am very glad that she has you in her life, Adolph. I want to discuss her health with you. Come in at one p.m. and we will talk."

Adolph was totally baffled. He had just been with Anna, and she had been well and happy. What could possibly have changed in so short a time?

Adolph left Doc Svenson's office feeling overwhelmed and confused. *Why had Anna not told him directly? Did she not trust him?* He took it as an insult to his integrity and leading.

Adolph returned to the boardinghouse. Mary met him. She waited for him to say something about his meeting with the doctor but he headed straight for his room. En route, he noticed the door open to Mary's bedroom and Anna lying on the bed. He entered and sat beside Anna. "How are you, Anna? I just came from the doctor's office. Why did you not tell me? Do you not trust me?" His voice sounded angry.

Anna sat up. She looked Adolph directly in his angry and confused eyes. "Adolph, I hope your meeting went well with the doctor. Thank you for your willingness to see him. As you

know, Adolph, I am pregnant. Do you still want to marry me, Adolph?" Anna bravely stated her thoughts. She fearfully awaited Adolph's answer.

"I do not understand why you did not tell me first, Anna. That does not sit well with me. You are not a child. Yet you acted like a child. I do not want to marry a child, Anna! When do you intend to grow up?"

"I am going to be the mother of your child, Adolph. I am ready and willing to be a wife and a mother. I will have this child either way." Anna was glad she had spoken her mind.

"Anna, did you not know how to protect yourself? Didn't anyone teach you anything?"

Adolph still felt anger and resentment toward Anna for her reluctant actions.

"No, I knew nothing. Does that bother you, Adolph?" Now, Anna felt like challenging this man, putting him to the test. Maybe it would be that *she* would not want *him*.

"When do you want to marry, Anna? And where?"

"First, I must know that you *want* to marry me, Adolph." Anna stood firm with her challenge.

"Yes, I do. I will let you make those decisions."

"In Moscow. In the summer." Anna felt a great sense of relief. She could now move forward, even though it was not the way she had always desired. For that, she blamed herself.

"Done. I will contact your father and let him know about the need for arrangements. I will not mention your condition. I will also look for work. How are you feeling, Anna?"

"Pregnant!" Anna smiled and winked at Adolph.

Adolph wrote to Johnn Albert for the wedding plan arrangements for June. *A father. He was to be a father. Was he ready?*

Papa wrote to both Adolph and Anna. He was ecstatic and could hardly wait to meet the man who had stolen his precious daughter's heart. A summer wedding was planned for the summer of, at the Swedish Lutheran Church of Moscow, Idaho. Johnn Albert would make all of the arrangements and post the information in the Moscow newspaper. He was filled with joy! He gathered the children—no longer children, really—together and shared the news.

Anna was now beginning her second month. Mary had helped Anna her choose a beautiful white gown with satin slippers. Anna had spent her days working on a hat to match. Wherever her world would take her now, she was ready to meet the challenges.

Where would they live? Where would she be delivering and raising this newborn? She prayed for a girl.

Pastor Nordgren welcomed Adolph and Anna. The church was packed with family, friends, and community, including those of the church. Albert was the best man. Selma was the maid of honor. The other siblings filled in as bridesmaids, groomsmen, and ushers.

Papa proudly escorted Anna down the aisle. Adolph looked at Anna. She was more beautiful than the day he had met her. She took his breath away. He felt sick at heart for his actions toward her. She definitely was not a child. She was a beautiful, mature woman.

"I now pronounce you husband and wife. You may kiss the bride, Adolph."

"Adolph, you may now *stop* kissing the bride!" Pastor Nordgren laughed along with the rest of the attendees!

Food was in abundance downstairs. Enough food for Papa to take home and feed the family for a week!

Adolph and Anna would spend the night in Moscow. Papa had everything ready for the honeymoon suite at the Lindquist home. Their sending off breakfast would be fit for a king and queen. Anna's baby sister, Lilly, had gathered her siblings together and planned the meal. Ida was ready to pamper her guests.

Papa wondered how his nice new Swedish son-in-law would support his precious wife.

June, 1910. Adolph and Anna arose, ate breakfast, and thanked Ida for the lunch she had packed for their enjoyment en route. Anna ate a light breakfast. She did not want problems the day after her wedding.

Anna hugged her family goodbye and climbed into their new automobile. They had their first auto and would soon have their first home. A permanent home.

"Write me, Adolph, and give me your new address. Let me know about your work there. I will be anxious to hear about all of it," Papa said.

They packed the abundance of wedding gifts. The siblings had placed "Just Married" signs all over the automobile.

"What's the name of that Idaho town where you are going to live, Adolph?"

"Mullan, Johnn Albert. Mullan, Idaho."

Anna would share the news about Papa's grandchild when the time was right.

Mullan

In Spokane, Anna had bade farewell to the Davenport family. She had said she was feeling much better and ready to meet the next challenge of her life—marriage and family.

In Moscow, she once again bade farewell to the Lindquist family.

The baby grew inside of her. She could feel it kick. "Are you ready to be a father, Adolph?" Anna was delighted with the new chapter of life that faced her—one she had been preparing for since childhood. Anna believed that all the bad things were behind her. Only good things were to follow.

The town of Mullan was set up in the mountains above Coeur d'Alene, Idaho. There were many types of mines there. Adolph would be working for the Morning Mine, working with silver.

Mullan was located in Shoshone County on the South Fork of the Coeur d'Alene River. The town was started by Lt. John Mullan, a West Point graduate who built a military road to what would become the town of Mullan. It was high up in the hills. The lack of oxygen made Anna feel dizzy and sick upon her arrival. Pregnancy was bad enough. Now she must get used to the heights. Anna had been used to the growing city of Spokane; Mullan was just the opposite. The town had been birthed in 1885 and was a progeny of the Gold Hunter and Morning silver mines.

"Where do I wash the clothes, Adolph?" Anna was hoping for a washboard and a good scrub bucket, at the very least.

"At the creek, Anna." Adolph seemed to think that was amusing.

"How do they get clean? What about soap?" Anna was used to city conveniences.

"You take the soap with you, Anna. You scrub them clean. Next question!"

"With what do I scrub them?" Anna could not grasp this new way of living.

"With a rock, Anna. Watch the other women. They will show you." With that, Adolph walked off.

Anna carried the heavy load of laundry down to the creek side. It was almost a weekly meeting place now with the other women. Kneeling down, she took each piece of clothing and pounded it with a big rock, rinsing each soapy item in the creek and carrying it back to the house to hang on the outside clothesline. As the months progressed, it became more and more difficult to carry the load. Adolph's clothing was filthy with dust particles.

As Anna met women at the creek, Adolph brought home men he had met at the mine. Soon, they were entertaining couples. A bond began to build with the miners that she had never before experienced.

One day, Anna shouted, "Adolph! Call for the midwife! The baby is trying to push its way out!" Anna felt both fearful—remembering her mother—and joyful.

Adolph ran for the midwife and rushed back through the house. So many women died during childbirth. *Where would a baby go if it died?* She wondered to herself. *Does it go to heaven, too? Will I see those who have passed before me? Babies are too small to make a decision for eternity.* She remembered hearing that from her mother. *Who had told her mother that?*

"Waa. Waa!" Phyl entered the world very vocal on that cold January morning of 1911, nearly ten pounds of squalling flesh. Anna did not enjoy the luxury of city life with scrubbed nurses, doctors, and a fresh-smelling room. Phyl had torn her pelvic flesh. Anna was bleeding profusely.

"Adolph, send for the doctor immediately. Anna is bleeding, and I cannot stop it."

Adolph remembered what Anna had told him about Wilhelmina's death after giving birth. He ran and pounded on the doctor's door.

The door opened. "Doc, please come quickly. The baby has been birthed, but Anna cannot stop bleeding. She is torn."

They rushed back to the house. Anna was loosing blood rapidly. The doctor gave her a sedative and proceeded to stitch up her wounds.

"Adolph, someone must be with Anna day and night to watch the bleeding. As she awakens, she will need medication for pain. I will bring that by for you and check on her daily. I know you must work in a very filthy, dusty environment. Be sure you scrub profusely before you touch her so she will not get infection in her wound. It will take some time to heal. You must find someone to be with her, to care for the baby, and to bring the baby to her to nurse. Right now, Adolph. Find someone before I leave."

Adolph walked to the church and asked for help. The pastor provided names. Adolph called each one. Finally, one young girl came to their aid. She would need to cook, clean, and attend to everything Anna needed.

Phyl was progressing beautifully. Anna was not. She began to hemorrhage. The doctor returned and sedated her, checked the stitches, and pulled them tightly together. He had Adolph drive her to the nearest hospital. Anna was beginning to turn blue.

Anna was rushed into the emergency ward. For the first time in his life, Adolph was brought to his knees. He set aside his bullheadedness, his pride, his demanding spirit, and he prayed.

Hours later, the doctor came out to see Adolph. "You can take your wife home now, Adolph. The bleeding has stopped. Her color has returned. She will need rest. The healing will take time, and she will feel discomfort. You must care for her or provide care round the clock. No sexual intimacy until I say so. Have your doctor visit her weekly. Bring her back here in a month."

Adolph had not recalled ever praying since he was a child. God had answered his prayers for Anna. *Maybe there was something to be said for praying after all.* He would keep that in mind.

Anna became strong again. Phyl became plump and laughed a lot. Adolph had seen his family through birth and near death. He was grateful that all was well.

Then one day, the sky was ominous. Thunder and lightning strikes resounded everywhere around them. Then the sounds changed and fear struck their hearts.

Crackle…crackle…crackle…

The air was stuffy and still. Hot. Sticky hot. There was a new smell to the air. Anna had opened two windows to bring in whatever breeze might cool the stale air inside their home. The air that began to fill the Nelson household did not quench the heat or purify the humidity. This air stung her eyes and made here baby girl cry. Still, the air was not just filled with a different smell. It was filled with a very unusual and frightening noise. Thunder deafened her ears. Lightning startled her eyes. But that other sound. What was it?

"Oh, my God in heaven!" Anna wailed. "Fire!"

Adolph and his family of three reunited in Spokane. Now, they needed a home.

The Homestead

Adolph searched the Spokane newspaper for ads. Something caught his eye, and he read the article closely.

Homestead Act

The Homestead Act is a United States federal law that gives any applicant freehold title to 160 acres (one quarter section or about 65 hectares) of undeveloped land outside the original thirteen colonies. The new law requires three steps: file an application, improve the land, and file for deed of title. Anyone who has never taken up arms against the United States Government, including freed slaves, can file an application for making improvements to a local land office. The Act was signed into law by President Abraham Lincoln on May 20, 1862. The South resisted for fear the increase in free farmers would threaten plantation slaves. Two men have stood out as greatly responsible for the passage of the Homestead Act: George Henry Evans and Horace Greeley.

"Anna, we have a place to go to build ourselves a home—a new life. It will cost us

nothing. It is called a homestead."

"What on earth is a homestead, Adolph? How do you get one?" Anna looked to Mary. Mary was nodding yes and smiling. "Adolph, what do we do to earn it?" Anna questioned.

"We live on it, Anna. We live on it and improve the land for a certain period of time. We file a deed, and we wait to hear that we own it. We can do that in Idaho. I am going to leave early tomorrow morning and look at the land. I will be back soon."

Adolph gathered up some essentials and placed them into the trunk. Mary and Anna packed a lunch for the trip. At least he would have one meal without expense.

"Anna, perhaps you could come with me as far as Moscow. You and Phyl could stay with your family. I would leave there the next morning. The journey for me will not be far, and I can return for you in a short time."

"Oh, yes, of course!" Anna said. She wanted to discuss this homesteading idea with her family.

Moscow welcomed them again. Papa was standing at the door, eager to see his beloved daughter and his baby granddaughter.

Adolph explained his intent to the family and left early for the homesteading properties.

Upon his arrival, he visited the land office. He was given directions and rules. He drove from one section to another until he spotted a beautiful piece of land with a view of the mountains and a small lake nearby.

I wonder if that lake has any fish in it. Best way to find out is to fish! Adolph got out his rod and bait and stood by the bank tossing his line back and forth. He played with it a short while before a fresh brown trout bit the bait. *Dinner.* Adolph smiled. He walked around the property lines. A view of snowy mountains was in the background. A forested area bordered the property. He looked again into the forest. A deer was staring back at him. Frightened, it quickly ran into the woods. *Hunting.*

No one was going to see him out here if he built a little fire and cooked his trout. *Delicious!*

Adolph drove back to the land office and filed his claim.

"Adolph, it is expected that you and your family will improve this land. That is one of the criteria to possess it." The official from the land office shoved the papers toward Adolph to sign and be filed.

In Moscow, Anna poured out her heart to her family about their loss of everything they had had in Mullan.

"Anna, dear," Papa began, "it is up to you to follow your husband. It is his responsibility to find a home for you, to provide for you and Phyl and to protect you. I believe that what he is doing is a wise thing. You need to support him, Anna." Papa had said his piece. There would be no more advice.

Anna took Phyl upstairs to the bedroom. She placed Phyl into the bed. Then, she went into the spare bathroom, knelt down beside the claw-foot tub, and sobbed. Between her tears, she prayed and asked God's forgiveness for her terrible fear of what was ahead for them. She begged for understanding and acceptance.

God, I don't understand why you would give us everything—and then, take it away. Why are you sending us to live in a primitive land? I want to live in the city, Lord. I want to make hats. I cannot make hats in the middle of nowhere, Lord. I cannot even buy the fabric. Who would buy them out there? I want my little girl to have playmates. It will be so lonely, Lord. I can't do it, Lord. I can't. I want to stay here, in Moscow. Let Adolph go live on it! Anna wiped away her tears and waited for God's answer.

Phyl cried out for Anna.

Anna opened the door and scooped up Phyl into her arms. Phyl placed her tiny hand on her mother's cheek, wiping the tear away.

"You wet, Momma? Why you wet?"

"I am all right, baby Phyl. Let's get to bed and get some sleep. Your papa will be here tomorrow with news." Anna placed Phyl onto the bed and crawled in beside her. Efforts to sleep evaded her. Fear gripped her heart.

Anna fell into a deep sleep somewhere late into the night or early morning hours. She awoke at the sound of a car coming into the driveway.

Adolph! Anna carefully climbed out of bed to let Phyl sleep a little longer. She placed a little water into the tub and took a rather chilly sponge bath. She did not want to awaken the family by going downstairs and heating up the water for the tub. She returned to the bedroom and began to dress when Phyl awakened.

"Mommy, hung'y!" Phyl placed her little arms around Anna's legs. They dressed quickly and tiptoed downstairs.

Adolph was standing in the kitchen looking for coffee. Anna walked over to her husband and gave him a big hug and kiss. Adolph took Phyl.

"Anna, would you fix me some coffee and breakfast? I'm starving!" Adolph placed Phyl on the chair and sat beside her.

Anna placed the water into the old blue-speckled coffee pot. She found a big pot, filled it with water, and waited for it to boil. She checked the cupboards for oatmeal, finally stumbling upon it. Milk was in the icebox. Sugar was in the sugar compote in the cupboard. She placed everything on the table and served Adolph first; then, spooning a teaspoon at a time, she fed Phyl, blowing on it to cool before it hit the baby's lips.

They sat in silence until Adolph finished his first cup of coffee and cooked cereal. "Is there toast, Anna?" Adolph expected this with a second cup of coffee. Then, he would be ready to talk.

Anna fixed two slices of toast and found some jam. She poured Adolph a second cup of coffee. She waited in silence for Adolph to be ready to speak.

"We will be packing up and moving to Idaho as soon as we can, Anna. I have made a land claim on a piece of property." Adolph dunked his toast into the coffee and ate.

"Where is it, Adolph?" Anna asked.

"Where is *what,* Anna?" Adolph looked at her, surprised.

"Where is this piece of property? What does it look like? Is there a place to live there? Are there other people?" Anna had so many questions.

"It has a lake with trout and some woods with deer. No other people that I could see." Adolph chewed his last bite and set his coffee cup down.

"Where will we live?" Anna knew she must be patient with Adolph. She certainly did not *feel* patient. She felt ill.

"Oh, we will find someplace in the nearest town until we get something built to live in while we work on a house. It will be primitive for a while." Adolph got up and walked out to the car.

"Oh," Anna said, to the silent kitchen.

Papa walked into the kitchen and greeted Anna and Phyl. Lilly followed and began the breakfast routine. "Any word from Adolph yet, Anna?"

"Adolph is back, Papa. Lilly, we have already eaten. Thank you."

"What did he find, Anna? You do not seem to be very happy. Are you all right?" Papa searched Anna's eyes.

"We're moving tomorrow, Papa. We have no house, nothing. We have land. We will have no neighbors—just a lake and a forest. It will be so lonely, Papa. There will be no playmates for Phyl, no church, no friends. Papa!" Anna put her head down on the table and cried.

Papa placed his arm around his beloved Anna and tried to comfort her.

"When I was home," Anna said between sobs, "at least we had each other. I miss you, Papa, all of you. I miss you so very much. I never knew married life could be so harsh."

Papa was silent. Adolph stood just inside the door.

"In that case, Anna, why don't you just stay right here with *this* family. Go back to your little girl roots. Maybe they can finish raising you so I can have a *woman* beside me when you grow up." Adolph stormed out the door.

Papa ran after Adolph. "Please! Please, Adolph. Do not go. We are men. She is a woman with a child—"

"She still *is* a child, Johnn Albert! She is a child *with* a child!" Adolph headed for the car.

"No, Adolph! You, too, are not being very grown up in *your* attitude. You are under God's laws to provide for and protect your wife and your children. God works through you, Adolph. Are you going to walk out on your family—abandon your responsibilities—just because you will not listen to your wife? I think you better get yourself right with God, then your family."

Johnn Albert returned to see Anna.

Adolph stood by the door of his car. It was packed and ready to travel. There was much to do before fall and winter weather set in—a home to build, fruit trees to plant, a vegetable garden, a storage shed for his supplies, a barn. He knew he could not do it all alone. He would have to secure help.

Back in the house, Papa said, "Anna, get up. I want to talk to you."

"What is it, Papa?" Anna stood up from the table, picked up Phyl in her arms, and looked at Johnn Albert.

"What if your brothers and sisters and I come out to the town and help Adolph with the building of the house and you with getting a home ready? Lilly and the twins can stay here with Pete. They will be fine. You are not going to be *that* far away. It will be just like the Amish do when they build a new home. We will bring food. There *must* be a town nearby with a hotel. We can afford to spend a week at a time there—or weekends—until you have shelter. What do you say? I will speak with Adolph." Papa looked to Anna for an answer.

Anna smiled at her papa and rejoiced at his conciliatory wisdom. "Yes, Papa. If Adolph agrees, I do also." Anna hugged Papa.

Johnn Albert walked out to where Adolph still stood next to the car and shared his ideas, then waited for a response.

"I think that might work. It would certainly help us to have a place of shelter. Once we have that, we can handle the rest. There is a town not too far from the homestead. It is where I contracted the land grant. I could secure the rooms for weekends until we are stable enough to be on our own. The children could help with plowing and planting. Yes, thank you, Johnn Albert."

Johnn Albert went into the house and headed for the parlor.

"Where are you going, Papa? Is everything all right?" Anna yelled after Johnn Albert.

"To the parlor to pray. I will be right back. God and I need to converse for a bit."

Lord, this has been such a difficult time for Anna. The road ahead is also very frightening. Would you bless her, Lord? Would you help us to help her and Adolph? It is in your name I pray. Amen.

Johnn Albert did not wait for God to answer. He knew the answer would come in his time. He walked over to Anna and Phyl. "We are going to come together as a team—a weekend work party—every weekend until you have a home, a barn, a storage shed, and a garden. Then, we will come and visit you when we can." Johnn Albert put his arm around Anna.

"Oh, Papa. Thank you. Does Adolph agree?" Papa could see the deep concern in her eyes.

"Yes, Anna, Adolph agrees. It is all set—except for the hotel reservations. I will bring Albert to help with the building. Selma will come from the hospital in Portland to help you with the women's work. We will also bring meals and extra food for your storage until you can produce your own. It will be fun. You must be content, Anna. It is the woman who sets the mood in the home. Remember that!"

Anna remembered. She had lost that mood when her mother died. Wilhelmina's loss had caused a deafening silence in the Lindquist home for a long, long time.

Anna walked out to the car where Adolph stood.

"I am ready, Adolph." Anna waited.

Silence.

Adolph put his arm around Anna and lifted Phyl into his arms. "We are united. We will make it through this, too. Mullan was not the end of us, only the end of a town we once knew. Now, we have a chance for new beginnings. That is what life is about, Anna—new beginnings, each and every day."

Papa, Albert, and Selma climbed into their own vehicle. Adolph, Anna, and Phyl climbed into the front seat of Adolph's car. The other siblings agreed to keep the home intact while they were gone for the day. Papa had contacted the church to look in on the children. He warned them that they might be gone a day or two because of the distance.

When they reached the last town before the homestead, they stopped and checked out the hotel. Adolph secured reservations for rooms for every weekend throughout the summer and into the fall. Adolph and Papa took Anna and Selma into the dining room.

"My treat!" Papa insisted. "We are going to have happy tummies before we start such a huge project." Papa leaned over to Adolph and whispered, "I brought along several commodes. Where else are you going to go in the wilderness! The ladies will be offended. We have to put up with being primitive until we get the outhouse built. That should be our first project. We will need to buy some lime."

After their meal, Anna and Selma stayed at the hotel while Adolph, Papa, and Albert purchased immediate supplies.

It was still early in the day when they arrived at the property. Papa and Albert took one look at the land, the mountains, and the lake and fell in love with the surroundings. Anna looked and saw barrenness and loneliness.

The men surveyed the ground. They placed posts and string to outline areas for each of the buildings. Albert took the fishing rod and caught a few brown trout. He built a bonfire and cooked the fish for a midday meal.

"I believe we are ready to cut trees and build buildings. What do you think, Adolph?"

"I agree. It will take the three of us a long time. Do you suppose we could get some helpers?" Adolph looked to Papa.

"The church. We have some wonderful builders at the Swedish Lutheran Church in Moscow. They dearly love Anna. I am certain we can get all we need. I will ask. Adolph, bring the family back to the house. I believe Anna and Phyl should stay there until we men have finished building and supplied the house with the necessities to make it a home. This is what I did when we moved from Massachusetts to Moscow."

"Thank you, Johnn Albert. I accept your generous offer." Adolph shook Papa's hand.

Anna looked at Selma with a sigh of relief. She could spend time with her siblings. When she moved to this isolated existence, at least she would have a home.

"I wonder if there is a church in the nearest town, Selma. I need a place to worship." Anna looked down at the floor.

"Anna, shame on you, big sister! We do not need a *place* to worship the Lord. Anywhere where we are, Anna, that is a place of worship. Perhaps you could build an altar to the Lord on the property—a little chapel by the woods." Selma ached for Anna's sadness.

Johnn Albert returned with Albert. Adolph drove up shortly afterward.

"We are all very pleased with the land purchase. It has a breathtaking view and is perfect for all your needs." Johnn Albert smiled with confidence.

Not all *my needs, Lord. Please fill my life with people—friends—church. My baby needs playmates.* Anna excused herself and walked out to the porch that surrounded the outside of the family home. She sat in the swing and rocked herself back and forth.

Anna awakened abruptly and looked up. There was the image of Jesus with his outstretched arms. Anna immediately raised herself up to go toward her Savior. He was gone.

His image was etched indelibly in her mind. She went upstairs to check on Phyl who was napping. Phyl was sleeping peacefully.

"Bless you, baby girl. You are not aware of disappointments or lack. You are content just to be loved," Anna whispered softly to Phyl.

Anna grabbed her Bible and headed back downstairs to the swing seat. Rocking back and forth, she turned to the book of John, reading 14:27. "Peace I leave with you, my peace I give unto you: not as the world giveth, give I unto you. Let not your heart be troubled, neither let it be afraid." Anna placed the Bible down beside her. She looked up toward heaven.

"Lord, thank you for making your presence known to me. Thank you that you are always with me and my family. My fears and trembling have not yet subsided. However, I know in my heart that you are here with me."

Johnn Albert called Pastor Nordgren at the Swedish Lutheran Church. He expressed his dire need for any help from the men to assist Adolph, himself, and Albert in building on Adolph and Anna's homestead. He told Pastor Nordgren about the breathtakingly beautiful land purchase and its primitive yet pristine conditions.

"Do you think you might approach the congregation Sunday about their need?" Johnn Albert sent up a quick prayer to the Lord.

"Yes, John Albert. I will see what I can do. I would also love to help. Perhaps the women can bring meals and come along with their men. I will get back to you on Monday. See you Sunday!"

Johnn Albert took Adolph aside and told him about the conversation. At dinner, they all discussed the property and plans with excitement and joy. Papa looked over at Anna, wondering if she, too, was full of joy.

Sunday morning, the entire family dressed and headed for the services. They were greeted warmly and welcomed into the liturgical services. The pastor spoke about Antioch, where the members of the congregation were first called Christians, how they had all things in common and shared what they had. Then he directed his sermon specifically to Adolph and Anna's needs and called for helpers. He had a sign-up sheet in the foyer.

The phone rang at the Lindquist home Monday morning. Johnn Albert reached for the receiver. "Johnn Albert speaking."

"Johnn Albert. This is Pastor Nordgren. We actually have *too many!* I will narrow it down to those men who have specific skills for the task at hand. The wives of these men will bring meals for each time they come to the property. I believe we should be completely finished with everything by the end of summer."

Johnn Albert was overwhelmed with joy. "Thank you, Pastor Nordgren. I will share the good news with the family. When do you think we might begin?"

"Most of the men are working. How about every weekend? Will that suffice?" Pastor asked.

"It should be sufficient for the task at hand. I will tell Adolph and Anna. Thank you, Pastor." Johnn Albert *ran* out to the front porch where the family was gathered and drinking iced tea. Lilly had prepared some scones and was serving the family.

"Johnn Albert, why are you out of breath? What's wrong?" Adolph asked.

"I have very good news. Every single weekend this summer—or

until the job is finished—men from the church will help us build. Of course, Pastor can only join them on Saturdays. He longs to be a part of it. The wives will take turns providing meals. When the house is finished, the wives will stock your shelves with canned goods, fabrics, and all the necessities."

Johnn Albert sat down on the front steps. He could not wipe away the smile that broadened his lips.

One of the twins spoke up.

"We can sell lemonade and cookies during the week to raise money for furniture. Can we do that, Papa?" Hilma was the first to express her idea.

"That is a wonderful idea! Do you mind if I put Lilly in charge?" Papa asked.

The summer was a busy time in Moscow. Lemonade stands were placed in front of the Lindquist home. Posters were placed around town. Lilly baked every kind of cookie imaginable. Some she created "out of her head." The posters indicated that lemonade could be sold by the quart jar, if the customers would supply the jars. Cookies could be purchased by the baker's dozen if they were given orders in advance.

Each one took turns manning the post outside the home. They decided to give it a name: "Lillie's Bakery."

Saturday mornings, each of the men in town, including Johnn Albert and Adolph, took turns loading men into the car and driving to the property. A wagon was connected behind the car and used to carry tools. A meal was provided to the men. The men told no one. Each one took along a fishing rod and tackle. They would have *another* meal before heading back to Moscow.

The summer was very hot. For the Lindquist women, that was a tremendous asset. People were thirsty! Moscow, Idaho must have sold more lemonade that summer than in all the history of lemon growing! Lilly cooked cookies in the coolness of each dawn and placed them in the cooler. People bought them by the dozen—the baker's dozen!

Anna's time with her family gave her confidence and joy. Phyl was growing to be a healthy little girl. Anna walked with her daily. Phyl was taking her first steps. She needed to walk off that chubby baby fat! She was a happy little child with an early independent streak. She loved lemonade.

"Phyl, lemonade is for sale for our new home. If you drink it all, dear one, we will be losing money." Phyl giggled. "Mo,' Momma?" It was obvious Anna was not communicating rationally with a baby!

The men arrived back home late Sunday evening exhausted. The outhouse was up with lime at the bottom. The frame for the house was up. They should finish it in a few weeks.

The work continued during the summer months. By the end of the summer, the temporary house was completed, offering a kitchen, dining room, two bedrooms, bathroom, pantry, and living room. Adolph would add a porch later. The barn was completed. Now, they needed to purchase a horse or a mule and a plow. A storage area had also been erected with an area for blocks of ice. An underground cellar was added to keep storage for meats and other cold-storage items. The women spent the summer canning meats, fish, fruit, and vegetables and took them to the house for their winter supply.

The siblings had raised five hundred dollars for furniture for their new home. Their efforts were honored and applauded at a special going-away banquet at the church.

It was Labor Day weekend. The church taped off an area for a picnic. Adolph and Anna enjoyed the fellowship and food.

It was now time to select furniture and appliances for the home. Adolph hired some college students and a truck. Anna and Selma went shopping for household furniture and items of necessity.

The church congregation offered various pieces of furniture from their homes.

The Nelsons bid their goodbyes to Moscow, thanked the Lindquist family for travel food, and were on their way. They should reach their property by noon.

Selma returned to her nursing position in Portland.

The college students drove up the long gravel road completed by the Moscow work crew. Anna directed the placing of the furniture while Phyl tried out her new walking skills.

By late afternoon, every item was in place, and the pantry cupboard was loaded with canned food. Tomorrow, Adolph would take Anna into town to purchase all the supplies she would need to complete her kitchen.

Adolph purchased bales of hay to place in the barn. On the next trip, he would locate chickens and a mule. He did not look forward to riding the mule back to the house. Anna would have to have a quick lesson in driving. The car must have *some* way to return to the house.

Adolph promised to build a highchair for Phyl. Some dear saint had provided them a used crib, blankets, and baby clothes.

They sat down at the meal given them by the church family. They placed the garbage in a huge bag and put it outside the back door. Adolph would need to dig a pit in the morning and use some of the lime to destroy it. Or, he realized, he could build up compost with the garbage to use on his garden next spring.

Anna fed Phyl and placed her into her crib. She remained with her until Phyl fell asleep. Anna boiled water taken from the pump. Adding some cold water, she dumped it into the tub and stepped in, testing it first with her toes. She laid back and soaked for an hour. Her muscles ached.

Anna thought about the work ahead of her. She would have to become creative in a way she had never before accomplished. For now, she stepped out of the tub, drained the water, and dried herself off with one of her new towels. She donned her nightgown and joined Adolph in their new living room.

"Do you hear a noise, Adolph? Outside the back door. Are you expecting someone? Who knows we are here?" Anna looked at Adolph, very puzzled.

Adolph walked over to the kitchen window and peeked out.

"Oh, my God in heaven! A black bear!" Adolph stood at the window paralyzed while the bear enjoyed the remainder of their dinner.

"Adolph? Who is it?" Anna got up to open the door.

"No! Anna! Stay put and be quiet. There is a bear dining on our leftovers." Adolph laughed.

Anna had shivers running up and down her spine. "Adolph, will he kill us?"

"No, Anna. Don't be dumb! The bear is just being a bear. He is hungry, and he found some food. Don't ever get near any wild animal if it has cubs nearby. Clanging some pots and pans would chase it away. It will go away if we just wait a while. It will eat and leave. Tomorrow morning, I will dig a pit to dump the garbage and place lime on it."

It was getting dark. They securely locked the house and crawled into bed. Adolph went to sleep immediately. Anna did not. *Bears…*

In the morning, Adolph said, "I need to go into town to get some chickens and feed. Eventually, I will get a cow and a steer to raise. You and Phyl can stay here." Adolph grabbed his jacket and headed for the car.

"We're going with you, Adolph. I am not going to stay here with bears around."

"Anna, the bears are not going to leave. Are you? This is home now, Anna, bears and all." Adolph looked at Anna with disgust.

"We're going." Anna grabbed a coat for herself and Phyl. The early mornings and late evenings were beginning to get chilly.

Adolph had built a chicken coop in the barn. Now, he placed a rooster and half a dozen hens to nest on the hay with some feed for them on the ground. Phyl was fascinated by the clucking noise and laughed.

Anna never lost her fear of the bears. Going outside the house was, for her, a traumatic experience. Adolph never lost his ability to laugh at her fear. One increased the other. Phyl was now fifteen months old.

Adolph took the mule to the plow and tore up the sod softened by the late winter rains. He tore grooves into each section of the ground. Anna followed behind with seed to toss in. She took more from her pocket and loaded it into her apron. Phyl trotted behind, kicking the dirt back in to cover the seed, just as Anna had taught her. She thought that was such fun.

In June Adolph began to see signs of harvest popping through the topsoil. Anna hauled in buckets of water that Adolph had provided from the lakeside.

"Look!" Anna pointed to a doe and her fawns drinking at the lake. "They are beautiful, aren't they, Adolph?"

"Too bad it isn't hunting season. But then, who is to know the difference out here?" He walked into the barn and got his rifle.

"Not the doe, Adolph! She has babies!" Anna couldn't look.

"Ah, Anna, there is the buck. That buck will feed our family for a long, long time." Adolph aimed the rifle and let the shot ring. The buck stumbled to the ground. The startled doe and fawns ran rapidly into the forest.

Phyl began to cry. "Noise, Mommy. Phyl cry!"

Anna picked her up and carried her into the house. "Papa is getting dinner."

Adolph pulled the buck into the barn and gutted it. He let it hang strung onto the rafters and closed the barn doors.

Adolph filleted the deer and cut the meat into pieces, identifying each piece. It was placed in the coldest portion of the underground cellar.

Anna canned and preserved their crops. It was harvest time, and the nights were getting very cool and crisp.

"Adolph, I think I am pregnant. Who will deliver this baby?" She looked at Adolph, waiting for a response.

"You will, Anna."

"Adolph, my mother died giving birth. I need to know a midwife. We need to find one soon." Anna's fears grew for herself and for the little human growing inside her.

The summer had been unusually dry. It was amazing they had had any crops at all. Now, the winds were whipping up and howling around the buildings. It frightened Phyl. It frightened Anna even more. Adolph stoked the wood in the fireplace. Anna pulled up her chair and wondered what next spring would bring.

Winter brought severe storms. Adolph could hardly get to the barn from the house. Everything was frozen over.

In early spring the rains became torrential. The lake rose and flooded the property before it began to return to normalcy.

Anna went about her chores that morning. Suddenly, she felt internal pains. She called Phyl into the bedroom and checked herself. Something was not right with the baby.

Anna fainted. Phyl tugged at her dress. "Momma. Momma. Sleep?"

Adolph walked into the log house for his morning coffee with Anna. He looked around the kitchen and called, "Phyl! Where's Momma?"

"Momma sleeping!"

Anna does not sleep in the middle of the morning, Adolph thought.

Adolph walked into the bedroom and saw Anna lying on the floor, bleeding.

He picked Anna up and laid her on the bed. He bent down to examine the mess on the floor and realized what had happened.

Adolph took Phyl by the hand. "Come with Daddy. We go 'bye bye.'" Adolph drove into the nearest town and located a doctor.

"Anna is in shock," the doctor said. "Let her rest in bed. Give her liquids when she awakes—some hot broths, water, and juice. She might be down for a couple of days. I will return in three days and examine her again. She should be all right by then. Emotionally, she may not recover immediately. She will, however, recover in time. You must take care of your wife and your home in the meantime. I am very sorry. The loss of a child is devastating. Would you like a minister to come out? Please bury the body with a little grave. Give the child a name. You will be glad you did. I gave her a sedative in a shot. She should sleep soundly." Doc left for town, stating his soon return.

"Come on, baby girl. Come with Papa." Adolph took Phyl by the hand. He walked out to the barn, picked up some wood, and began to build a tiny coffin. He lined it and returned to the house. He then picked up the tiny fetus as best he could and placed it gently in the coffin. Then, Adolph cleaned up the floor, so that when Anna awakened, the stained floor would not be the first thing she saw.

Adolph took the tiny box outside and dug a hole in the ground.

"What shall we call this little one, Phyl?" Adolph placed a cross beside the grave. "I will call her Heather because of the heather we grow." A swatch of heather was placed on the baby's grave. Adolph knelt beside the grave and invited Phyl to do likewise. Phyl knelt beside her daddy and took his hand. Of course, she did not understand why.

"Lord, I do not understand your ways, especially now. You gave us life. Then you took it away. Why is that, Lord? Please take care of Heather in your heaven. Will we see Heather some day? What do you do with babies that die?" Adolph began to sing "Jesus Loves Me." He shoveled the dirt back onto the grave and stood up.

He knew he must tell Anna when she awakened and before the doctor returned.

Adolph took Phyl's hand and walked around the property. He returned to the house and checked on Anna. She was still asleep.

Doc had given her quite a bit of medication. He grabbed his fishing gear, scooped up Phyl, and said, "Come on, baby girl, your daddy and you are going to get tonight's supper."

"Go fish, Papa?" Phyl smiled back.

"Go fish!" *I understand that is what Jesus did, too. Maybe he will meet us there.*

The Decision

Adolph looked in on Anna. She was responding. She had suffered such a traumatic shock that she had temporarily forgotten.

"How are you feeling, Anna?" Adolph sat down on the bed beside her, placing Phyl on the bed.

"Momma sick?" Phyl crawled to her mother.

"Just resting, baby. Why am I here, Adolph? I don't usually sleep in the middle of the day."

Just then, the doctor knocked on the front door. Adolph picked up Phyl and went to answer it.

"Good afternoon, Doc. Come in. Anna just awakened."

"How is she?" Doc asked.

"I don't know for sure. She does not seem to understand why she is resting. Should I tell her?" Adolph asked.

"I will," Doc replied.

"Good afternoon, Anna. How are you feeling?" Doc smiled at Anna.

"Just fine, Doc. Why on earth are *you* here?" Anna said.

"Anna, you have suffered quite a shock that has caused you to forget momentarily. You lost your baby, Anna. The baby was stillborn."

Anna touched her stomach.

"My baby! Not my little baby! Where is it? What happened to it?" Anna demanded.

"I buried the baby this morning," Adolph told her. "I built a small casket for it and placed a headstone at the top."

Anna burst into tears.

"Let her grieve, Adolph. She needs to experience this in order to heal. If she does not come out of it in a few weeks, call me. For now, just let her rest. She will recover and regain her strength. In the meantime, Adolph, you need to assume her chores.

"Mommy cry, Papa. Why Mommy cry?" Phyl tried to crawl on the bed.

Adolph took her tiny hand. "Come on, baby girl, we will go fix some supper for you and me and Mommy." Adolph walked them all into the kitchen.

The doctor said his goodbyes. "Call on me if you need me. Otherwise, I will return in a month. She should be back to normal in a few weeks."

Adolph shook the doctor's hand and bade him goodbye. Phyl waved.

Normal! Just what is *normal?* Adolph wondered.

Adolph took a few leftovers and made some dinner for himself and Phyl. He saved a portion for Anna—just in case she would eat.

The next morning, Adolph looked over at his sleeping wife. He tiptoed out of bed, cleaned up and dressed, and got baby Phyl ready for the day. He fixed a pot of coffee and some porridge. Phyl ate heartily.

"We are going out to gather some eggs," Adolph told Phyl. "Let's go say good morning to the chickens."

Some kind of animal had ransacked the henhouse overnight and killed two of the hens. The eggs were there—some broken with pieces lying on the ground. So were feathers—everywhere! Adolph disposed of the dead chickens, placed the eggs in a basket, and let the cow out to graze.

Adolph brought the eggs in the house and placed them in the cooler.

Anna was up, washed, and dressed. "Have you had breakfast, Adolph?" she asked. Then she spotted the extra bowl of porridge. "I guess that answers my question."

"Adolph, what was the baby—a boy or a girl? Did you give it a name?" Anna sat down at the table and poured milk on her porridge.

"It was a girl, Anna. I named her Heather and wrote that name on the top of the cross. She is home, Anna. I believe we will see her again, don't you?"

"David said that about the son he had with Bathsheba. That baby died and David said he would see him again. Yes, I believe we will see Heather. I want to see the grave, Adolph," Anna said.

Anna finished her porridge and followed Adolph and Phyl to the gravesite. She knelt beside the tiny grave and stirred the dirt on top. She picked some flowers and placed them on the grave. Then she noticed something odd. "Something has been digging here, Adolph. Some animal. Or has Phyl been playing with the dirt?"

"Phyl has been with me every minute, Anna," Adolph said.

"Then, what could it be?" Anna looked quizzically at Adolph.

"An animal. Something smelled the body and began to dig. It must have been scared off. I will move the grave to a higher place where no animal can get it."

Adolph carefully dug up the small grave and placed it into a larger, more secure box. He took it and the cross and placed it on an elevated site.

"Anna, I have made many improvements to this land. It has served us well. However, there have been many unhappy events. Not just the death of our baby, Anna. The weather has not always been on our side. Animals have destroyed crops and chickens. I have had enough of homesteading. I have applied to work in Washington State for the Northern Pacific Railroad. Do you think your father would put us up for a few days again until we—I—locate a place for us to live?" Adolph looked over at Anna.

"Yes, Adolph. I know he would be happy to do that. It is always a good opportunity to visit. Shall I write him?"

"I already have." Adolph chuckled to himself. "Here is his letter, Anna. He understood perfectly. He seemed to know that we would not take this very long before deciding to vacate. He is a wise man."

"He always has been," Anna said.

Adolph placed an ad in several papers, locally and beyond. He waited.

A letter came in the mail from Northern Washington State.

Dear Mr. Nelson:

I saw your ad in the King County Newspaper for the sale of your Idaho homestead. My wife and I live in a camp where I have been working for the Northern Pacific Railroad. Of course, I have no idea what your further pursuits and plans are beyond homesteading. However, would you be interested in an exchange? I would offer you my job and camp home here in Northern Washington for your homestead in Idaho. We would, of course, pay you the cash balance.

Also, it would be necessary for you to apply for this position. I am working on building railroad trestles and snow sheds. If you are interested, you may write to me at the address listed.

Enclosed is a photo of the campsite and railroad. There are some fantastic plans forthcoming for work here. We would just like to try a different lifestyle. Thank you for sending a photo of your land and its surrounding beauty.

Yours truly,
Mr. Emil Peters

"There it is in a nutshell, Anna. I have building experience from Sweden. I believe I can do the work. It would be a change for us and a quick release from here. There would be a home and job already provided. I must write quickly and let him know. Plus, I must apply for that position and wait. Anna, how do you feel about it?" Adolph folded the letter and placed it back in the envelope.

Anna sipped her second cup of coffee and took a quick bite of the skorper she had sliced and toasted from the cardamom bread. She dunked it in her coffee and pondered Adolph's request.

"I long for a place with roots, Adolph. I also desire a good place for my children to live—one that is safe and offers them a good education. Do you feel the camp offers that?" Anna picked up their coffee cups and headed for the sink.

"Maybe, Anna. Maybe not. It would be a well-paying job. Right now we only have one child who is just over a year old. We have five or six years before they need to be in school, assuming we have more children. It would give me the opportunity to make a lot of money in those few years before we would move to a more suitable surrounding with schools and a better place for the children to grow up." Adolph leaned back in his chair and waited for Anna's answer. He was getting impatient.

"Yes, Adolph, if that is what you want, and if you are willing to move to a suitable place for our children within four or five years, I would be willing to go. How much do you want for the homestead?" Anna washed the cups and saucers and cleaned up the crumbs.

"With the offer of a small camp home and a job, probably five hundred dollars. That would give us the money to move our things and have something to live on while I wait for a paycheck." Adolph stood up, indicating to Anna that he had chores to do.

"Why not leave the furniture and take what is in their camp house? That would save a lot of money for moving expenses. You could use that for travel and meals." Anna did not relish the idea of packing again.

"Excellent idea, Anna. We will pack the baby things in the car. I can lower Phyl's little crib and place it in the back seat. She can sleep and play in it while we travel. I will write Emil today with our offer. Thank you, Anna." Adolph lifted Phyl. "New home for Momma and Papa, baby girl."

"Home?" Phyl picked up words to repeat. She had no idea what they meant!

Adolph sat down after lunch and wrote a letter to Emil. He had about an hour before the postal delivery man was due along their route. He and Phyl would walk down the long gravel road to the postal box. He would help Phyl put up the flag.

Dear Emil,

Thank you for your very welcomed letter and offer. My wife and I are interested in your offer of exchange. The balance of payment for you would be $500. We have a huge parcel of land here with forest and lake bordering the property. The forest offers an excellent choice of wood for building. Already, I have a two-bedroom, one-bath home with a living room, dining room, and kitchen. On the property, I have built a two-story barn, an outhouse, a storage shed, and an underground cold storage for food.

The lake offers excellent trout. There is an abundance of birds and deer for your food as well. It is pristine property and well worth every penny. Please let us know whether you accept or reject our offer. Please also let me know where to write about the job and to whom.

Regards,
Adolph Nelson

"In the meantime, Anna, there is still work to do." Adolph shut the door and walked to the barn to gather chickens and milk the cow. He chopped wood for the stove and stored it alongside the house in the bin.

Anna fed Phyl and placed her in her crib for an afternoon nap. Then she gathered up her large basket and walked to the garden to pick vegetables for supper. She sat in the chair Adolph had built and basked in the sun, hoping the vegetables would not wilt before she took them inside.

Very loud wailing came from inside the house. Adolph reached the bedroom first. Anna was close behind. They ran into Phyl's bedroom. A huge rat was sitting on Phyl's tiny chest peering at her. Phyl's loud noises made the animal move, but it did not leave the crib. Adolph grabbed it by the tail. The rat, in turn, bit him on the hand. Adolph took an object and hit the rat on the head. It fell limp in his hand. He took it out and buried it deep into the ground. He washed his hand thoroughly with soap and water. Then he placed a disinfectant on the wound.

Anna picked up Phyl and held her in her arms until her crying stopped. "Shh, baby girl. It is all right now. The big bad rat is all gone. It will not hurt you anymore." Anna sat in the rocker and rocked Phyl back and forth until she calmed down. When she fell asleep again, Anna placed her back into the crib.

Adolph is right, Lord. Thank you for giving us this property. We have been blessed by your generous love. Thank you, too, for the offer of a home, a job, and cash for this property. If it be your will, we will move. Please work through this young couple for your decision for our lives. In your name, I ask and pray. Please work also in my heart for another move.

I ask you for roots, Lord—permanent roots in a safe place that offers growth and stability for my children and husband. Amen.

Anna took the cow's milk and placed it in the cooler. That evening, after the thick cream had risen to the top, she skimmed it off and placed it into the huge jar. She inserted the wooden ladle and began to churn. She churned one hundred fifty strokes and Adolph churned one hundred fifty strokes. It was now a ball of butter. Rolling the ball out of the jar, she placed it into a huge bowl, adding a little salt to mix in. The she placed the ball on the cutting board. Next, Anna formed the ball into a huge square and cut it into long pieces. She wrapped each piece and placed the extras into the cooler for future use. Fresh butter for dinner.

Phyl awakened. Anna was fixing fresh brown trout from the lake that Adolph had caught that morning, fresh green beans from the garden, fresh corn on the cob, and wild berry pie with homemade ice cream. Phyl was learning to handle a small glass of milk and eating with a spoon. Anna would transition her to a fork in a few months.

The postal man drove by and waved from the road. He saw Adolph outside. Mail delivery was slow and very welcome when anything arrived. Anna was grateful that her Moscow family wrote often. They gave her news about the Moscow Swedish Lutheran Church—even sent her the Sunday bulletin.

Anna deeply missed going to church. She wanted to raise her children in a Christian environment. There was no church in the nearby town. *Would the camp have a church? Probably not. What kind of environment would that be for a young child? What could she do to enhance the spiritual life of her family?* Anna decided to start reading the Bible to Phyl. She decided she would draw picture stories and create her own storybook for her children, attempting to bring God's Word to life for their little minds. *They. Them. Would there* be *more children? Please, Lord, please do not take more life from me. I want babies, Lord, babies that live and grow. I want them to know and follow you.*

Anna picked up her Bible and placed Phyl in her lap. When she came to a particular story, she sketched out a picture of that story, one page at a time. Phyl studied the picture and listened to her momma's words. It was not long before the story came to life. Later, when Anna mentioned a Bible story, Phyl would find it and point to it. Soon, she was able to name it.

A letter finally arrived from the railroad camp and Emil. Adolph opened the letter and read:

> Dear Adolph:
>
> Thank you for your answer. My wife and I have discussed the offer. We would like to come there and see the property before we make a final decision. I have three days off the weekend after next. If this is an acceptable and convenient time for you, we would appreciate viewing the land and buildings. At that time, we will discuss our terms.
>
> Regards,
> Emil

"Adolph, why don't we have them stay here, with us? We can put Phyl into our room and let them stay in that room for the weekend. That would give us time to know them a little better. For them, it would give an opportunity to see the land and buildings and make a decision. What do you say?" Anna read the letter to herself while she awaited Adolph's response.

"You do realize that I would have to *build* another bed!" Adolph said.

"You can do that, Adolph. I know you can!" Anna winked.

"All right. For the sale of the homestead, it is worth the task. What do we plan to do for bedding?" Adolph asked.

"I will sew together a quilt and some material for sheets. We already have a couple extra pillows. They will be fine for one weekend." Anna began to plan her menus and sat down to sew.

Adolph returned the reply to Emil and their offer of hospitality for that weekend. A decision would need to be finalized before they left to return to Washington State.

The offer was accepted. The weekend arrived. Adolph had put together the bed. Anna had sewn together a quilt and sheets and a pillow covering. Her menu was set for each day.

Emil and his wife Erika arrived on schedule. Anna had the second bedroom looking spic and span. Phyl was delighted to move in with Momma and Papa. Adolph was not as enthused about it as Phyl. The aroma of home-cooked food and the wood crackling in the stove permeated the rooms and drifted outside. Adolph welcomed the young couple into their home.

"Please, sit down here, Emil. I have a glass of wine for us that I brought from Moscow. Will you join me?" Erika joined Anna in the kitchen.

"May I help you, Anna?" Erika seemed like a warm and friendly young woman. She was a perfect age to handle the many chores that came with this very difficult way of life.

Emil discussed the work he performed and the camp conditions. "The town—the camp—is very small, Adolph."

"It could not be smaller than here, Emil. We are only three people—maybe two and one-half!" They laughed.

"There is a small grocery that handles a gas station, a bar as part of a hotel, and that is about it. My job takes me away during the week. I am home on weekends. We men sleep in bunks up in the mountains and cook our meals, taking turns. It gets lonely for the wives and families. However, they do have each other, their children, and their chores. They survive." Emil looked at Adolph to see his reaction.

"Emil, it would be no different. Here, there is no one to talk to but each other and the animals. We have no neighbors, just the forest, the lake, and the animals," Adolph said.

"Animals. What *kind* of animals, Adolph? Wild animals?" Emil asked.

Adolph decided he was not going to mention rats, bears, and other wild things. He wanted to sell the land. "Deer," Adolph responded.

"That's it? Just *deer?*" Emil looked surprised.

"Fish." Adolph thought that should be a sufficient answer for this wilderness place.

"Is the fishing good, Adolph? Does it provide?" Emil asked.

"We have plenty of venison and trout. We have eggs and chickens. The steer will be big enough soon for butchering. You might consider a pig. It looks like it is time to eat. Let's join the women in the dining room, Emil. Then, we will go look at the land. Did you bring your fishing rod?" Adolph asked.

"Yes, I did. I look forward to catching trout for breakfast." Emil joined Adolph in the dining room with Anna, Erika, and Phyl.

Lord, please hold back the bears for the weekend. Amen. Adolph silently shot up a quick prayer.

"Emil, is there a church at the camp?" Anna asked.

"I'm not sure. There might be a church there or nearby." Emil said.

"Some of the ladies have started a Bible study, Anna. Perhaps you might want to join them." Erika smiled at Anna.

It depends on what they are studying, Anna decided. *I have my catechism, Sonda Skolbok, Psalmbok, and Daily Food for Christians.*

"There is quite a diversity of religion there. Some are Catholic, Mormon, Jehovah's Witness, and Protestant." Erika offered her knowledge of the study.

"Good heavens, Erika. What do they use for study with such a diversity of religious beliefs?" Anna was dumbfounded that anything productive could come from that mixture.

"They use the King James Bible, Anna. The majority agreed on it. They just read passages and pray." Erika sipped her glass of wine.

"To whom? To whom do they pray?" Anna inquired.

"Anna, for crying out loud. What difference does it make? Just enjoy the meal!" Adolph retorted.

"To God, Anna." Erika was tired of the questions too.

When they had finished dinner, Erika and Anna cleaned the table and did the dishes while they talked. The men went out to look over the land.

"Adolph, this is absolutely beautiful! You even have a view of the mountains! Do you know which mountain range that is?" Emil stood in awe of its breathtaking view.

"Sawtooth, I think the people in town said. Very rugged. Lots of snow in the winter." Adolph was anxious to show Emil the rest and get on with the negotiations.

"Let's try out the fishing in the morning, Adolph. I want to see if they bite." Emil gave a twist of his arm as if he were already fly-fishing.

Adolph knew he must be patient with Emil until the decision was made firm in writing.

With a pretty good night's sleep—Phyl was very excited to be sleeping in the same room with her parents—they got up to face the next day with Emil and Erika. Phyl made certain her parents awakened early.

"Oh my, baby girl, you *do* rise early, don't you?" Phyl giggled with delight. She lifted her arms. "Up, Papa. Up, p'ease."

Adolph lifted her out of her crib. Anna got up, washed and dressed, and took Phyl into the kitchen. She made a pot of coffee and cooked porridge. She took the day-old bread and toasted it in the oven and placed the fresh butter and homemade jams on the table. After feeding Phyl, she sent her off to play with her toys.

Adolph came into the kitchen for a fresh cup of coffee. "Are our guests still sleeping?" he asked. "Emil wanted to go fishing."

"I believe they are awake. I heard some stirring. I think I will take this opportunity to show Erika how to quilt and sew. I wonder what they have decided." Anna washed Phyl's dishes and sat down for coffee with Adolph.

"So do I!" Adolph responded.

"Good morning, Adolph and Anna." Emil and Erika came into the kitchen. Anna handed them each a cup of coffee.

"Did you have a good rest? Breakfast is ready. We're having porridge and toast. I have some homemade butter and jam on the table." Anna put the milk into a pitcher and placed it on the table. All was ready.

"Did you still want to fish, Emil?" Adolph asked.

"All ready, Adolph. All I have to do is bait the hook." They ate and visited. Then the men excused themselves, donned their boots, and set out for the lake.

Anna and Erika washed the dishes. "I would like to show you how to make a quilt and sew. Or do you already know how?" Anna set out the materials.

"I do sew, Anna. Quilting I have never learned." The women took up their project. Erika was a quick learner. "What do you think of the homestead, Erika?" Anna pushed for an answer.

"I love it. It is perfect for us, I believe. We will see what Emil decides. We need to leave for Washington early tomorrow morning." Erika picked up her needle and thread as Anna instructed her.

The men brought in a bountiful supply of trout. They gutted them, scrubbed off the scales, and prepared them for the cooler until it was time to cook dinner.

Adolph took the scraps and buried them outside the back door.

During the night, they heard a rumbling and awoke. Emil got up to investigate the noise. So did Adolph. "Go back to bed, Emil. It is just the wind rattling things around." Adolph did *not* want Emil to see bears on the last night before he made his decision.

"Odd-sounding wind." Emil walked back to the bedroom and slept soundly until morning.

In the morning, over a breakfast of trout and fresh eggs, accompanied by toasted cardamom bread and homemade jams and fresh butter, Emil spoke.

He lifted his coffee cup and took a long swig, then placed it down on the table. "I have come to a decision, Adolph. We will accept your offer. Since this is already the end of summer, I would like to be here before winter. Have you had a response about the job yet?" Emil asked.

"Not yet, Emil. I am not concerned about the employment. I have excellent experience and skills to offer. With a house to live in and some cash to survive, I believe we will be all right." Adolph looked at Anna and winked.

Adolph made out a contract for Emil to sign. He placed two lines for "witness" where Anna and Erika could sign and a place for him to sign in agreement to accept the offer. He had a place for the date and a place to fill in for the cash amount of $500. Adolph handed the contractual agreement over to Emil to look over and sign.

Adolph and Anna watched as Emil signed the agreement. Then Adolph signed and dated it. Anna and Erika signed as witnesses.

Adolph waited.

Emil took out his wallet and handed Adolph five hundred dollars in cash.

They shook hands and loaded their vehicle. Emil expressed his thanks for the hospitality. Erika gave Anna a hug and thanked her for a wonderful weekend.

It was settled. They waved goodbye. Adolph would contact Johnn Albert for their move.

Adolph's hand was hurting badly. Something must have bitten him. *The rat!*

Doc came by that afternoon to check on Anna, but it was Adolph who needed medical attention.

"Adolph, I want you to come back with me to my office. I am going to test you for rabies. You may have to begin shots in your stomach. They are very painful, but if you do have rabies, you will die without them."

Adolph tried to argue with the doctor. He knew he could not win. The pain was excruciating. Could shots be worse?

The doctor confirmed after testing that Adolph had rabies. He began the first of many shots.

"I just sold the homestead, Doc. We will be moving by winter," Adolph said.

"Not before you complete the shots, Adolph, or there won't be any move!" Doc gave Adolph a very firm look.

Adolph went for the length of time for all the painful rabies shots. When it was over, his thoughts went elsewhere.

North Washington. The Northern Pacific Railroad? Will I have friends? Dangers? Joy? Spiritual growth? Where is stability?

Lester and Loneliness

Adolph and Anna were grateful for their return visit and stay with the Lindquist clan. Yet it seemed to be God's will for Anna to move constantly.

Lester, Washington, was a tiny town near Stampede Pass. It was located just south of Snoqualmie Pass in King County by the Northern Pacific Railway.

Adolph located the house. He took out his key and opened the squeaky door. Anna followed behind him with Phyl.

Anna took one look at the tiny house and let out, "Oooh! When Erika said it was small, she certainly did not lie! At least it has a bedroom and a bath separate from the rest of the house." There would no separate bedroom for Phyl.

"Anna, it will be a while before I begin any work here. I will begin to add on a room so we can have it for Phyl before winter and before I go to work."

They settled in. Adolph went downtown

for groceries and other supplies and greeted the owners of the businesses. He inquired about work. There seemed to be always a need for builders of the railway and snow sheds.

They busied themselves on their first night there. At sunrise, there was an abrupt knock on the door. Curious, since they knew no one yet, Adolph opened the front door. It was the sheriff's posse. He showed Adolph his badge. "You are under arrest for the robbery of the Great Northern." He placed handcuffs on Adolph and led him out of the house.

"Yust one minute! I yust arrived here yesterday from Idaho with my family. I haven't the slightest idea what you are talking about. Uncuff me, right now!"

Anna came into the living room and saw the handcuffs. "Adolph, what have you done?"

"I have not done anything, Anna. They think I am a train robber."

"Please, let my husband go!" Anna found herself yelling at the sheriff.

"You look exactly like one of the robbers. And they are still on the loose. The robbery happened not too far from here. Do you have proof of who you are?" the sheriff asked.

"Anna, get my passport. Hurry!" Adolph tried to wriggle out of the cuffs to no avail.

"Papa, who he?" Phyl ran to be by Adolph's side.

"Phyl, honey, go find Momma." Adolph did not want his daughter to see him in handcuffs, which he would have to explain.

Anna walked over to the sheriff and handed him Adolph's passport.

The sheriff looked at the passport, back at Adolph, and at the picture of the robber. "All right, Mr. Nelson." He unlocked the handcuffs and apologized. Then he showed Adolph the photo of the bandit. It was an amazing similarity.

"Very handsome man!" Adolph replied.

The sheriff laughed, tipped his hat to the family, and walked away.

"That was close! Too close! It isn't good to look like the wrong person. Maybe I should color my hair!" Adolph was half-serious.

"I could send away for a wig or make you a hat," Anna laughed.

"Papa bracelet, Momma." Phyl looked at both of them.

"Yes, baby girl, a bracelet." Anna winked at Adolph.

"Bad man took, Papa!" Phyl felt bad for her daddy.

"It's okay, Phyl. I did not like the color or the size. Let's have breakfast and get on with the day."

Adolph gathered all the lumber he could find and began to add a room onto the house. After a full week of hammering nails from dawn to dusk, he finally completed the outer walls. Then he walked to where the inside door needed to be and cut a doorway through what had once been the wall to the outside. Cleaning up the debris, he added a small closet. Next, he placed Phyl's crib in the corner with a small chair. That would do for now. Tomorrow, Adolph would paint the room and add a window. At the end of the next week, he stood back and looked at his work, satisfied it was ready for occupancy.

Anna decorated Phyl's room with pictures, a baby quilt for the bed, and a play box for her toys.

Adolph walked into town and found the supervisor for the railroad.

"I would like to place an application for employment." Adolph took out his necessary information and a pen.

"For what position?" the man at the desk asked.

"Any position," Adolph said.

"What experience do you have? We don't just take anyone!" the man retorted.

"I'm a builder. I can build railroad trestles and snow sheds. I am a Swedish immigrant. I am also a citizen of the United States. Here is my passport." Adolph handed over the necessary identification and information. "I would like to speak with the supervisor," Adolph said.

"Would you, now? Well, he ain't in right now. He'll be back about four thirty. Where can he find you?" the desk clerk asked.

"I'll find him. Four thirty. I'll be back then." Adolph took his legal documents and walked out.

"Let's have an early dinner, Anna—or a late one. I have an appointment at four thirty with the supervisor of the Northern Pacific Railroad here.

"I will have it ready by six. That should give the two of you enough time to talk. I'll feed Phyl early, bathe her, and put her down so we can talk when you come home."

"You might try one of your prayers, too, Anna. We cannot live here forever unless I have work."

"Adolph, I always pray for you. I will especially be in prayer today. You will do just fine, Adolph. I believe in your ability." Anna grabbed Adolph's hand and gave it a squeeze.

Adolph dressed for the appointment and walked up to meet the supervisor. He opened the door and introduced himself.

"My boss will be out in a minute, Mr. Nelson. Have a seat."

Adolph waited. He wondered what he was going to say. He needed to choose his words well.

"Good afternoon, Mr. Nelson. I understand you are new here and looking for work." The man reached down his hand. Adolph stood and shook hands.

"Yes, sir. My wife, child, and I have just moved here from Idaho where we had a homestead. I heard about the opportunities awaiting railroad men and decided to take my chances." Adolph waited.

"As a matter of fact, Mr. Nelson, I have a spot open right away. It will require you to be away from your family during the week. We have a bunkhouse up in the hills for the men to sleep and a chow room for their eating. Restrooms are outhouses. If this is acceptable to you, you can start tomorrow. Bring clothes for a week and all your toiletries. We provide the bed rolls. They are cleaned weekly and brought back up by mule train. You will need to be here at five a.m. tomorrow. We will transport you to the train. It will take you to the bunkhouse. From there, you will eat and ride a mule train to your work location. Is that acceptable to you, Mr. Nelson?" The supervisor held the contractual agreement in his hand.

"Yes. I will need to notify my wife. Are there any women's activities here for her?" Adolph was concerned for Anna's being alone and knowing no one.

"Does your wife go to church?" the supervisor inquired.

"It depends on the church, sir. She is of the Protestant faith." Adolph began to feel better already.

"The women meet each Wednesday morning at the little church down the road. Babysitting is provided. I believe they meet about ten a.m. to noon. She might want to start with that." The supervisor handed Adolph the contract.

Adolph signed. "See you tomorrow morning."

"Dress warm, Adolph. It gets mighty cold up there. I hope you have boots," he said.

"We homesteaded, sir. We're prepared for everything." Adolph walked back home.

He sat down with Anna and ate a delicious meal. Anna was an outstanding cook. He would miss those weekly meals. He wondered what he would be eating. Pork and beans? Probably every night!

"What did the man say, Adolph? Will you be able to work?" Anna looked quizzically over at her husband.

"Tomorrow, Anna. I start tomorrow. I will be gone all week, every week. Home on weekends." He told Anna about the church and hoped she would join the women. He placed a bunch of cash on the table. "This is for your necessities, Anna. If you need something, just take a portion of the money with you. For any emergency, it would probably be a good idea to contact the pastor. That seems the best choice for now. There is a sheriff here. I'm sorry, Anna. It's difficult for both of us. I'll try to make it up to you someday. At least we will have food on the table."

Anna looked away from her husband. Her lip began to tremble. She was used to having her husband with her every day—every minute of every day and night. And Phyl. He would not even see her except weekends. Anna did not want Adolph to see her despair.

She took Adolph's hand. "We'll make it through this, Adolph. We will scrimp and save. One thing I ask. I ask that we move to a better place when Phyl reaches school age."

"I will try to keep that promise, Anna—for all of us. I will be home each Friday night and will have to return each Monday morning. There is a bank here in town. Always keep a little cash on hand. Don't take too much with you when you go out. I will show you where you can safely hide the rest." Adolph had an ache in his heart. Homesteading looked good to him right now. Yet it had provided no income. He must have income to support his family. A few years on the railroad. He could do that.

Monday morning came. Anna rose early and fixed Adolph a hearty breakfast. She had packed a lunch for him. She kissed him goodbye and waved until she could see him no more.

Then she sat at the kitchen table, placed her head down, and bawled.

Tuesday Anna decided she would begin to teach Phyl. She began by building a children's Bible study book that she hoped to publish. She taught her the alphabet and a few numbers. Phyl responded successfully. Anna felt very fulfilled that day.

Wednesday, Anna took Phyl and walked to the little church at the opposite end of town. The pastor and women were warm and welcoming, inviting Anna into their circle of study. Phyl joined a few other small children in the nursery. Anna appreciated their taking time to hear her story. They began a study on the book of John, encouraging one another to invite those who did not know the Savior.

"Ladies, I have a question. Do you really believe that unsaved women will come to a women's Bible study inside a church?" Anna looked around at the reactions of the other ladies.

Anna continued, not waiting for a verbal response. "Ladies, what do you think about the idea of having a luncheon in our homes and offering a Bible study as a part of it? Or we could have morning coffee and refreshments. Perhaps our pastor would create a basic Bible study on the book of John that we could use. We could open it up to the community of women. What do you think?"

One lady spoke up. "Thanks for your input, Anna. However, we are used to having a study here and have been for a long time. I don't think the women want to give up what we have had." Others nodded affirmatively.

"But isn't it the point of the Bible to proclaim his Word to others?" Anna asked.

"They can come here, Anna." They seemed closed to the idea. They also seemed to miss the point.

As Anna went through the study that morning, she decided she would pick a different morning and spread an invitation to other women of the community to come to her home once a week for coffee and refreshments and a Bible study.

Adolph had warned Anna about grizzly bears coming down from the hills looking for food. They would wander the streets as if they were a part of the population.

Anna finished her morning study, picked up Phyl from the nursery, and began her trek back to the little house. When she was about halfway home, she looked up and saw a grizzly coming down from the end of town toward them. She had been warned never to panic and run. She took Phyl's hand firmly in her own and immediately opened the door to the first business she could find. Her face was ashen.

"Mommy, you hurt my hand." Phyl withdrew her hand from Anna's and shook it. "Ow!"

"I'm sorry, baby girl. There is something very bad outside that could hurt us. We must stay in here until it is safe to walk home." Anna feared the thought of stepping back out into the street and possibly facing instant death.

"Good morning, Ma'am. May I help you find anything?" the clerk asked, walking toward the two of them.

"Oh, no thank you," Anna said.

"Then I'm sorry, Ma'am, I must ask that you leave if you have no business here to attend." The clerk was extremely abrupt. That surprised Anna and gave her additional fear.

"There is a grizzly bear in the street. My child and I are walking home. Please, please let us stay here long enough for our safe walk home," Anna pleaded.

"Ma'am, I sympathize with your concern. However, I need people here who want to *buy.* I am sure you understand." The clerk firmly stood his ground.

"When we finish with you, no one will buy here," Anna said.

"That sounds very much like a threat!" The clerk's jaw tightened.

"Very astute of you!" Anna took Phyl's hand and walked out. She was scared to death and just as furious in her emotions with the clerk.

Anna looked up the street, down and across. She saw nothing. She *had* to know where that bear was before she could risk their lives. She tightened her grip on Phyl. She decided she would go from storefront to storefront. That way, if she saw it, they could dash inside. When she reached the end of the town, the situation became more dangerous for them. They must make it from the edge of town to the inside of their home. *Lord, I need your help. Please, Lord, would you send your hedge and army of angels and place them round about us as we walk. Please get us safely inside our home. In Jesus' name. Amen.*

Anna turned to Phyl. "I am going to carry you, child. I must walk quickly but not run. Jesus is sending us his angels to walk us home. Up now, in my arms, little girl." Anna took that first dangerous step away from town. She walked as slowly as she could. She finally reached the door of their home. She reached into her satchel and pulled out the key. The key would not turn. She tried again, more slowly and determined. She heard a noise and did not look behind her. She opened the door and slammed it shut, wedging a chair against the knob.

Anna looked around the kitchen to make sure no food was out that a bear could smell. She stood in the middle of the room with Phyl. Again, she heard a noise. There was something scratching at the front door. Anna did not move. She held Phyl in her arms.

"Down, p'ease," Phyl said.

"Shh, baby girl. Let's be very quiet." Anna hugged her closely.

"Why, Mommy?" Phyl looked into her momma's eyes and gave her an odd look.

"Bad animal outside." Anna rocked her back and forth.

"Animal hurt us, Mommy?" Phyl questioned.

"It could. Shh!" Anna was shaking.

The sound ceased. Anna waited awhile longer. Then, gently, she placed Phyl on the chair at the table. She reached for the sandwiches already made and in the icebox. They sat quietly and nourished themselves.

Anna turned to Phyl. She wanted to change the subject to more pleasant things. "Did you have fun this morning? Did you meet other children?"

"Yes, Momma. We talk about Jesus."

"What did you learn, Phyl? What did you learn about Jesus?" Anna asked.

"Jesus in heart."

"How?" Anna wanted to be sure the teaching was accurate.

She pointed to her heart. "We ask." Phyl looked at Anna for approval.

"Very good. Did you do that? Did anyone do that?" Anna asked.

Phyl nodded yes and smiled at Anna.

"Good girl, Phyl. Now, let's get you ready for your nap in your new room." Anna took her hand, wiped her face with a cloth, and placed her in her crib. She went to the window to close the blinds. Then she saw the grizzly. This time, though, it was running toward the woods.

Anna returned to the kitchen and cleaned up from lunch. She sat down at the table and prayed. *Lord, not only am I extremely lonely and depressed in this place, I am a prisoner in my own home. Please free me, Lord—free* us.

Anna and Phyl remained inside the house for the remainder of the week. Friday evening, Adolph returned to them. Anna shared their experiences.

"Anna, I have a terrible boss and worse working conditions. I know it is unthinkable to ask you to move again, but I am going to apply for a transfer to the Cascades to work for the Northern Pacific Railway. I would be doing the same thing. I will say it is because we want to be closer to Idaho and Moscow."

Pneumonia

Adolph's coughing had grown steadily worse as he had worked in the silver mines and had persisted even after he had changed careers.

"You must have a doctor look at your lungs, Adolph." Anna had heard him coughing ever since Mullan.

"You worry too much, Anna. I'll be yust fine!" Adolph never gave up his "y" sounds to the English "j." It was a permanent part of his Swedish heritage.

Adolph continued to cough.

"Adolph, I beg you to see a doctor. Before you begin another outdoor job, please let them look at your lungs." Anna would persist even if Adolph saw her as a nag!

"I'll go tomorrow, Anna. Now stop your worrying, *please!*"

Adolph drove into town the next morning to visit the doctor. He caught him early.

"Morning, Doc!" Adolph greeted the Coeur d'Alene doctor.

"Adolph, what brings you to my office? You are as healthy as a horse! It must be for another member of the family. What is your concern, Adolph? Please sit down."

The doctor listened to Adolph's lungs. When he finished with the stethoscope, he sat down beside Adolph.

"I want to meet you over at the hospital this afternoon to run some further tests. I am concerned about one of your lungs. One p.m., Adolph."

"Of course, Doctor. I don't see that there is that much to be concerned about though." Adolph said.

"The patient never does, Adolph. I want to be doubly sure. I do not like to guess!"

Adolph drove back home and told Anna.

"You'll be in my prayers, Adolph."

"Anna, I am not dying. I yust have a cough!" Adolph insisted.

At the hospital, the doctor met with specialists and tested Adolph's lungs.

"Adolph, I am afraid we are going to have to remove one lung. Were you ever a smoker?"

"For a while. I just smoke a pipe now. No cigars." Adolph was not excited about giving up his bad habits.

"I am scheduling you for surgery. I would tell you not to ever return to the mines. However, since Mullan burned, that will not be necessary. You can never return to that type of work again, Adolph. It is surgery or death. No more smoking. Your choice."

"I'll take the surgery. I am applying for work with the Northern Pacific Railroad in the Northern Cascades. The outdoor air should be good for me. It should clear my lungs."

"You're right, Adolph. However, nothing will save your one lung now. It must be removed."

"I begin my job next week. I do not want to lose it. I will wait. My lungs will be yust fine once I am in the fresh air. If I still have a problem, I will let you know, Doc. Thank you." Adolph started for the door.

"You do have a wife and child to think about, too, Adolph." Adolph's mind was on provision. Protection would take care of itself.

The work was difficult and demanding. Anna knew many months of loneliness. What a difference from a small town to a big city, then to a mining town and now total isolation. Thank God for her little girl to bring her comfort.

Adolph loved his work in the Cascades, near Spokane. Anna longed for people and conversation.

It was Thanksgiving Eve. She had spent the day cutting the kindling and stoking the fire for the living room and kitchen stoves. She was grateful for the turkey given to them by Adolph's company. The rest of the meal they had grown or she had canned and prepared for the family. Everything was ready. It was past time for Adolph to come home.

Anna watched as the sun descended beyond the hills. She stoked the fire and checked the meal, which was getting overly-done.

No Adolph.

Anna fed Phyl and read to her in the rocker.

Still no Adolph.

It was now dark. Anna placed Phyl down on the rug with some toys. She heard a thud at the door and ran to open it.

"Adolph! Adolph! What's wrong?"

Adolph dropped inside the doorway, exhausted.

Anna helped him to the bed. By morning, he was no better. She placed Adolph, Phyl, and herself in the family automobile and drove to Spokane's hospital. They rushed Adolph into emergency and called the doctor.

"Anna, Adolph has a very severe pneumonia. Another day, I believe he would have died. We saw on his chart that he was supposed to have a lung removed. We will be doing that now. He will be in the hospital for several weeks recovering. Do you have a place to stay?"

"Yes, I will call my Aunt Mary. She will put us up for a while. I must contact Adolph's employers and let them know."

Mary was delighted to see them, yet she was sorry for the news about Adolph's health. "Anna, he might not be allowed to return to the Cascades. I think you had better plan on another move and another line of work for Adolph. I'm sorry."

"Mary, it would be a relief. It is so lonely there, I cannot stand another year of it."

The doctor called Anna into his office. Adolph was recovering nicely and should be able to go home in a few days. That was the good news. The bad news was that he could never return to work in the Northern Cascades. He needed sunshine.

Adolph and Anna returned to the mountain cabin and collected their belongings. He found a place for them to stay in Spokane. They would live on their savings. Anna knew very well how to scrimp and save.

Mary kindly accepted them into her boardinghouse until Adolph could find gainful employment elsewhere.

It was now 1914.

Anna had given birth to another beautiful baby girl. She looked just like Adolph. They named her Harriet. She had straight fly-away, tow-headed blonde hair and the bluest eyes. They were like the ice blue of Crater Lake, nestled in and formed from a volcano that erupted many years ago and imploded. Anna was pleased that Phyl and Harriet could grow up together as playmates.

Adolph read the news and discussed it with Anna, Mary, and the boarders.

"America has entered the war—the Great War, they are calling it. It is worldwide. Anna, we received a letter from your father. Albert has been called into service. He needs our prayers and support. We can send food packages to him. Because of my health and the fact that I have family, I am not being asked to serve."

"How is Papa doing? This news must be devastating to him. After all, there are more sons than just Albert. Elfin's health is too frail. The others could be called, too. Why must men war with one another? Why can't they get along or settle their differences peacefully?"

"Your papa is concerned, Anna. He is surrounded by family, church, and friends. He will be all right." Adolph laid down the paper and grabbed his spoon.

"Mary, this tomato soup is delicious. It feels good on my lung. Good hot broth!" Adolph savored every sip and let it slip slowly down his achy throat.

Adolph looked for work daily. His concerns grew as their funds lowered. They had plenty. However, wherever they moved, he wanted to be able to buy a home for the three of them.

"Anna? Anna! What's wrong with you? Are you ill?" Adolph caught her as she nearly dropped to the floor.

"I'm not ill, Adolph. I believe I am pregnant."

Adolph saw it as a financial disaster. Anna saw it as a blessing. She hoped for another little girl to grow up with Phyl and Harriet.

Adolph found some part-time employment with carpentry in the city. That would keep their savings in tact.

They would remain in Spokane at least until after the baby was born. Adolph might have to go on ahead if he found work.

Anna knitted and sewed for the baby. Names. What would they choose for a name? She decided on Peggy.

At Home and Abroad

Peggy came into the world in 1916. She looked like Adolph. She was tiny and sickly. Her health was a constant concern to Anna.

A letter arrived from Elfin.

Dearest Anna,

I am excited to inform you that I have been accepted to play for the Paul Whiteman band. Just in case you are not familiar with his music, he is the number one jazz band at present! He started out playing viola for the Denver and San Francisco Symphonies. He also played in a navy band during the war. Now, he is into ragtime jazz. He is one of the best-known bandleaders, Anna. I am so proud to be a part of his group. I feel honored. Some find his music controversial—a sign of the times. Times are changing. I trust everything is well with you, Anna.

You probably heard about my marriage—

or rather, divorce. I married a lovely girl from Montana a few years ago. She did not approve of my travels and left to return to her mountainous home. Since then, I seemed to have made a turn for the worse in my health. I do not mean to burden you with my problems, only the good news of the Paul Whiteman band. He is becoming a national icon.

I am in hopes that you might write me soon. It is exciting times. It does get lonely, though.

Your loving brother,
Elfin

It was now 1917.

The men were coming home from war, seeking employment and places to live. Mary's boardinghouse was filling up fast.

Mary fixed breakfast and was just cleaning up the dishes when she heard a call from upstairs.

She walked quickly up the stairway toward the sound of the voice.

"Anna, Adolph, come quickly!" she called back down the stairs.

Adolph bolted up the stairs.

"Call Doc Adams. Karl is so pale. He is regurgitating everything. There is blood coming up and he has diarrhea."

Adolph rushed back downstairs to the phone.

"Anna. Stay down here. I do *not* want you upstairs for any reason. One of the men is very ill. I'm calling the doctor.

"Doctor's office," the receptionist answered on the other end of the line.

"Please send Doc Adams over to Mary Olson's boardinghouse right away. We have a very sick man here who needs attention." Adolph tried to sound as emphatic as he could.

"I'm sorry, Doc Adams has been on calls all morning. I don't know when he will return."

"Do you have another doctor there? Will Doc Adams phone in? We have an emergency."

"I expect the doctor to phone when he can. He has had an unusually heavy schedule out of the office this morning. Give me your number, and I will have him call."

Adolph looked at the number on the wall and relayed it back to the office girl.

"Adolph!" Mary was calling from upstairs. "Can you come up and help? Did you call the doctor?"

Adolph raced back up the stairs. Karl was heaving uncontrollably. He was so pale. He fainted on the floor. Adolph pulled him up onto the bed.

"Is the doctor on his way, Adolph?"

"No, Mary. He is not on his way. He is not even in the office. The girl said he would call. She also mentioned that he has been out on numerous calls just this morning."

Another one of Mary's boarders, JoAnna, began to vomit and groan.

There was a knock on the door. Doc Adams did not wait for someone to answer it.

"Doc Adams here!"

"Up here, Doctor. Hurry!" Mary yelled from the top of the stairway.

Doc Adams opened his kit as he walked over to Karl. Doc was wearing a facial mask.

"He's dead, Mary. Your boarder has expired. Adolph, would you call the morgue? Mary, you must act quickly and scrub down everything with disinfectant. Throw away the sheets and his clothing. Open the windows and air out the room."

"Doctor, there is another boarder who is also ill." Mary pointed down the hallway.

JoAnna lay in her bed moaning. She was as white as the sheets upon which she lay.

"JoAnna? I am Doc Adams. Are you able to tell me what you are experiencing right now?" The doctor tested her lungs and heart. "I am going to send you to the hospital, JoAnna. Adolph, would you make a call to the hospital for me? Have them pick up this lady."

"Mary, you must do to this room what you have done to the other." Doc treated JoAnna and left for his next call.

It was called the Spanish influenza pandemic and lasted through 1919, causing fifty million deaths around the world. It was exceptionally severe. Nearly one person in every household lost a life to the devastating epidemic.

Soldiers returning home from The Great War, exhausted from their tour of duty, and in much need of rest and recuperation, were met with the horrifying and devastating disease. Many who had survived the trenches did not survive this disease.

Harriet

"Harriet has the flu," the doctor explained. Harriet's flu went on for several weeks without improvement.

Harriet was just a tiny child of three—soon to be four.

"Mommy, my head hurts. My neck won't turn very well. Please turn down the lights, Mommy, my eyes hurt." Harriet was vomiting continually. It seemed as if she was complaining about her whole body.

The doctor said she has the flu. He should know. After all, he is the doctor. It has just been going on for such a long time and it does not get better, Anna thought.

"Adolph, Harriet is so feverish. I am very worried about her. She just wants to sleep. She throws up anything I try to feed her. She seems confused. It just does not seem to want to go away—or even diminish. I'm scared, Adolph."

Adolph wanted a second opinion—anything to make his beautiful little blue-eyed towhead better. The hospital doctor examined Harriet.

"Adolph, Anna," the doctor began. "Harriet has spinal meningitis. She is gravely ill."

Little Harriet who always said, "Don't worry about me, Momma," as she rode her tricycle down the sidewalks of Spokane, "I can find my way home. I count the light posts!" Harriet was not responding to treatment.

"I wish you could have brought her in earlier," the doctor said to Adolph.

"We didn't because our doctor kept saying she had the flu. We believed his diagnosis until Harriet did not respond to his treatment." Adolph hung his head and stared at the floor.

"I want you to go home. I will call you every few hours and keep you posted." The doctor spoke to both of them.

"Thank you, Doctor. We will be praying for our baby girl continually." Anna's face was tearful. She took Adolph's hand and called for Phyl to follow her.

It was a long and silent drive home, though the distance was not far. Phyl asked when Harriet was coming home. Adolph and Anna chose their words carefully.

"When she is well, Phyl." Adolph could only give her a brief answer.

The doctor called every few hours as promised. Harriet was not improving.

Two days passed. The doctor called and asked for Adolph. Anna called him to the phone while she looked on, deeply concerned.

For the first time in Anna's life she saw Adolph cry. He sobbed. Anna picked up the phone, "Doctor? How is Harriet?"

"Anna, Harriet just died." Anna heard no more. She dropped the phone. Her wails could be heard throughout the house. Phyl came running to her momma's side.

"Mommy, what's wrong?" Phyl looked up into her mother's tear-strained eyes.

"Your sister will not be coming home any more."

"Mommy, why? Doesn't Harriet like it here?"

"She did not get well, Phyl. Harriet died."

"What's *died,* Mommy?"

"Phyl, remember when your kitty cat was hit by a car and it did not breathe anymore?" Anna tried to explain death to her and could hardly speak.

"Yes, Mommy. Did Harriet get hit?"

"No, Phyl. She just stopped breathing. She is with Jesus now. He is taking care of her until we see her again."

"Is she coming back, Mommy? Will she come back and see us?" Phyl was trying to picture all of this in her mind.

"Phyl, we will see her again, someday. When we die, Phyl, we will go to be with Jesus, too. He will bring us together with Harriet. We will not see her again here. No more questions today, Phyl."

"But, Mommy, *why* are you crying if we will see her again?" Phyl continued.

"We will talk about it again another time, Phyl. No more today. I am crying because we cannot see her again right now. We must wait." Anna was too distraught to continue the question and answer session. She knew her child's questions were justified, but so was her deep grief.

She decided to take Phyl to God's Word, to Ecclesiastes 3: "…a time to be born and a time to die…" and to the Psalms where David says he will see his dead son again, that the son cannot come to him, but he will go to the son. It would help *both* of them, she hoped. "Phyl, I believe David was saying that God takes babies to heaven. They cannot return to us. We can someday go to be with them when we die."

"Are we going to die, Mommy?"

"Someday, child. Someday every person dies."

"Do they all go to heaven, Mommy?"

Anna felt exhausted from Phyl's unending questions. Yet this was a good opportunity to explain life and death issues to her child, especially when they were experiencing it.

"Some go to heaven, Phyl. Some do not. God the Father sent Jesus the Son to earth to die on the cross for the sins of all of us. Jesus did not sin. We did. We were born that way. We had no way to do anything about it, but Jesus did. Jesus gave us a choice to either believe in him and what he did for us on that cross, or to reject him and the cross. If we accept his offer of forgiveness, he forgives us and saves us. Otherwise, those who reject him go to a place of eternal darkness. Do you understand, Phyl?"

"I think so, Mommy. I believe in Jesus."

"So do I, child." Anna hugged Phyl close to her. *God, please save this child. Please keep her well and safe and save her for your heavenly home. I know it must be* her *decision to accept you or reject you.*

The next few months were difficult for all of them. Anna took each of Harriet's items and gave them to the church for others to wear and use.

Moving again. It helped Anna emotionally to be removed physically from difficult memories. She knew, however, that grief over Harriet would always follow her.

Ocean Breezes

It was 1921.

Adolph had applied for the position to supervise the building of the Chetco River Bridge in Brookings, Oregon.

"They hired me, Anna! They need me there next week. I will go down ahead of you and the girls and find a home for us. Please advertise the furnishings for sale and pack. I will send for you as soon as I can."

Adolph found a little house in Harbor. It was just what they needed. He had fresh air, sunshine, and best of all, he had warmth and the healing touch of salty air in his lung.

Anna sold everything, packed, and got the girls ready to travel. Mary and her husband drove them to the train. The girls were now in the first and fifth grades. Adolph would meet them in Portland and drive them along the Oregon Coast highway to Brookings.

"It's a perfect fishing spot, Anna. We'll pack a lunch while the girls are in school and row out until we get our catch."

"I don't know, Adolph. That's really taking a chance trying to get back before the girls come home."

"Anna, you worry too much! We will have plenty of time. And we'll have fish for dinner tonight!"

They parked the car by the dock and took a rowboat into the bay waters near the ocean.

"The tide is out, Anna. We will be fine. Just a few hours and we will quit and come home with our catch!" Adolph placed Anna, his equipment, the lunch, Thermos, and blankets in the boat and began to row out.

They fished for several hours, finally catching their limit.

The tide changed. A riptide—unnoticed—began to pull the rowboat out to sea. They fought the pulling waters.

"Keep rowing, Anna. We must get this boat turned around and headed back to shore." Adolph was rowing fervently and feverishly to overcome the pull of the tide.

"The children!" Anna could not help but fear death and loss.

"Keep rowing, Anna. Together. We must work together to turn the boat around."

Anna fought with all her strength. She took the extra set of oars to work both sides.

"We're making progress, Anna. The boat is beginning to turn around!" Adolph felt such relief. "Keep rowing. Harder, Anna!"

Hours passed. Dusk was beginning to set in. They lost the progress they had made. The riptide was winning.

"Pray, Adolph. Pray that our girls are safe. Pray that we can turn around or that someone will see us. Maybe someone will miss us and come looking." Anna's fear gave her extra adrenaline to row harder.

Peggy and Phyl were home from school. They searched the house and yard. No Papa or Momma.

"Why would they leave us, Phyl? Maybe they don't want us anymore." Peggy clung to her sister.

"Don't be silly, Peggy. Papa and Momma would not leave us. They love us! How strange. They are always here. Momma always has supper ready."

"I'm hungry, Phyl. I want something to eat." Phyl thought it was just like a six-year-old to think of her stomach first!

"I'll fix us a sandwich as soon as I find the peanut butter. Here is a glass of milk to get you started, Peggy. There's an apple over there for your dessert. I want you to stay right here and eat your supper."

"Where are you going, Phyl?" Peggy did not want to lose her parents *and* her sister.

"I'll be right back. I am going to check with the neighbors to see if they know anything. Stay put."

Phyl went from door to door, inquiring of each if any had seen their parents.

"I saw them go out to the car this morning with their fishing gear and lunches. What can we do to help?"

"Do you know where they went to fish?" Phyl was desperate for some immediate answers. Her parents might be in great danger.

"No. We'll get our coats. You and Peggy can go with us while we look."

Phyl went back home, grabbed a sandwich and milk, and told Peggy to get her coat. She told her they were going to look for Momma and Papa. And pray.

What would I do, thought Phyl, *if I lost my parents? How would we survive?*

"Look, Adolph!" They could see the lights of the harbor and Brookings in the background. "Row toward the light!" They continued to row. They were so exhausted.

"I don't know if I have the strength to keep on rowing, Anna. I am so tired."

"What choice is there, Adolph? It's that or die. Think of the children. Then, you will."

A light began to appear in the distance. It was slowly coming closer.

"Adolph! They're going to hit us. They can't see us. We have no light!" Anna was frantic.

Adolph took his flashlight and pointed it in the direction of the other boat. He flashed it on, then off, then on again. He continued to do this until the flashlight began to dim. The boat continued to move forward in their direction. Again, Adolph tried to use the flashlight. The battery had died. Panic struck his heart.

"Good heavens, Anna, they're going to ram us!"

Anna reached into her bag and pulled out some long matches. She struck one against the side of the box.

"Cup your hand around this, Adolph, so the wind does not blow it out." Adolph took his hand and placed it around the lit match so the light would shine toward the oncoming boat. Anna continued to light match after match.

A foghorn sounded and repeated itself. They had been seen! The boat slowed and changed its path to come alongside theirs.

"Is there anyone aboard?" they heard someone yell from the deck.

"Over here!" Adolph shouted.

Pulling alongside them, they dropped anchor. Next, they dropped a rope ladder. One by one, two of the men climbed down the ladder and extended a hand, first to Anna, then to Adolph. They helped each of them climb into their boat, then secured Adolph's boat alongside their own to tow. Reaching shore, the men assisted Adolph and Anna onto the dock.

"You two are very lucky. You could easily have gone out to sea. No one would have ever known you were there." The captain spoke to them sympathetically.

"God knew we were there, gentlemen. He was watching over us and protecting us. He brought you to us. We have two daughters waiting for us at home. I'm sure by now they are very frightened—and hungry!" Adolph was not going to accept a reprimand from this "prophet of doom." He knew that God had answered his and Anna's prayers.

"We're eternally grateful to all of you for your help to us. Now, we must hurry and get back home to our daughters and dinner!" Adolph shook hands with each of the crew. Anna gave the captain a big hug.

They threw their belongings into the trunk and climbed into the car. As they approached home, they could see lights in the windows. *The girls are home and safe. Thank God for their safety and protection.*

"We're home, girls! Phyl? Peggy? We're here!"

No one responded. Where could they be? Adolph was so exhausted. He did not want to go looking for them. He just wanted to eat and to rest.

Anna began to make phone calls to neighbors with brief explanations to each about their adventure.

"Adolph," Anna began, "the girls have gone with one of the neighbors to the dock. What should we do?"

"You stay here, Anna. I'll take the car and drive down there, look around, and come home." Adolph grabbed his coat and hat and walked out.

Anna began preparing some dinner. She prayed for their quick reunion.

"Momma!" The girls came running to her waiting arms. "Oh, Momma. We thought we had lost you. Where's Papa?"

Anna hugged them tightly, not wanting to release them. "He's out looking for you down by the dock. He said he would be right back. Come now, girls, help me with dinner. We'll talk about the whole ordeal when Papa arrives."

"We prayed for you and Papa." Peggy looked up at her mother with fearful eyes and tears.

"Yes, Peggy, I know. God answered them, and we are here. Thank you. You were both very brave. I'm proud of both of you."

Adolph came bounding in, looked around, and seeing the girls, dropped into a chair, exhausted and relieved.

He wondered, *What would these little children have done if we had not come home? Who would care for them in their absence?* Then he realized, that was not an option. *When God answers a prayer, there is no Plan B!*

Anna and the History Lesson

The months of bridge-building passed. The bridge over the Chetco River was a work of art and an asset to the community. Its completion brought an end to Adolph's work there.

The girls walked home from school on their last day of school. Their minds were totally occupied with summer activities and how they were going to get everything in before school began in the fall.

They did not see the two men walking behind them, exposing themselves.

The men came alongside each of the girls.

Phyl looked at Peggy.

"Run!"

The girls ran down the street toward their home.

The men—startled that the girls had gotten away from them—began running after them.

The gap was closing between them.

They were nearly home now.

The phone rang, and Anna answered it. "Oh, Ericka, thank you for telling me." Anna hurried out the door and ran toward the girls. The girls looked up, startled that their mother was not inside waiting for their return with cookies and milk as usual. Phyl was crying.

"Momma!"

Peggy grabbed her sister's hand. Together they ran to meet Anna.

The two men turned and ran off.

"Momma, did you see those men?" Peggy asked.

"Yes, girls, I saw them. Come along. You are safe now. Let's go inside." Anna grabbed their little hands and led the way.

When Adolph arrived, she told him about the incident. Adolph decided it was time to leave Harbor. He had already applied for work in Portland with the Northern Pacific Railroad.

"Pack up, Anna. We're going up north to look for a house. It is time to find new territory."

To Anna, it simply meant another move, another home, another school, and new friends. How she longed for roots. Permanency. Anywhere.

They sat down for a last meal in their seacoast home. Adolph turned on the Sunday sports on the radio that Anna had given him on his last birthday. Grantland Rice was at the microphone reiterating the first world series. The first World Series had been October 4, 1903. Twenty-five thousand had been in attendance. Boston played Pittsburgh. Boston won. He heard that was a great game. The score was topsy-turvy. Unfortunately for Pittsburgh, it was on their home turf!

"Adolph, I was just reading some statistics about things that were going on during the early years of this century. Washington's population was 581,103; Idaho was 161,722; and Oregon had a census of 413,536. Pretty evenly distributed, except for Idaho. It's a good thing we moved there and had Phyl, just to help it grow!" she chuckled.

"I think it is the mining that helped it grow, Anna." Adolph laughed heartily. "But the fire of Mullan did not help increase its statistics." Adolph remembered how they had barely escaped with their lives. He turned away from Anna to wipe away a trickling tear. After all, his father had always told him that men don't cry.

Adolph gave Anna another remembrance.

"Remember the World Fair in St. Louis in 1904? Do you still recall the song, 'Meet Me in St. Louis'? Anna, can you sing those words? I first heard that song, Anna, when I attended the World's Fair. It was packed. There were so many, many exhibits of every kind, people from all over the United States and different countries. It was unforgettable. If there is ever another one, Anna, I will take you.

"My sister had accompanied me to North Dakota because we had relatives who also had emigrated from Sweden. My sister married, but when I decided to leave for Spokane, she returned to Sweden—just the opposite arrangement from our decision when we left Laholm.

"It was after that, Anna, that I worked some odd jobs around the area and then booked the train for Spokane. The rest is history!" They giggled and their eyes met. Memories passed between them, unspoken and cherished.

"The Seattle expo was in 1909. I read where one of the games was a contest to guess one's weight. There was a scale. Before the person stepped on the scale, the operator would guess the person's weight. If he failed to guess within three pounds, the game was free to the participant. It was so close by, I would have loved to have gone. Work kept me from it. Seattle has such an interesting history. Did you know that it was named after an Indian chief, Anna?" Adolph looked to Anna for her expression.

"No, I did not. I'm sure I missed that with my lack of high

school education." Again, Anna felt more than slighted by a lack of education. She felt intimidated by Adolph's vast knowledge and having to explain everything to her as if she were a child.

"Well, Anna, it is time to clean things up and get going. It's about a six-hour drive. We will spend the night in Portland and then look for a home near the city. Are the girls ready?"

"Momma, Momma!" Peggy yelled for Anna. "I don't feel good, Momma."

Anna came running to her side. She looked at her ill child and fear consumed her.

Peggy at Death's Door

"Doctor, this is Adolph Nelson. Peggy is very ill. I prefer *not* to take her out of the house. Can you come over right away?" Adolph was pacing the floor. It was her *heart* that paced in Anna.

Dr. Dennison arrived within the hour. He examined Peggy and prescribed some medicine for her.

"This should help calm her down. If she isn't better in a couple of days, give me a call. I might have you bring her into the office," Dr. Dennison said.

Adolph had decisions to make. He was all packed and ready to move. He had a daughter who was ill. It was already past midday.

"Anna, I am not going to call Dr. Dennison any further. Wrap Peggy warmly. I will make a little bed in the back of the car. You and the girls can sit back there. We are leaving for Portland immediately and will check out a specialist if she is worse. Better pack some overnight clothing for yourself and Phyl and me."

In Portland, Adolph stopped to see if Peggy was better or worse. She had thrown up several times along the way. Her forehead felt as if it was burning up. Adolph drove straight to a hospital. "I have a gravely ill child. We have been traveling all day. I want her examined by a specialist immediately."

"Bring her in. We'll see if we can find a doctor for you."

"Peggy is a very sick child," the doctor said, after examining her. The doctor told them the name of the disease, but it was so long and complicated, they forgot it the moment they heard it. "And it is very rare," the doctor continued. "My advice: take her home, make her comfortable. She is too far gone to make her better. Prepare yourselves for the worst. I am very sorry." The doctor tried to comfort Anna who was nearly hysterical. Adolph stood abruptly to his feet.

"Anna, I will search for a specialist until we find the right one. We will *not* lose Peggy!" Through much insistence, Adolph convinced the doctor to leave Peggy under hospital care. She would be better off there in an emergency.

"Adolph, find Phyl and me an apartment close enough where I can walk to the hospital."

Adolph complied. He then found three specialists who agreed to work with Peggy. Then, he focused his attention on finding them a home, settling in their furnishings, and contacting his new employer.

Leaving Anna and Phyl comfortably settled in their new apartment near the hospital, he said he would be house-hunting and would return by nightfall.

Anna called Emmanuel Hospital in Portland, Oregon, and asked for her sister Selma, who was employed there as head nurse.

"Anna! How wonderful to hear your voice. What are you doing in Portland?"

Anna explained everything in detail. "Selma, will you look in on Peggy? Phyl and I will be there as soon as we can get settled here this afternoon. Please call me immediately if there are any changes—either way!"

Selma promised.

Adolph found an ad for a home in Metzger. He called the sellers and met them at the house. He was satisfied that it was a good buy. He next went to the bank and transferred funds from Brookings and gave a down payment. Then he contacted his employer. They wanted him to begin work Monday. He explained about his sick child. "Monday," his employer stated firmly.

Anna took Phyl and walked to the hospital. Peggy was getting worse.

"Anna, there is nothing more we can do. The other specialists concur. Peggy is too ill to recover. Do you want to keep her here?" The doctor took Anna's hand and expressed his sorrow.

"I am taking her home. I will care for her myself! She is *not* going to die, Doctor. She is *not!*"

"I will send her there by ambulance, Anna. Here are medications you can give her and a prescription to refill them. I wish you well. You may call me anytime."

Anna and Phyl went home to the apartment.

"Mommy, is God a doctor?" Phyl looked up into her mother's tearful eyes.

"Why, yes, Phyl. He is." She said it to comfort Phyl, but did she really believe it herself?

"Then he could make Peggy well, Momma, couldn't he?" Phyl waited for an answer.

"If that is his will." *What is God's will? Harriet died. Did he want Peggy, also?* Anna wasn't certain she wanted to know his answer.

"Then why don't we pray, Momma, and ask him?"

"All right, Phyl. You pray. I'm too upset." Anna knew that was not good mentoring, but it was how she felt right then.

Phyl took her mother's hand and began praying a very childlike, simple prayer to her heavenly Father and called him a doctor. When she finished, she looked at Anna and smiled.

"Peggy is going to get well, Momma. God said so." Anna gave Phyl a big hug. She wished her beliefs were as simple and strong as her little girl's.

The ambulance delivered Peggy to the apartment, and the two gentlemen placed Peggy into her little bed, which Adolph had put together before he left. Anna thanked them and went to her daughter's side.

Anna began to whisper to Peggy. There was no movement or response.

Adolph came in late that evening. He brought with him a huge lunch from Rose's Restaurant. He even had a huge slice of cake—their specialty. "Did you know they put gelatin in their icing to keep it stiff and flavorful?" He then knelt by Peggy's bed. "Any changes?"

"None."

Anna stayed by Peggy's side through the night, while Adolph cleaned up the apartment and readied Phyl's room so she could go to bed.

Anna listened as she heard whimpers occasionally from Peggy. She medicated her, wiped her brow, and gave her broth and tepid water.

After several days, Anna awoke to Peggy's crying for her mother. Anna sleepily looked down at her daughter. The fever had broken.

"I'm hungry, Momma." That was the best news Anna could have heard.

Anna continued to feed her broth, with bits of bread in it. She put a salve on Peggy's mouth to ease her fever-blistered lips. She gathered her up in a blanket and placed her in a chair while she changed the bedding.

Several more days went by before Peggy could sit up by herself. Anna walked her a little bit at a time around the apartment.

"Anna," Adolph began "I have the house ready for us to move in. Do you think Peggy is well enough to make the trip?"

Anna nodded.

"Where are we, Mommy?" Peggy asked, looking around her new home.

"We are near the city of Portland, in your new home."

"Why didn't Papa like the other home?" Anna looked at Peggy and laughed.

"Peggy, dear, your papa finished his work there. Now, he has a new job near here. And you, Peggy, have a new home, a new school, and soon you will have new friends."

"Are we near the beach and the ocean?" Peggy inquired.

"No, but we *are* near the zoo!" Anna waited for Peggy's questions.

"What's a zoo, Momma?"

"That is where they keep animals so people can pay to go see them. You just get well and we will go there."

Peggy was up and walking very soon.

Once again, Anna knelt and thanked God that his will had been to save her child.

The Squirrel Cage

Phyl and Peggy spent the rest of the school year in Metzger. Anna liked her house. It had been an atrocious mess when she moved in. Wilhelmina had trained her to excel in homemaking skills. She could take any kind of ugly house and make it into a comfortable, livable home.

One day, Adolph came to Anna and said, "Anna, we will be moving to Linnton, just outside of Portland. I will be closer to my work that way. Get packed, Anna."

"God, you and I need to talk," Anna mumbled to herself through her tears. "I want to be settled. This is not good for me, for the girls, and not even good for my husband to move and move and move again. Please, God, find us a place where we can live and stay—where all of us can have roots and friendships that last."

"Good evening, Anna, girls." Adolph came rushing through the Metzger home door. "Here, Anna, I will help you get packed. We will go house-hunting in Linnton. When we find what we want, I am going to take all of us to dinner and a movie in Portland! How does that sound to each of my family?"

What makes Adolph so cheerful under such irritating circumstances? Anna bit her lower lip and tried to be cheerful for the sake of the family.

Up the hill they went when they arrived at Linnton. Straight up a high hill. The home was for sale at a price Adolph could afford. Anna looked through the house. It was filthy. It was tattered and torn with newspaper on the walls.

"Oh!" She turned away from its awful appearance. Adolph had already negotiated with the owners for its sale. *Adolph,* she thought, *How can you keep doing this to us? Do I have the will to keep fixing up filthy, rundown homes and then moving from them again?*

"Anna!" Adolph called to her from the dining room where he had just signed the papers for its purchase. "Anna, welcome to our new home!"

"Uh-huh." Anna turned away and coughed. There was dust everywhere—and trash.

Phyl began the sixth grade, walking from atop the high hill down to the busy highway and to the school. She was so scared every day. Anna met her at the bottom of the hill at the close of each school day, so she would not have to walk alone *up* the hill, too.

Adolph's job was ending. A letter arrived in the mail. The girls had just come home from school. Anna began fixing supper.

"A letter for you, Adolph, from Vernonia."

"Dinner smells wonderful, Anna. What are we having tonight? I'm starving! Will you be including a dessert for us, too?"

"Roast beef, roasted potatoes and carrots. Fresh green beans for our green vegetables that I just had Phyl pick from the garden. They were so good at stemming them for the pot. I put in a little fresh bacon and some chopped onion. I have fresh tomatoes from the garden, too. For dessert, I have Swedish Fruit Soup (Fruktsoppa).

Anna poured the fruit soup over a delicious rice pudding. It was almost a meal in itself! Anna always did her best to cook what Adolph loved. Whatever he liked the most was what she always served. He especially loved dishes that represented Sweden. She tried her best to duplicate these and introduce him to the American dishes as well.

Did he love her? She had always mulled that over in her heart and mind ever since their hurried wedding plans. He did not ever say it. She longed to know.

"Adolph, what does the letter from Vernonia say?"

"They are ready for me to supervise the building of the railroad trestles and to do some logging and building of snow sheds for the coastal highway. You know, Anna, you have never complained no matter how many times we have had to move. I thank you for that."

If you only knew! Anna thought. "How much time do we have, Adolph? Will the girls be able to finish school here?"

"They'll adjust just fine, Anna. Quit worrying. They have asked me to be head of the Oregon American Lumber Company. I need to be there by September. That gives us the summer to move and find a new home. We'll find a place near Vernonia. Then we can move into town."

"That's *two* moves, Adolph."

"We'll be settled soon, Anna. Be patient."

"Uh-huh." Anna turned away.

During those years since Mullan, Anna had suffered several miscarriages. *Where are my other babies, Lord? Will I ever see them? Have you named them? Are they with you?* Anna suffered grief from every loss. She loved those unnamed children. She yearned for the chance to

know them, name them, raise them, love them, and pamper them. *Would they recognize me if I could see them someday?* Anna prayed that God would allow her that privilege. *You must have had something you wanted them to do for you in heaven,* Anna thought. She also grieved for Harriet. She hoped to see her again someday, too.

Life seems to mean a lifetime of blessings and tragedies, Anna thought. *It is a play. We are the characters. Life is full of scenes and acts. What is its final curtain?*

"Will this be the last time, Momma?" Phyl asked. "Will I have to keep leaving my friends?"

"Your papa says we will have one more move. Pray for a place to settle down, dear daughter." Anna realized *she* had no friends. She did not even have any neighbors. She longed for just one special, lasting friendship outside her family. What would that be like?

Adolph found a rather run-down house in Trehorn, near Vernonia. The girls would go to Pleasant Hill School, a one-room schoolhouse up on the hill.

Adolph was working in the woods one day when a lightning strike caught some trees on fire. It was only late spring. However, the leaves were already tinder dry. He recalled the conditions that set off the Mullan fire and became concerned. Mullan had begun with a lightning strike. He knocked on a neighbor's door and called the fire department.

Adolph shared his concern with Anna. "There is another side to forest fires—the animals. Let me tell you about this one. I saw a mother squirrel carrying her baby by the neck, running as fast as its little legs could go. I was about to do the same thing. The mother squirrel dropped the baby and continued on its way. It never looked back. I picked up the baby squirrel and carried it in my coat pocket while I, too, ran out of the woods. Here, Anna, is the baby squirrel." Adolph pulled the nervous little critter out of his pocket.

"I'm going to build a cage and have it ready when the girls get home. Do you think you could hold onto it while I build, Anna?" Adolph began looking for his tools.

Anna had cared for many babies, but never a squirrel!

"Yes, Adolph, I'll try. What shall I feed it?"

"Get some nuts and seeds, Anna. That should keep it occupied until I finish."

Anna petted the baby squirrel as if it were her own child. It was so cute and helpless.

Adolph sawed and nailed until he completed his project. He carved out a little wheel and placed it inside the cage. Anna placed a tiny container for water and another for food.

The girls came running home, ready to share their school-day events with Adolph and Anna.

"Girls, I have a little surprise for you two!" Adolph announced and waited.

"Oh, it's so *cute!*" Phyl screamed.

"May I hold it, Papa? I'll be careful!" Peggy was feeling especially motherly.

"Don't squeeze it, Peggy. It's just a tiny little baby. Be *sure* you watch out for the cat. Cats eat squirrels!"

"Don't worry, Momma. We'll be really careful." Peggy felt like she had just given birth.

Peggy gently placed the squirrel into its new home and giggled as she watched it play.

"It needs a name!" Phyl now took charge.

"What should we call it, Phyl?" Peggy looked up to her big sister.

"Pete! We'll call it Pete!"

Anna had a quilt she had made several years ago to put on the bed. It had a hole in it from so many washings.

"Peggy, let's put Pete on the quilt and let it run around. We'll watch it carefully—and the cat!"

Pete had a great time until he found the hole in the quilt.

Phyl and Peggy watched as Pete scrambled furiously around the inside of the quilt. It ran and ran and ran. Finally, after what seemed like hours, it found the hole again and crawled out. The girls were relieved it didn't suffocate.

The girls threatened the cat within an inch of its nine lives! It didn't dare get near Pete.

One day Adolph was walking through the house, totally preoccupied with his thoughts. He never saw Pete. He stepped on him and crushed his tiny skull. Pete died instantly.

Phyl and Peggy cried. Adolph cried too. Anna comforted them all.

Phyl found a matchbox. She placed some soft cotton inside and placed Pete on the cotton, closing the matchbox. She recalled the stories of her mother's birth and that she had been so small, she could have slept inside the matchbox.

Then Phyl dug a hole in the ground and buried Pete. Peggy shoveled dirt into the little grave and placed flowers atop.

It was one of the biggest funeral services the girls ever recalled even hearing about.

The cat sat on her haunches, smiling discreetly.

Two Hills

It was 1924.

Vernonia. It was primarily a one-main-street town. At the end of town was a little bridge to cross over the river.

"Anna," Adolph said one day, after he came home from the logging company from which would come the building of the trestles. "I believe we should live in town. Phyl will be starting high school. She would be able to walk to school. I have located a nice home on the hillside overlooking the town of Vernonia. It's called Corey Hill. I am making a lot of money now—more than I have ever made. It is time to upgrade our living status and live within our new means. I found a wonderful house at the opposite end, closer to the school. However, the wealthiest man in Vernonia lives there. He is head of the Oregon Electric Mill. We do not need to be on the same hill! I will be the other millionaire, Anna, at the opposite end of town. That is close enough in a town this size!" They both laughed heartily and agreed that Adolph had made a wise decision.

"Anna, I placed a down payment on the house. I did not want to lose something that is so perfect for our family. I must give them a decision tomorrow."

Moving day—again! Anna was most familiar with the tedious job of moving. This time felt *different,* though. This time felt *permanent.* She delighted in the home. A doctor and his wife had occupied it previously. How refreshingly different to be moving into a home that had already been maintained. Love had resided there!

Phyl checked out the high school. Oh, how she longed to have four years in the same place. The family checked out the grade school in the middle of town. They were delighted with what they found.

So once again, Anna packed for another move. This time, however, she did so with eager anticipation and a real home, a place to know people and have lasting friendships, a place in which to stay. *In this place, I believe I will find myself.* Anna was ready for the task ahead.

It was the mid-1920s. Movies filled the minds of most adults and school kids.

"Anna, this weekend, how would you like to stay at the Heathman again and go to see the *Jazz Singer?* There is a new actor named Al Jolson who will be starring in it. Remember hearing him on the radio? This will be the first full-length movie with talking sequences. It is to be premiered tomorrow. The theatre will be packed. I will call and get reservations at the hotel. Perhaps, when we arrive, we can all walk down and get tickets early. You know there will be a line a mile long!" Adolph was so happy to provide special events for his adored family.

"Do you mean it, Adolph? I'll tell the girls as soon as they get home from school and tell them to get things packed. City-life, here we come!" Anna bustled about finding outfits for each of them for such a special occasion. She hugged Adolph. He was so good to them.

"Girls, get yourselves packed," Anna told them when they came home.

"Momma, are we moving *again?*" Peggy's smile turned to sadness.

"Oh, no, girls. We are going to Portland to see the sights with a weekend at the hotel, a movie, and wonderful meals served to us that we do not have to prepare. We don't even have to make up the beds! This time, we will be seeing a brand new showing of a movie with sound!" Anna felt like a young girl herself.

"Adolph, there has been something on my mind for a long time. Now that we have a nice big home that is easy to find and a town where we can walk around, the girls growing and in school..."

"Anna, for gosh sakes, get to the point!" Adolph's mind began to wander toward the day's activities.

"Adolph, I would like to have a family reunion." Anna waited for Adolph's response.

"Your relatives or mine?" Adolph inquired.

"Adolph, I do not think your relatives want to come clear from Sweden to see us. And *who* would pay their way? While I still have some family left, Adolph, before they all die, I want to see them again." Anna knew Papa did not have many years left.

"I'll think about it, Anna. Where would we put all these people? How would we feed them?"

"When you love someone, Adolph, you find a way." Anna loved them that much.

"I'm not sure I do." Adolph laughed.

"Oh, come on, Adolph. You like them enough, don't you?"

"I think I am about to find out soon enough!"

When they returned home from Portland, Anna began to plan. She had already made so many friends at church and in the community. Offers poured in to house the members of her family.

Anna felt loved and accepted. She believed she was gaining back a portion of her identity that had been lost over her many moves.

The day arrived. They talked, ate, laughed, and cried together as they remembered old times and what each family member had experienced since seeing Anna last.

Papa looked over at Anna. "My dearest daughter, Anna," Papa began, "this will undoubtedly be my last visit with you. You have been the backbone holding the family together since your mother died. You have earned at least one heavenly crown, dear daughter. When I leave in the morning, I will take all of these cherished memories with me and keep them in my heart. I love you, Anna. You have blessed my life."

Anna was speechless. She turned aside and wiped the tear moistening her cheek.

"I love you, too, Papa," Anna said through her tears. "I believe it is *you,* Papa, who has been the glue holding us together. Remember when the townspeople wanted to divide us and raise us after Momma died? It was you who put your foot down and said, '*No!*'"

"Family takes care of family—always, Anna."

Morning arrived much too soon. Spring meant life. She also remembered it could bring death. "Death is not a respecter of persons," she recalled.

"Goodbye, Papa. *Au revoir, mon ami!*" She waved until she could see him no more.

Six months later, Anna received a phone call from Moscow. "Papa died this morning, Anna." It was Lilly. "The memorial service will be Friday. Will you be coming?"

"Yes, Lilly. Tell the family we will be there Thursday afternoon." Anna walked out to her garden, looked toward the hills, and let the tears and remembrances flow.

Holidays and Angels Unaware

Adolph was extremely busy with his new business. The girls were doing well in school, and it was their first time for the holidays in their new hometown.

The girls had enjoyed the summer activities with their new friends. They loved the town of Vernonia with almost everything on one street, including their schools and their home. One of the best places was the local ice cream parlor at the end of town. They had the best shakes and sodas.

Now summer had ended, the girls had returned to school, and it was nearing time for Thanksgiving. For Anna, this time of year meant checking out the decorations for the tree—just to be sure she had enough and to determine what replacements she might have to buy for the next holiday.

A shopping list of food was made, always checking those special recipes for homemade cookies, fruitcake, pies, and all the traditional dinner items the family enjoyed. The turkey was always purchased fresh from the grocer. The bread would be broken into small pieces and toasted in the oven. Then sage, salt, and pepper would be added. Just before stuffing the turkey, fresh turkey or chicken broth would be added to cover the cubes. The stuffing would be carefully placed into the turkey cavities, with leftovers placed into a baking dish and put into the oven alongside the turkey.

The turkey was always the biggest they could get. They would invite any family who could come, and friends—as many as the house would hold. Anna would make cardamom bread and fresh rolls. Before the stuffing was complete, Anna would place a little butter in a large saucepan and add sage, chopped celery, onion, and walnuts. She would simmer these until the ingredients were tender, then add some of the chicken broth. This she would add to the bread mixture, pouring more chicken or turkey broth over the mixture to make it moist. She placed this into the cavities—all she could squeeze in.

For the pumpkin pies, Anna would steam the fresh pumpkins, peel off the skins, place the cooled pumpkin into a large bowl and add eggs, milk, spices, sugar, and a little bit of maple syrup and maple flavoring. She would mix these together and place them into the unbaked piecrust shells. She would flute the piecrust edges with her fingers.

From the store, Anna would buy sweet potatoes. She could keep those in the cooler a while. Steaming them until tender, Anna peeled off the skins, cut each potato in half, and placed them onto a skillet that had melted butter and brown sugar. Occasionally turning each slice, she would slow- and low-cook these until they were candied.

Weather permitting, she would be able to have fresh green beans with a little added bacon, onion, salt and pepper, and a dab of butter. If not, they would settle for any green vegetable available.

Anna had made special dresses for the girls with aprons to don the outside while they helped her with the meal. She had knitted Adolph a pair of warm winter gloves and socks—even a cap to keep his head warm under his hat.

The girls were such a tremendous help to her. Phyl had only one more year left of high school. She was already talking about going to college. There was a wonderful teacher's college in Monmouth, Oregon, called Oregon Normal School.

"I think I have always wanted to teach, Momma. I hear they have an excellent school. And it is only two years. Thank you for making it possible." Phyl was grateful to them both.

"It has been our dream to educate both of you toward your desired goals." Anna did not want either one of them to be stuck without a good education. She knew firsthand how humiliating that could be.

Peggy had not decided what she wanted to be—probably a hairdresser. She wanted to stay at or near home. She did not feel the ambitious nature of her older sister.

"Maybe you will find a good husband there, Phyl. You never know what God has planned for you." Anna prayed silently that her girls would stay pure and presentable.

Thanksgiving passed. The days of being all together had been relaxing and fun for the entire family. They had had a few friends over from Adolph's workplace. The children and adults had played board games. The had men settled into the living room after dinner and discussed business. Anna wondered if men ever stopped working!

It began to snow, lightly at first. Then the flakes became larger and larger. Soon they had several inches on the ground. Adolph walked into the house early one morning.

"Too wet and cold to work anymore until the snow stops. Too dangerous, also. I am going to change clothes and go chop some wood for the wood stoves, Anna. You should place a pan of water in a couple of rooms to keep moisture in the rooms."

It was the week before Christmas. Anna, Adolph, and the girls had purchased all their gifts on their last trip to Portland. Good thing! The heavy snowfall kept them all home. Anna had purchased wrapping paper and ribbon. The girls made tags. They also loved to use old wallpaper, catalog sheets, and newspaper for wrapping.

Adolph cut down a tree from the forest. They set it up Christmas week and decorated it to the fullest. It looked so beautiful with ornaments handed down from generation to generation, the old-fashioned lights, candy canes, and the popcorn strung by the girls. They placed a red holly berry in between the popcorn pieces. It looked so festive and smelled wonderful. In Sweden the tree was put up Christmas Eve. Candles were placed on the branches and lit.

As Anna finished stirring the cranberry sauce she had made with fresh cranberries and a little sugar added for sweetening, Adolph stirred the gravy from the turkey drippings. Then he added the chopped giblets.

"Everyone come to the table. Dinner is ready." The aroma permeated the house. Adolph said the blessing: "Lord, we thank thee for thy provision. On this, the eve of thy birth, we remember thee and the sacrifice you made for our salvation. Please bless this food to our bodies. Thank you for this abundant provision. In your name we thank you. Amen."

They passed each dish that had been lovingly prepared, scooped out servings too big without any apology, and stuffed themselves until they were hurting in their tummies and groaning.

The fellowship began with Adolph and moved from Anna to each of the girls and their guests. They spoke about the year and its challenges and blessings. They talked about the year to come and what they hoped for. Adolph read the second chapter of Luke aloud.

When dinner was finished, Anna, the girls, and the female guests cleared the table and talked while they washed and dried the huge stack of dishes. Finally finished, they joined the men in the living room. It was time for passing out the presents that beautified the fragrant tree.

"Peggy," said Papa, "how would you like to distribute the presents this year?"

"Oh, Papa, could I?" Peggy smiled appreciatively. "Thank you, Papa."

One by one, each of the family piled their gifts high. Peggy finished and sat beside her abundant supply.

The doorbell rang. They turned and looked at each other. They were not expecting anyone else to come. Adolph answered the door.

"Is this the place that invited me for Christmas dinner?" the disheveled-looking man said.

"No," Adolph replied. "Everyone here is accounted for and has eaten. Did you try the other neighbors? Do you have a name? Perhaps I can help you find the person who invited you."

"My name? My name is not important. What is important is that I find where I was invited for Christmas. You did not invite me? Then, I must go."

"Wait!" Adolph yelled out. "I will drive you around town. It is too cold for you to walk around tonight. Besides, if you were invited for dinner, you will want to find them quickly."

The man crawled into the passenger seat of Adolph's car. Adolph drove down every street, inquiring of his passenger, "Is this where you were invited?"

The response was always negative. Finally, Adolph asked his passenger where he would like to be dropped off. Adolph needed to return to his waiting family.

"Anywhere is fine. Thank you. Merry Christmas."

Adolph said goodbye to the man. "I'm so sorry. Good luck to you. I hope you find the right home. Merry Christmas to you, too."

"Adolph," Anna began, after he returned home and she found out what had happened, "have you ever heard about 'angels unaware'? It is in the Bible. God sometimes sends angels from heaven to earth.

They take the form of a person. They are sent to minister or deliver a message. We are to invite them in—as God's sent servants."

"Anna, I had no idea." Adolph bent his head and looked down humbly. He felt bad that he had missed such a heavenly opportunity. "Should I try to find him again, Anna?"

"I think we should continue with our evening, Adolph. If God intends for him to be here, he will return."

Anna and the girls thought about him for many days and nights. They believed that God had sent him to their home to be warmed and fed—even clothed. They also believed they had missed a very great opportunity to serve him.

Christmas vacation was over for the girls. They each loved their new coats, hats, and winter gloves. They felt very stylish as they walked to school. The new snow boots were a great asset to their winter wardrobes in the frigid winter weather.

One day, there was a knock on the door. Anna felt surprised. It must be one of the neighbors paying a visit. She opened the door and saw the owner of the ice cream parlor.

"Good afternoon. What a surprise! Would you like to come in for a cup of tea? We just baked cookies."

"Yes, I would, Anna. I have an important matter to discuss with you. Thank you." He seated himself in the living room near Anna. The girls were in their rooms doing homework.

"Anna, I would like to have Phyl work for me at the ice cream parlor, behind the counter. I would train her. We have had many applicant responses to our inquiry. However, Phyl is the one we want."

"Phyl has no experience working outside the home. Did she ask you for this job?"

"She hasn't, Anna. But that's who I want to work in my store. I trust her handling customers and cash."

"Do you mind waiting here a moment? I will go ask her." Anna walked to Phyl's bedroom and knocked lightly. "Phyl."

"Yes, Momma. Come in, please."

Anna opened the door. "May I sit down a moment, Phyl? I'm sorry to interrupt your homework, dear. I have something to ask you. You remember that nice man who owns the ice cream shop?" Phyl nodded affirmatively. "He is here. He wants you to work for him."

"I never applied for the position, Momma. It would be fun, though. Would you mind if I did? I could use the money for college."

"If that is what you would like to do, Phyl; then by all means, come and tell him so."

Phyl came out and greeted Mr. Nicholsen. "Momma said you would like to have me work for you. Is that correct?"

"I would be honored, Phyl, if you would consider coming each day after school for a few hours. There are times when my wife and I would like to get away for a few days. We want someone who is dependable and trustworthy. At those times, you would be handling the cash and taking it for deposit to our bank. We thought about you. How do you feel about such a responsibility?"

"Honored." Phyl was delighted for the opportunity.

Adolph did not react kindly to the news. "Anna! You can be so stupid! What are you thinking having our teenage daughter left alone to handle customers and cash? She would have to walk that money to the bank. Why did you not check with me, Anna? You are not to make decisions on your own. You are to ask me first! Don't you ever again do such a stupid thing! You can be so dumb sometimes!" Adolph walked out of the house angrily.

Anna was devastated. She began to think differently at that moment. *There is a vast gap between Adolph and myself. It is because of the difference in education between us. He is smarter and wiser than I can or will ever be.* The only way Anna would be able to overcome her insecurity would be to show him that she could do things for herself. She wanted to make him proud of her, but how?

Railroad Trestles

Railroad trestles and snow sheds needed to be built in the coastal communities of Northern Oregon. Snow sheds were needed to prevent avalanches along the railways.

Adolph's new work as head of the Oregon American Lumber Company in Vernonia, Oregon, was a tremendous responsibility. He formed his work crew and carefully chose his men. The crew operated about three miles from the Sunset Highway on Wolf Creek Highway on the logging bridge for the Oregon American Lumber Mill. It was ninety-five feet high and ready for stringers. Adolph Nelson was the supervisor of his crew and company.

"Adolph, I always knew you were meant for greatness," Anna said. Her heart could be no more proud of him than at that moment. As a Swedish immigrant, he had come here with a high school education and gained experience toward this top position.

Anna became acclimated to her new surroundings rapidly. She soon met a nice ladies' two-table foursome that played the game of 500. Although cards were not her favorite thing, she wanted to be a part of the community and socialize with other women. In all honesty, she would rather have been cooking, cleaning, and sewing for her family. That was the role she had always played. It was comfortable to her. Her identity was as a homemaker, mother, and wife.

Anna was both proud and envious of Adolph's high school education. She felt very much in his shadow and hoped she did not embarrass him by her lack of education.

Adolph began with the woods around Vernonia. There was such a rich forested area. The harvest was plenty for the lumber business.

Anna's Lesson

Phyl had been offered an after-school job at the soda fountain. Anna agreed to let her work. It would help her with college income and give her some independence. She had seen no need to consult Adolph.

Phyl began working for Mr. Nicholsen on a Monday.

"Momma, you wouldn't believe the interesting people I am meeting. I love the job! Mr. Nicholson has taught me so much each day about making shakes, sodas, and all the necessities of the soda fountain. Thank you so much for letting me work there."

Anna thought, *If you only knew the sacrifice of making that decision.* For now, Phyl would not know the heartache she had experienced.

"Phyl, my wife and I are going to be gone for a few days. We are taking a trip to the coast. I will give you a phone number where you can reach us if you have a problem or a question. I trust you, Phyl. You are doing an excellent job. Any questions?"

"Yes, Mr. Nicholson. Where do I take the money? Do I take it every day? How do I take it? Will I be safe?"

"Let's do a trial run today, Phyl. About four thirty each day, you will put someone else in charge while you take the cash in the cash bag to the bank. It is just up the street. Make the deposit, get a receipt, and place the receipt in the lockbox in my office. You will lock up each night and do the same procedure each day. On a weekend, you will deposit on Friday and again on Monday. Very simple. Do you think you can handle that?"

"Yes. I will do my best." Phyl felt very grown up and confident.

Friday morning the Nicholsons left for the beach. Phyl enjoyed serving the after-school crowd and chatting with all her friends. She began to feel uncomfortable when one of the high school bullies, and his buddies came in just before bank time. She served them. They began to tease and harass her. She ignored them, asked her assistant to take charge, and prepared the cash for banking.

Phyl had nearly reached the bank when she noticed the three students behind her. She began to pick up her pace. They moved faster. Her heartbeat became very rapid. She felt panicky. One young man grabbed her from behind and pulled her into the alley. Another grabbed the cash purse and ran. The third was on top of her.

Phyl screamed at the top of her lungs. Across the street, an officer had stopped a vehicle. He quickly turned around and stared into the alley. Running toward the screams, he pulled out his gun, ready to fire if necessary. The driver of the vehicle ran into the nearest building and phoned the police department for help.

The sirens screamed. The two men who were accosting Phyl took off in different directions. The officer fired into the leg of one young man, felling him to the ground. The other continued to run away from the town. Another officer put on his siren and began the chase. A third came to the first officer's aid, taking the suspect into the police car and to the hospital.

Phyl lay in the alley, crying and bruised. She had failed her employer. The gentleman who had made the call to the police ran to her assistance. He pulled her up and politely looked away while she pulled herself together.

"Where do you live?" the man asked her, looking at her with such sympathy.

"Up on the next hill," Phyl said.

"Would you trust me to take you there?" the gentleman asked.

"I must close the business at the end of the day at the ice cream parlor. My assistant is waiting for me. My employer left town. I have failed him. The money is gone," Phyl cried.

"The officers will get the students *and* the money. I will contact the police to close business at the end of the day. You need to go home. You might need a doctor to look at you. Will you allow me to take you home?"

Fearfully, Phyl agreed.

The gentleman first drove to the ice cream parlor. He walked in and told the assistant what had happened and instructed her to have the police help her lock up. He told her to call her employer and let him know what had happened and that Phyl would be all right. Then he drove to the police department.

"I have the young lady with me who was attacked. I am taking her to her home. She may need medical attention. Would you assist the young lady at the store to lock up at the end of the day?"

They agreed. "We will need to talk to the young lady. I will walk out to the car with you to get her name and address."

When they got to the Nelson home, the gentleman walked Phyl to the door. Anna opened it in shocked surprise.

"Anna, I had no idea this was your daughter."

"Phyl, what happened to you? Please come in, Harvard." Anna grasped her daughter and led her inside.

Harvard told Anna the story. Anna put her arms around Phyl and sat beside her as Harvard talked.

"How can I possibly repay you?" Anna trembled as she saw Phyl's scratches and scrapes. She could also feel her inner pain.

"By making sure she is all right. She might need a doctor." Harvard then said goodbye.

"I will tell Adolph about your rescue of Phyl." Anna shook his hand goodbye. "Would you join us for dinner next Sunday, Harvard?"

"Yes, of course. I would be honored. I trust that Phyl will be recovered by then. Is there anything I can bring? How about some beverages?"

"Thank you, Harvard. See you then."

Phyl went into the bathroom and began to pour a tub of water. She felt so dirty inside and out. Anna came in with a solution to place on her wounds.

"Phyl, I am so very sorry this happened to you. Did they harm you *inside,* Phyl?" Anna began to feel sick.

"I don't know what you mean, Momma."

"I mean did they *penetrate* you?" Anna realized that, just like her own mother, she had never discussed this with her girls. She would make that a priority when Peggy arrived home today.

"I don't know what you mean, Momma." Phyl looked at Anna quizzically.

"I mean, Phyl, did anyone place a part of their body inside of you?" Anna looked into Phyl's eyes.

"No, Momma. It was all over before that ever happened. Mr. Malmstein came to my rescue and the boys ran. They took the money and ran in two different directions. I hope they have been caught. I had better clean up. The police want to come by and speak with me." Anna walked back to the living room, ashamed.

Phyl bathed, dressed, and came into the living to sit beside her mother.

The police arrived shortly afterward. Anna could feel the neighbors' stinging stares and gossip. *How will I ever live this down? How did I ever let this happen to my own child?*

Phyl and Anna sat in the living room answering questions. The boys had been caught and placed in jail. The money had been recovered and placed in the bank with a receipt for the owner. One of the officers handed the money bag to Phyl. "Is this the correct amount?" The officer looked at Phyl while she counted it.

"Exactly! To the penny! Thank you, Officer." Phyl could finally smile.

"Did the boys harm you sexually? It is something we have to ask you, Phyl." The officer looked sheepish for having to ask such a young girl.

"No. I thank God they never had that chance. Mr. Malmstein intervened before that could happen." Phyl looked at the officer and Anna.

"That is all the questions we have for now, Anna. Will you need medical help, Phyl?" The officer turned to Anna. "She might want to be checked out with a doctor. It is your choice."

"I will be all right," Phyl said. "I am just bruised and scratched. It will take some time to heal, but I am not concerned about my health. Mostly, I was scared to death!"

"Understandable!" said the officer. "Call us if you have anything new. The boys will not be bothering you. The school has been notified."

"Thank you, Officers. I am grateful to all of you and to Mr. Malmstein," Phyl said.

They shook hands at the door.

"Anna!" Adolph erupted later, when he and Anna were alone and he had been notified of the day's events. "Anna, you are one of the stupidest women I have ever known! How could you allow this to happen? You did not even *ask* me if Phyl could work there. Now, because of *you* and your lack of concern, your daughter was nearly raped and killed. You put her in *dire* yeopardy!" Adolph stormed out of the house.

Anna sat by the window for hours. Peggy came home and talked with her sister. Neighbors called to inquire about what was wrong.

"Nothing," Anna responded to their never-ending calls. "Everything is just fine."

Finally, Anna turned to God. "Lord, I ask your forgiveness. You tell me in your Word that I am to come *under* the headship of my husband, and that he is your protective shield over me. Please forgive me, Lord, and please restore the relationship with my husband."

Anna prepared dinner for Adolph and the girls. They sat quietly and ate. Adolph retired to the living room. Silence. The girls went in to help Anna in the kitchen.

Evening. Anna dressed for bed. *Do not let the sun go down on your wrath.* Anna remembered these words from God's Word. Anna crawled into bed beside her husband. She lay there quietly praying.

"Goodnight, Anna." Adolph did not look at her or touch her. He turned over and went to sleep.

That's a start, Lord. Thank you.

"Good night, Adolph. Forgive me." Anna also turned over, but lay awake.

Phyl Goes to Monmouth

It was June. Phyl was graduating from high school. Adolph and Anna drove her to the school and watched their baby girl walk down the aisle toward adulthood. They were so proud of the woman she had become.

Peggy would enter high school that fall. Her plans differed. She wanted to stay near home and go to beauty school.

"They are so completely different," Anna mumbled to no one in particular. Phyl—the always stable, dependable daughter. Phyl called herself pleasingly plump. She was not fat. Next to Peggy, she always looked bigger. Peggy had been thin since birth and a sickly child. She resembled Adolph more than Anna. She was very flirty. She was not interested in personal achievement through education or work. She just wanted to stay in her hometown with the people she knew. Her goal—if there was one—was to have a good time. Phyl had goals with a determination to achieve them. *What will their lives turn out to be?* Anna thought about her dear daughters. Then she reflected upon her own goals that had been abruptly changed. Again, she grieved her Harriet. *What would she have become had she lived?* Anna would never have that answer.

The four of them climbed into the car. It was loaded with luggage and some memorabilia for the trip to Monmouth. Phyl was in a flurry of excitement. She always seemed to be confident. The drive took a few hours, giving them ample time to chat and sing familiar songs.

"There it is!" Phyl exclaimed as they arrived. Here was a new life for a woman, a chance for independence, challenges, and *maybe* a chance to meet the man of her dreams! Monmouth was a tiny town. A girl could walk safely anywhere by day. It was only for two years.

Bidding the family goodbye, she watched as they drove away.

"I'm Sylvia," her roommate said when Phyl reached her dorm. They have assigned me to share a room with you for the year."

They soon became very good friends even though they had opposite personalities.

A scheduled summer class for a cruise had been cancelled. Greatly disappointed, they returned to the schedule. There was a class at U of O. They enrolled and found openings. They would find a place to live on campus and walk to class together.

"Let's check out the library, Sylvia. We can do our research and homework there."

Mig and Cece were two University of Oregon students seated in the campus library doing their research when they became distracted. "Look at those two gorgeous women over there!" Mig said to Cece, whose name was short for Cecil. "I don't think they attend school here. At least, I have never seen them before. Let's make ourselves known. I like the brunette." That was just fine. Cece liked the blonde.

"Good morning, girls. I'm Mig. This is Cece. Who are *you?* And why have we not had the pleasure of meeting you before now?"

"This one is a little too suave," Phyl mumbled to herself as she looked over at Sylvia, then into the eyes of a very handsome Mig. Her heart skipped a beat. She remained cool and collected.

"We're taking a summer course," Phyl said. "We attend school at Oregon Normal School in Monmouth. We are studying to be teachers. We'll be returning soon." Phyl was not impressed.

"We would like to take you out," Mig said.

No response.

"Would you go out with us?" Cece inquired.

No response.

"Are you available for dinner tonight?" Mig was getting nowhere. *These girls are really playing hard to get!* he decided. *Are they worth the pursuit?*

"We're busy tonight," Phyl said.

"Tomorrow night?" Cece inquired.

"I believe we have plans for tomorrow night, don't we, Phyl?" Sylvia continued their independent stance.

"We would like to take you on a picnic this week. How about Friday? What time may we pick you up?" Mig continued, getting a little impatient.

"We have swimming Friday." Phyl looked up at Mig and Cece.

"Skip it!" Mig was emphatic.

"No," Phyl continued. "We don't skip our classes."

At this point, Mig and Cece did not know whether to play the game or bail out.

"How about *after* swimming—after you return and clean up? We will pick you up and bring the entire picnic lunch." Mig had decided that would be his final offer. He was very interested. He was not interested in rejection.

"Sylvia, what do you think? Do you want to go on a picnic after we swim Friday?" Phyl asked.

"Yes, I think that would be fun."

They had better be worth it! Mig thought. He wasn't sure if he had won or been manipulated.

"We'll leave you to your studies. Please give us an address and we will pick you up at two thirty on Friday. Please be hungry."

"We'll meet you right here." Phyl did not want to give out addresses.

"See you then." Mig gave Phyl a big smile and left with Cece.

The men were there to pick them up promptly. They had every kind of picnic item imaginable. No one would starve.

They drove to a spot by the river and spread out the blanket and a few chairs. The food was fit for a king—or a queen: fried chicken, fresh fruit, potato salad, tossed salad, chocolate cupcakes, and a bottle of wine with four wine glasses.

They visited for hours until it was time to return and have an evening meal. They had thoroughly enjoyed each other's company.

Summer ended and so did the class. The girls returned to Monmouth. The men returned to the girls. Romance was blooming. Cece had fallen for Sylvia and Mig for Phyl.

During Phyl's senior year, she did her student teaching at Rickreall. She absolutely knew she was destined for this career. A letter came in the mail at the end of the year.

"Sylvia! They have invited me to interview for a position at Banks, Oregon, to teach the primary grades!"

She called home and told Anna, "Momma! I have news! I am now officially a teacher. At Banks. I will be near home. We can see each other often. How is Papa? I will be looking for a place to stay in Forest Grove, Momma. It is too far to drive daily from Vernonia." Phyl did miss home. Now she must continue her independence. "We have been informed that, if we want to complete our five years

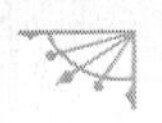

for a lifetime certificate in teaching, we cannot marry until that time ends." Teaching was everything she had set her sights on.

One day a little boy and his third-grade friend went swimming down at the river. Becoming overconfident, he dove into the deepest part. His buddy waited on the bank. He waited and waited. His friend did not surface. He walked back home and told his parents. They

drove to the river. His little friend never was seen again.

When his friend reported the incident to Phyl the next morning, Phyl knelt down beside the young friend. "Billy, why did you not run to the nearest house instead of going all the way home?"

Billy looked down at his feet, then up at his teacher. "I never thought about that, Ma'am."

Phyl hugged Billy. She went into the restroom to shed her tears for this dear lost classmate. The whole town attended his funeral. He had been such an asset. Very smart and loyal.

Phyl realized that being a teacher was not going to be easy. It was an opportunity to form minds for the future. She mentally thanked Anna for giving her a good foundation and strength to pursue her dreams. Anna was her role model.

Her love for Mig was growing. It appeared to be mutual. *How am I going to stay unmarried with so much love?*

Depression

Adolph walked down to the coffee shop in downtown Vernonia. He enjoyed having a cup of coffee and a biscuit with the men who worked under him. He considered them family. He admired and respected his men. He had an hour before work began to talk to them about the country and the issues of the day. They shared local gossip and the stock market news.

One day, Adolph walked in to meet and greet his friends, as usual. No one looked up at him or greeted him. They looked very grim.

"You guys look like someone just died! Adolph continued to look warily at the men. He ordered his coffee and a roll and settled in the chair. "Okay, gentlemen, what seems to be bothering you?" Adolph dipped his breakfast roll into his hot, steaming coffee and leaned back.

"Have you checked the stock market, Adolph?" One of his friends spoke without looking up at him.

"Not lately," Adolph continued.

"It has taken a huge dip," one of the men said.

"Oh, that happens all the time. It'll bounce back. Stocks go up and down daily." Adolph showed no concern.

The months went by. The economy had turned for the worse.

Adolph checked his stocks daily. They were definitely reversing. Thank God his income came mainly from his work and not the stock market. But still, he had appreciated the padding it had given his savings account.

Unemployment was reaching a record high. Twenty-five percent of the workforce was without gainful employment.

Then the banks closed. Not having listened to the news, Adolph again joined his coffee group of employees.

"Morning, men." He turned to the waitress. "I'll have the usual—coffee and a breakfast roll." Hungrily, he dipped the roll into the hot coffee and took his first bite.

"Is there something wrong, men? Don't like the way I dunk my roll?" He laughed.

"Adolph, have you heard the news? The banks are closed."

"What do you mean, 'the banks are closed'? I was just on my way over to my own."

"No, you're not. You won't find them open. You cannot withdraw or deposit. They will not open for you or me or any of us. They're closed, Adolph!"

Adolph's face turned ashen. "I will be in touch with you. Don't panic. We will work things out. I will not let you be unemployed. Take the day off and wait to hear from me." He abruptly left for home.

"Adolph, what is wrong with you?" Anna asked when he came in the door. "Why are you back home? Are you ill?" Anna's deep concern for her husband was revealed in the tone of her voice.

"Anna, I just received the news that the stock market crashed. The banks are closed. We cannot even get our money out of the bank. I'm not sure there will be any money when they do open. This will change our lives, Anna—perhaps, forever. I am going to go in to work, tell the men to take the day off, arrange a meeting with my superiors, and make some life-changing decisions for work and home. Our home is secure, Anna. I paid off the mortgage just last month. However, our style of living must change. No more extravagant times. We must learn to be very frugal. We will survive this, Anna. I have some cash here at home."

"I have cash, too, that I continue to save. I will go to town and purchase necessities. We will live off what we have for as long as possible. I'll talk to Peggy when she comes home. I'm sure Phyl has heard about it. I'm so grateful that Phyl is now teaching and has a secure job. They will always need good teachers. Peggy wants to be a hairdresser. I doubt women will be getting their hair done like they used to. She could train to work at home and give haircuts, perms, and styles in exchange for food or services. There is nothing wrong with barter.

"People are killing themselves because they are losing everything. Suicide is not a solution. This is not permanent. We will recover and move on. For now, you and I must find ways to change our habit of living—and to help others. I must make my men secure." Adolph looked distraught and heavily burdened.

Anna walked over to Adolph and put her arms around him. "Whatever sacrifices need to be made, Adolph, we will do it together."

Phyl read the devastating news. She placed a call home. Anna answered.

"Yes, Phyl. Your father just came home and told me the news. We are okay here. We have plenty of everything and some cash on hand. Papa is meeting with his supervisors today. He said he will keep the men working and pay them what he can. And, you, Phyl. Are you all right? Do you have enough to eat and some cash? That's good. How is Mig? Are you in love, Phyl?"

"Momma, love cannot be a determining factor right now. I have to complete my five years first. It is good to talk to you and know that you will get through this."

"It isn't just us, Phyl. It is this community of people who are in shock. We must find a way to help them."

"You're very resourceful, Momma. I know you will find a way. Love you. Bye now."

Anna thought about what Phyl had said. *"Resourceful." I believe that I have been placed here for such a time as this.*

The phone rang. "Anna? It's Marge. I hope no one can hear me on the phone. We are devastated here. My husband just lost his job. We have no money and no food. I cannot even feed the children. I don't know what we are going to do, Anna." She began to sob.

"Marge, I want you to come up to see me. We will have some tea and talk. Good. I will see you shortly." Anna quickly made a coffeecake and put on the tea water. She gathered together some food items for the family. The doorbell rang.

"Marge, please come in." Anna gave her a hug and sat her down for a snack, tea, and a long conversation. "I have some ideas. I am going to discuss them with Adolph. I believe we can be of help to our community."

As Marge was leaving, she handed her a little money. "Stick this in your pocket and spend it when you need it most."

Anna later sat down with Adolph. "I want to teach the women of this community how to use what they have, to stretch their resources, and to barter. I want to teach them how to knit and sew and grow. I want to teach them how to can and become self-sufficient." She waited for Adolph's response. Never again was she going to do something without checking with Adolph first. She had learned her lesson.

"Anna, I think that is an excellent idea. In fact, I want to have a meeting with the men up here and discuss finances. I believe I can teach them how to manage the financial resources they have and make them stretch. We will discuss ways of service to one another and barter."

"It seems as though God brought us to this community to be here for these crucial times."

Adolph looked at Anna. "That was a very wise choice, Anna. Thank you for consulting me."

Anna knew she had found her niche.

Over the months ahead, they worked together with the community. They were always there for each other's needs.

Anna opened her Bible to the book of Acts. She read again how the early Christians had shared what they had. *Sometimes God has to take us through hard times to get our attention.*

There would probably be a wedding soon. Anna knew that the bride's family always paid for the wedding. *How will we manage with so few resources?*

Love in Bloom

Anna longed for the day when she could help Phyl make wedding plans. She remembered how rushed her own wedding had been. She believed she might make up for that with her daughter.

Phyl and Mig had been dating steadily ever since they met. They knew they were in love. It was December. The snow lightly covered the countryside. It was a picture only God could paint. The freshly-fallen snow had not yet been tainted with footprints or car tire tracks or debris.

Mig picked up Phyl for their next date. He brought flowers. They ate at a cozy little restaurant in Forest Grove. When he took her back to her living quarters, he got on his knee and brought out the box. Looking up into her beautiful blue eyes, he said, "Phyl, I love you. Will you marry me?"

Phyl was taken by surprise, despite their closeness. She knew she loved Mig.

"Honey, I cannot teach and be married. The

rules are very strict. In order to receive my lifetime certificate in teaching, I must remain single until the five years have been fulfilled. Yes, I love you, too. And, yes, I will marry you—then."

"Phyl, Christmas vacation begins for you next week. I have a plan. I have vacation the twenty-seventh through the New Year. We will drive to Stevenson, Washington, and get married by a justice of the peace there. There is no waiting period. All we need are two witnesses. I will ask Cece and Sylvia if they will join us. No one in Oregon need ever know. I will hold your ring for you until the ceremony. And Phyl, I *promise* to keep our marriage a secret."

Phyl's five years would be completed by the end of this school year. She thought about her love for Mig and her desire to marry him. She also thought about her mother. *What would Momma say? Would it hurt her if I run off and do not have a big wedding—or even tell them I am getting married? How will I feel about that after I have done it? Will I regret my choices? But I love Mig.*

"Mig, I have no desire to deceive my boss. Yes, I love you, and I want to marry you. How do you feel about keeping this a secret when it could be a compromise ethically? I have worked very hard for this certificate. I do not want to lose it."

"I believe we can do this, Phyl. I ask you to consider it. I am comfortable with not waiting as long as we tell your employer about our marriage after you have reached next September. It will work, Phyl. We will make it work."

"And my parents? It will devastate them, especially my mother." Phyl tried to imagine how Anna might feel.

"They'll recover. It's our life, Phyl, not theirs," Mig said.

Phyl wasn't so sure about that.

"All right." Phyl felt love, fear, and hesitation. She would have to play a role she was not sure she could.

"Let me take care of telling your folks, Phyl. They do know about us, don't they?" Mig placed the ring back in the bag for safekeeping. "I was taught, Phyl, that if you really want something badly enough, you go after it. You do not let obstacles stand in your way." Mig smiled. He knew he could win. Now, to wipe away her feelings of guilt.

"Where would you like to honeymoon?" Mig wanted to focus her attention away from her concerns.

"The beach. I love the coast. Do you think we can go there, Mig?" Phyl felt like a young schoolgirl again.

"The beach it is!" Mig turned and smiled. He had won!

December 27, the four of them climbed into Mig's Model T and headed for Washington.

"Sylvia, why don't we make it a double wedding, as long as we are here, anyway?" Cece looked at Sylvia for an answer.

"Might as well," Sylvia replied.

They said their vows to each other in front of the chaplain, and he pronounced them husbands and wives. They exchanged rings, kissed, and were off to the coast.

"I think I'll give Phyl a call, Adolph. She is so close to graduating. She must be extremely busy and excited. I wonder how her relationship is going with Mig. I think we'll be planning a wedding very soon." Anna picked up the phone and dialed.

"Adolph, I cannot get anyone to answer!" Anna looked at Adolph with great concern.

"Didn't you say that she and Mig are in love, Anna? Why would she be home? She was just here for Christmas!" Adolph felt exasperated with Anna.

"Of course," Anna said. "I'll wait until tomorrow."

"Give her a break, Anna. Call her during the New Year. Your calls are getting expensive. She isn't a child anymore, Anna. Leave her alone."

Anna walked away. She wanted someone to nurture, someone to

love her in return. She would wait to hear from Phyl about future wedding plans. It would give her a reason to dream again.

"Momma?" Phyl struggled with how she was going to tell them.

"Phyl, how wonderful to hear your voice. How are you? How's Mig?"

"Momma, Mig and I would like to come over New Year's Day and visit with you. I have something I want to tell you. Will you be home?" Phyl paced the floor.

"Of course. I'll have dinner ready for you. What time will you be here?" Anna was already planning the menu.

"About eleven a.m.," Phyl said.

"That's pretty early for such a long drive. You must be leaving after breakfast." Anna was adding the miles and time.

"We're not that far away." Phyl tried to catch herself before Anna figured out how close they were. "See you then. Love you. Bye." Anna hung up the phone and went in to tell Adolph.

Mig and Phyl drove up to the house. Cece and Sylvia had taken a bus back home. They all hugged and kissed. The dinner was superb. They retired into the living room.

"What's going on in your lives? How's school?" Adolph looked to Mig.

"The news is that Phyl and I just married December 27. We drove up to Stevenson, Washington and married in the chapel."

Adolph was furious. He refused to speak to Mig or his daughter.

Anna burst into tears and walked into the bedroom. Phyl followed her. "Momma, what's wrong? Mig and I are very happy, Momma. Momma!" Phyl put her arms around Anna.

"Why, Phyl? Why couldn't you wait and have a wedding? A big wedding? Why couldn't we plan this together? How could you?" Anna continued to sob.

Mig walked into the bedroom. "Come on, Phyl. We're leaving. Adolph won't even speak to me." Mig grabbed Phyl's arm. "Come on." Mig led Phyl out to the car.

"We can't just drive away. They're hurting. I should have told them in advance. I cannot leave them like this, Mig." Phyl wiped away a tear.

"We are not going to solve anything with them tonight and I am *not* going to stay here any longer under these circumstances. We'll take care of it later." He started the engine and backed out.

Phyl's week of joy ended. Heartbreak and guilt replaced it. How would she heal the bond between herself and her parents? Between her parents and her husband? It was *not* the way a marriage should begin.

The CCCs

Weeks went by with no word from Anna or Adolph. Phyl prayed that time would begin to heal the wounds caused by her hasty decision.

The school year ended. Phyl entered the principal's office and requested some time.

"Come on in, Phyl! I'm so glad you stopped by for a visit. What's on your mind this morning?"

"A confession," Phyl said.

"Oh? Did you kill someone? I'm the wrong department! Do you need a priest?"

"I'm married. I've been married since just after Christmas. I'm sorry. It was the wrong thing to do not to tell you. We kept it secret because we both wanted our lifetime certificates in teaching." Phyl looked down at her hands.

"I know."

"You *know?* How could you know? We eloped and never said a word to anyone! Did my parents tell you?" Phyl knew it would not be from Anna. But Adolph had been furious with Mig.

"I just knew, Phyl. You cannot get much of anything past a principal. Your demeanor was different. And by the way, it's all right. I decided I would not say anything either. I knew you would eventually tell me."

"I'm very grateful. And the certificate?" Phyl stopped herself from sounding assumptive.

"It's yours, Phyl. You earned it. You have done an outstanding job as a teacher here. We are very proud of you. The students have learned well under you. I would like to have you stay. Do you and Mig have plans?"

"Yes. Mig has signed up with the Civilian Conservation Corps. We will be leaving immediately for Idaho."

"I have heard about that. Would you tell me a little about it and the role Mig will play? What will you do? Teach?"

Phyl recalled what Mig had shared. "The Civilian Conservation Corps was begun under the planning of Franklin Delano Roosevelt. It was the first of its kind. It gives people jobs. It helps build America with hands willing to work and move wherever the army—the CCC is under their auspices—tells them to go. It pays them well for these times. Mig will be in Company 603 for a while, then Company 1647. He reports for duty June 14 of this year—1934—as Educational Advisor.

"We will begin at Ojai, California. Mig will be coaching, also. One concern is that sometimes there are fires. I will stay in Idaho during that time. Harsh living conditions exist in the mountainous terrain and the isolation can be very difficult.

"I hope and pray that there are no fires. I believe I told you about my being born just before the Mullan, Idaho, fire and that my parents and I barely escaped with our lives."

"You are newlyweds. I'm sure you will weather any storm that comes your way. How did Adolph and Anna receive the news about your wedding?" He looked into Phyl's eyes and detected pain.

"Papa will not speak to Mig. Momma burst into tears. There has been no healing yet." Phyl's heartache rippled through her again.

Fire and Other Surprises

"Fire! Run for your life!" Mig directed the men toward an opening at the top of Pot Mountain. They fought the fire for thirty days until they thought they would drop. The tinder-dry forest was consumed by any little spark, and the dry winds whipped it very near the camp. Some of the boys were young and inexperienced. Mig trained how to fight fire with fire by burning a path so that the fire could not jump across when it reached the edge.

"Run!" one of the kids called out, as he saw the flames approaching. They jumped across the burn line just in time. It seared their lungs. Mig had a pocket full of lozenges to soothe their raspy throats. He had them stop every hour to consume water and take a bite to eat from their food supply in their backpacks. That gave them some additional strength to continue.

Mig recalled Phyl's account from her parents about the Mullan, Idaho, fire where they had barely escaped with their lives, only to have everything they owned burned behind them.

One of the men was badly burned. He was carried out of the camp area to the nearest hospital for treatment.

Having completed their work, they headed for Camp Pine Creek at Pierce, Idaho, on April 28, 1935. There was snow on the ground. Living conditions in the mountain terrain were harsh. Difficult, too, was the isolation. Mig was relieved that he had chosen Lewiston for Phyl's residence.

She was waiting for him in the upstairs apartment.

"I read about the Ojai fire. You were daily in my prayers, Mig. After what Papa, Momma, and I went through in Mullan, I am terrified of even the thought of a fire."

By the time Mig returned, the snow was melting into a suddenly warm spring.

However, it was not the weather that was on his mind these days; he had something he must explain to Phyl. He hoped she would still want to remain with him.

"Phyl, let's fix some sandwiches and coffee and go down by the creek side. It's been a long time since we have been able to enjoy a picnic lunch and have a lengthy conversation. Besides, I have some news I want to share with you." Mig, always confident and self-assured, always in control and able to manage, now felt a lump in his throat. He did not want to lose Phyl. He loved her too much.

"News? Tell me now while I get a lunch together!" Phyl had not heard any kind of news for months. What could it be that Mig was so anxious to share? Perhaps they were to relocate. Why couldn't he tell her now?

The sandwiches were packed. Mig had fixed a thermos of coffee. Freshly-baked cookies were carefully placed on some waxed paper at the top of the lunches.

Walking down to the creek side, Mig grabbed Phyl's hand and

gave it a squeeze. "I love you. You do know that, don't you?" Mig's heart was racing.

"Of course I do. We made a vow to always love each other, Mig. Nothing will ever change that." Phyl squeezed his hand and gave him a wink.

"I hope not," Mig said.

The look in his eyes said something very puzzling. Phyl wondered what could possibly be troubling him so deeply.

The blanket was spread by the creek, under a big oak tree with its deep roots stretching down to the water for a drink. The shade felt soothing to their skin warmed by the heat and humidity of an unusually hot day. They took off their shoes and splashed their toes in the water like little kids again.

"Hungry?" Phyl spread out the sandwiches, fruit, and cookies. She hoped she would not have to compete with the ants.

"Let's begin with a cup of coffee." Mig unscrewed the top and poured each of them a hot cup of coffee.

"Now, Mig, what is it that is so deeply on your mind?" Phyl was anxious to get right to the heart of the matter.

"Phyl, I have something to tell you that might be very troubling to you. I should have told you before we married, but I did not think you would say yes to me if I did." Mig looked down at the ground as he spoke.

All kinds of unimaginable thoughts crossed her mind. "What is it, Mig? Can anything be so devastating that I would not have married you?" Phyl looked over at him, puzzled, and took her first gulp of coffee. She thought she might need the stimulant first.

"Phyl, I have a son. I have been married before. His name is Earl. We lived in Idaho. I became very ill. My wife took everything except my son and moved out. When I came home, she was gone, as was my bank account, furniture, except Earl's and my beds, and most everything else. She left a note saying she had met someone else. Then she divorced me. I was devastated, as, of course, was Earl.

I was still very ill. I explained it to Earl as best I could. I decided to leave him with his maternal grandparents who lived nearby. They were as upset with Winnie as we were. That is where Earl is now, Phyl. I hope you will forgive me." Mig awaited her answer.

The silence between them was deafening. Phyl stood up and walked away. She walked across the meadow, the words reverberating in her ears, tears streaming down her cheeks. The lack of trust between them devastated her. Their first child would not be theirs together. She was already a mother without even having given birth. What did he expect of her? Was she to raise this child she had never met? Would he even like her? For the next twenty minutes, she walked in silence. She knew she must have an answer for him and that she must return to him soon.

Mig lay back on the blanket, the food lying beside him untouched. He had had to tell her. She would have found out eventually. He was not a man of emotion or tears. Now, lying there and hardly breathing, he wiped away a trickle of a tear. Had he lost her forever? He carried no love for Winnie. He loved Phyl with every ounce of his being.

Lying down beside him, Phyl turned to face him. "How old is Earl? What is expected of me, Mig? Will he even want a stepmother?" Phyl waited for answers.

There was hope. "Earl is eight. He is a bright, loving, and trusting boy. He needs a mother—like you, Phyl, if you are willing to accept him—and me."

"Mig, I do not think I will ever understand your lack of trust in our relationship. Why did you not think you could trust me? It was not very responsible of you to not tell me. Now that we *are* married, it is for life. I do not believe in divorce or even separation. What are your plans for Earl?"

"I would hope that you would accept his living with us, Phyl. I realize that I am asking a lot of you—and of him—for you to begin our life together with an eight-year-old boy who is not even your own. I am hoping you will make him your own. He needs his father, too. I feel like I, too, have abandoned him and I feel very guilty. Grandparents should not have to raise their grandchildren. That is a parent's responsibility. I left him there so I could go to school and have something to offer him when I graduated." Mig felt a heavy burden lift from him. Phyl would not also leave him. At least he had that much.

"I'll accept him, Mig. I am willing to raise him. After all, he *is* your son. And if he is *your* son, he is *my* son, too. What other surprises do you have for me? Is there more?" Phyl thought she had known this man whom she had married. Now, she was not so sure.

"No more surprises. When I complete the CCCs, I hope to teach. Then I would like to drive to Idaho and get Earl, if that is acceptable to you," Mig said.

"Yes, it is. Let's eat before the ants have our lunch instead of us. Besides, I am starved!"

Mig poured more coffee. Phyl divided the lunch between them. "There is one more thing." Mig looked over at Phyl and smiled.

"Oh no." Phyl was not smiling.

"How would you like to spend the summer in San Francisco?"

"San Francisco! What does that have to do with the CCCs or teaching?" Phyl looked over at Mig, astonished.

"I have been invited to play for the San Francisco Seals. They need a first baseman to replace the one who is injured. It would just be for the summer. I have contracted with Beaverton Union High School to teach or coach for them starting in the fall." Mig could not hold back the excitement from his voice.

"It sounds wonderful! It sounds like we will be leaving soon. Shall I start packing?"

"I will notify the CCCs that I will be leaving the end of March. The season has already begun, and they are into their practice sessions. Yes, you can begin to pack. That shouldn't take more than an hour!" They both laughed.

"It will be a little out of our way. I have been depositing money into a bank north of here, and I will stop by and take out what we might need for our expenses." Mig bade Phyl goodbye as he headed back to camp. "See you in a week. Be ready to see The City by the Bay!"

Driving north, they both admired the breathtaking scenery of spring in bloom. Parking at the bank, Mig noticed that the parking lot was empty and there seemed to be no sign of life anywhere.

"Bank closed until further notice," read the sign on the door. The federal government had closed the bank. It was the final blow to the Depression years. Mig returned to the car. "It looks like we will have to live on the cash I have with me until we hit San Francisco. I have my final paycheck, and I will cash it there. Once I begin baseball, I will have an income again. Phyl, my life savings is in that bank. I hope to God I get it back. At least I have a job starting in the fall. I will try to convince them that I am capable of handling both the teaching and coaching positions. I know I can." Mig knew their lifestyle would be drastically different for months to come.

"I can teach, Mig. That way, I can help out and get us on our feet again," Phyl said.

"I want you to be home, Phyl. Earl will be coming to live with us in Beaverton. Once I sign the contract and find us a home, we will travel to Idaho to pick him up. I'll call him during the summer to prepare him. Midvale isn't that awfully far away. We may have to rent for a while. When I save up enough again, we can make a down payment on a home."

Mig found it interesting, indeed, that the first baseman he was to replace for the summer had the last name of Cook, matching his own!

❦

"Earl, this is Dad." It was good to hear his son's voice again. He explained to Earl his re-marriage and his plans to teach. He told him he would be coming to get him soon.

"Dad, I miss you, too. I love it here, Dad. All my friends are here. I don't want to leave Midvale." Earl sounded so disappointed.

"You'll meet new friends in Beaverton, Earl. Phyl and I will be picking you up next weekend. Please be ready. Bye." Mig couldn't understand how anyone could be that attached to such a little town.

"Bye, Dad." Earl hung up, disappointed. He had said his goodbyes—at least in his prayers—to his mother. Now he must leave his town, his grandparents, his friends, and everything familiar. It did not seem fair. He did not want new places. He wanted home.

❦

"Climb into the backseat, Earl. We have a long trip ahead of us. This is your new mom. Her name is Phyl." He waved goodbye to the grandparents and thanked them for the lunch they had provided for the trip.

Phyl spent most of the trip getting to know Earl. It was awkward for both.

"As long as I am still in Idaho, I am going to drive by that bank one more time." Mig had hopes for positive changes.

He drove into the parking lot and was relieved to see some activity.

"We can give you five thousand dollars. The remainder is still uncertain. We will have to let you know." The message was final—at least for now. It was *something*. It would give them a start. Mig had lost twenty thousand dollars of his life's savings, unless the government gave it back. The bank had not been federally insured.

Mig decided that would never happen to him again. He would see to that!

By the time they reached Beaverton, Oregon, Phyl and Earl were well-acquainted and fairly bonded. Mig was grateful and relieved!

Mig met with the Beaverton School Administration and argued his case. He felt fully capable of completing both the contract for teaching all the upper math courses *and* coaching football, basketball, and track. They weren't as convinced.

"We will place you on a one-year contract trial basis. If, at the end of that year, you find that it is too much to handle, we will reduce your contract to teaching *or* coaching." Their decision was final.

"Acceptable!" Mig signed the contract.

They had found a little rental just a couple of blocks from the school. It was perfect for all three of them. Earl quickly made friends. His academic adjustment was another matter. He felt intimidated by having a coach as a father. His growth spurt had not yet begun. He was only able to be a water boy for the team, too small to play.

One day, Mig received a phone call. "Mr. Cook, I am holding your son here at the jail. He has gotten himself into some trouble. Do you want to come and post bail?" The call from the police department infuriated Mig and saddened Phyl.

"It will be a good lesson for him. He can come home tomorrow." Mig could not be convinced by Phyl to bring him immediately home. *Discipline,* thought Mig. *That's what he needs right now, not forgiveness.*

The relationship between Mig and Earl became strained. Mig was constantly busy with such a heavy teaching and coaching load. There was no time for nurturing anyone else.

"Doctor, my wife has been throwing up all week. Would you please examine her and tell me what I need to do?"

Mig sat in the waiting room, awaiting Doc Mason's orders.

"Mig, you don't need to do anything. Your wife is expecting." Phyl walked out to the waiting room, beaming.

"I think we need to begin looking for larger quarters! Want to go house-hunting today?" Mig asked.

Just a quarter of a mile south of the high school, they found a two-bedroom house with a circular driveway. "I'll take it." Mig signed the contract.

"Honey, where will Earl sleep? He has to have his own room." Phyl now cared very much for Earl and thought of him as her own son.

"I'll clear out a room for him in the attic. It'll be fine." Mig felt he had more important things to think about.

Anna called and invited them for dinner. She wanted to hear the latest news about their home, Mig's job, and her soon-to-be grandchild.

Mickey, a girl, was born in March of 1937. Phyl decided she would put off teaching until Mickey was old enough for school.

World War II was causing everyone to scrimp and save. Phyl's sister, Peggy, had now joined the working women in the shipyards at Vanport. "Rosie the Riveter" was a new job description for women working in the war effort. Rations were given to each family for shoes, sugar, and other necessities. Families saved tin and other necessary items to give toward the war. There were scarcities. People learned to do without. They grew their own vegetables and saved. Neighbor helped neighbor.

"Get ready to move again. I have just contracted a coaching position with Klamath Falls High School. We'll be leaving at the end of summer."

Earl was devastated. The year was 1944. He had looked forward to graduating with his friends in 1945. He begged to stay behind with friends. Mig would not listen. He told him he would adjust.

Husky, their dog, would have to go to the Humane Society. They were not going to travel with a dog that many miles.

Mickey cried all the way. She had loved that dog with all her heart. She prayed he would find a good home. She recalled the day Husky and a neighbor's German Shepherd had fought. They had nearly killed each other. No one had dared intervene. Husky was part wolf—a Malamute. Each dog was capable of ripping anyone apart who interfered. One of the neighbors had brought a huge long stick and finally divided the dogs. Both were bleeding and had huge teeth marks in their necks. The family dropped off Husky without even a goodbye, except for Mickey. She cried all the way home.

By the end of the Klamath Falls coaching position, the war had ended, Earl had graduated and joined the navy, and Mig, Phyl, and Mickey headed back to Beaverton.

Mig contacted his former assistant coach. The two of them opened up a hardware business in downtown Beaverton. Phyl began teaching in the Beaverton schools. Mickey was beginning the third grade that fall. All seemed well.

A Betrayed Trust

The new home on Southwest Farmington Road was just enough out in the country to not be too crowded. It was only one-half mile to the grade and high schools and a mile to town. In no time, Mig and Phyl had become acquainted with neighbors. Mig busied himself remodeling. Phyl developed the garden into a showpiece. Now it was ready for entertaining guests.

Mickey was nine years old.

Phyl found a neighbor who agreed to take Mickey when Phyl and Mig had a night out. They were religious people and had a teenaged daughter. Mickey could even spend the night on those evenings when her parents would be out late.

One such evening, Mickey had gone over quite early in the day. Mrs. Culley was a sickly, quiet woman who kept to herself. Mr. Culley invested a great deal of time in Mickey's life. He took her along when he cultivated his garden, handing Mickey a rake or a hoe. She enjoyed digging and planting and reaping the harvest for lunches or dinner. He would sit for hours with her on the front steps and teach her string art. It meant that he must sit very close to her while their fingers entwined with the string.

One evening, Mickey requested permission to stay up later and finish listening to the baseball game on the radio. Mrs. Culley had gone to bed early. Their daughter was out with friends. As she listened to the game, Mr. Culley occasionally showed her pictures of women in underwear from the magazine ads. Mickey felt very uncomfortable and puzzled.

The game ended. Mickey went into the bedroom and closed the door. She sat a while recalling the strange events of the evening and trying to make sense of it. The door opened and Mr. Culley walked in. Mickey stood up—surprised and confused. Mr. Culley continued to walk toward her, grinning. Mickey felt frightened and trapped. She backed against the wall. Mr. Culley pressed himself against her. Mickey tried to let out a scream. Nothing came out of her mouth. It felt like her heart was going to jump out of her.

Desperate, she said, "I need a glass of water!" Mr. Culley ignored her.

Again, she pleaded, "I need a drink of water!"

"All right." Mr. Culley backed away and let her pass.

Mickey headed for the kitchen and stood in the middle of the room, thinking. Desperately, she wanted to go home. Fearful of being outside in the pitch black of night and meeting what might be a worse plight, she stayed put. Neither did she know how to reach her parents by phone. She waited, unmoving.

Mr. Culley came to the doorway of the kitchen. He looked angry.

Mickey did not move; she just stared at him.

Finally, Mr. Culley spoke. "All right." That was it. He walked away.

Mickey stood there for a long time. Finally, believing it to be safe to move, she cautiously walked back to the bedroom. Inside, she waited. No one entered. She waited some more. Then she dressed for bed, crawled under the sheets, and waited awake for the daughter to arrive home.

Mickey told no one. The next day after breakfast, she walked home. She did not say a word to anyone.

"Mickey," Phyl said, "your father and I are going out tomorrow night. You will be staying with Mr. and Mrs. Culley.

Mig had gone to bed.

"Mommy, can I talk to you?" Mickey asked.

"Sure, honey. What do you want to talk about?" Phyl sat down in a living room chair. Mig had already gone to bed.

"May I sit on your lap? Please turn out the light." Mickey knew she *had* to tell her mother. She could never go to that home again. Next time, it could be worse. She was only nine years old. She had begun already to experience the signs of growing up just a few months earlier, after school had ended.

"Why do we need the lights out?" Phyl inquired.

"Please, Mommy," Mickey pleaded.

"All right." Mickey sat down and began to tell Phyl the horrifying happenings of a betrayal of trust by their neighbor.

"Mommy, do I have to go there again? I'm afraid."

"No, Mickey. You never have to go there again. We will either stay home or find someone else. You go on to bed now. Everything will be all right." Phyl waited until Mickey went to bed, then walked into their own bedroom to tell Mig the story.

"I'm going to get a gun and go over there and shoot that man. Tomorrow! How *dare* he touch our daughter! How *dare* him!"

"No, Mig. No! I will take care of it. You are *not* going to shoot anyone. What good would that do? Then you would be in prison, and we would be without a husband and father!" Phyl had stated her case.

Weeks later, Mickey was sitting in the tub. She heard a knock on the door and her mother speaking to someone.

"You get off my property and don't you *ever* come to this house again. You *snake!*" Phyl angrily slammed the door shut in Mr. Culley's shocked face.

The gossip began. One neighbor swore that Mr. Culley was incapable of such an indecent act. After all, she said, "He is a Sunday school teacher!"

Phyl was shocked and dismayed to hear that. *I guess there are wolves in sheep's clothing even in the churches. How very sad.*

To soften Mickey's painful experience, Phyl decided she would tell her about the mischievous things Mickey used to do as a little child and make her laugh. There were some incredible stories.

Childhood Antics

At age four, Mickey had looked like an angel. She had towhead blonde hair and beautiful green eyes with blue rims around the green. She was a beauty. Her antics were not!

One evening Mickey's uncle was babysitting Mickey while Mig, Phyl, and their neighbors took in a movie. Mickey wanted to explore. She took her tiny chair from her bedroom and lowered it gently through her window to the grass outside, grateful that it did not tip over. She listened for any movement. All was quiet. One leg at a time, she climbed out of the window onto the chair and to freedom. She then ran to the neighbor's house and let herself in. She would not get caught because they had joined her parents at the theater.

First, she found a chair and placed it in the bathroom. Opening the medicine cabinet, she discovered all kinds of treasures. One by one, with the tap water running, Mickey poured the contents of each bottle down the drain. Completing that task, she took the chair and headed to the kitchen. There she opened up the cupboard and found more bottled things awaiting her destruction. She emptied each container down the kitchen sink. She stepped down, pushing the chair back the few feet into the dining room, and heard a car coming up the driveway.

Mickey ran frantically into the living room and found the perfect hideaway behind the couch. No one would ever find her. When she could, she would make her getaway back to the bedroom chair and crawl back into bed.

Mickey listened to the conversation in the kitchen. They knew someone had been there! Mickey's uncle came over and exclaimed that Mickey was missing.

The search began. They called her name. They searched everywhere. Smiling, Mickey knew she would not be found. Then someone saw a piece of clothing sticking out from the back of the couch. Frightened, Mickey crouched even more.

"Mickey, you come out from behind that couch *right now!*"

"The troubles did not begin there, Mickey," Phyl continued.

"One day you came over to the same place and killed all their chickens. In fact, you wrung their necks. We never did understand how someone so little and cute could do such a horrible thing." Phyl shook her head.

"I don't like chickens, Mommy. They're stupid!" Mickey felt that was a reasonable explanation.

"You got a good spanking, had to apologize, and spent time in your room," Phyl continued.

"Another time, you were staying with the neighbor on the other side. I came home from work, and they said I would have to get a different sitter. When I asked why, they told me you had drowned their kittens in a rain barrel, washed their dishes in milk, and beat their son with a teddy bear. He had just returned from World War II and was resting on the living room couch. You determined he would not sleep. You wanted him awake. That was the last time you were there."

Phyl continued, "Once I was visiting a dear friend who had two sons, one your age and one younger. Dottie was in the process of having the house painted. While we were visiting and having coffee together, you three finished painting the house—and yourselves. It is amazing I have any friends at all.

"Remember when we gave you piano lessons. You were faithful to walk to your lessons. When it came time to practice, however, I would find you sitting up in the walnut tree. We finally gave up and sold the piano.

"There was another sad time. I wonder if you remember. I was working in downtown Beaverton at a department store. We found a sitter for you a few blocks from the downtown area. They had two teenagers—a son and a daughter. Everything went well until one day the parents had to go somewhere. The daughter was there. She took good care of you, but she had to leave and the only person left was the son. You were in the kitchen. He picked up a butcher knife from the drawer and began to chase you. You ran toward the stairway and started up, making lots of noise so he would hear you. Then you turned around and hid in the coat closet downstairs. When the son ran up the stairs, you ran out the front door and down to the department store. I was so surprised to see you and noticed you were panicky. When you told me your story, I took the rest of the day off, took you home, and contacted the parents responsible for taking care of you, letting them know how irresponsible they had been and that you would not be returning."

"I remember, Mommy. I was very scared. I thought he was going to kill me with that knife. I waited until he got clear to the top of the stairs. As soon as I knew he was up there looking for me, I ran as fast as I could. I was afraid he would chase me down the street. I was so happy to see you."

"Me, too, Mickey." Phyl gathered Mickey in her arms and

hugged her. "Mickey, maybe you are old enough now to stay at home by yourself for a few hours. How do you feel about that?"

"I'm still afraid, Mommy. I'll try if I know you can come home if I need you. What if Glen tries to come over here? What if he sees you leave and knows I might be alone?"

"That will never happen, Mickey. I promise you. And, wherever you are, you will always have our phone number to call."

"One time, when I was in the first grade, I was walking home from school and three high school boys tried to run me down with their car. I ran into a ditch and they came close to me and swerved around the ditch. I was so scared. Then, I saw a lady standing on her porch motioning for me to come there. She took me inside and called you. You walked down to get me and walk me home. Do you remember that one?" Mickey looked over at her Mom.

"I sure do, Mickey. Your father found out who the three were and took care of them so they would never do that again. They did not know they were messing with the coach's daughter! The lady who took you in got the description of the car. Your father asked Earl if he knew who it was. He did. That was the end of that!"

Mickey settled into Phyl's arms and felt at peace.

Ghost Stories

It was 1938.

The world was at war. The economy was unstable, at best. One thing the war did provide was jobs, especially for women.

Peggy was working in the shipyards in Portland. She had moved with her daughter, Dee, to Vanport. It was a community full of shipyard workers who could find economic housing by the river.

Anna worried about her brothers who were serving. She got out her Bible and read. She prayed for their safety, protection, and provision. There was nothing she could do about the war or them. God would have to intervene.

Adolph had served the lumber business twenty-seven years. It was time to retire.

"Anna, grab your coat. We're going to look at some property out on Timber Route." Adolph walked out to start the car.

Why? she thought. Anna loved it where she

was—a beautiful home, garden, friends, church. She could walk everywhere. She had finally found stability and lasting friendships. Peggy had her business downtown and could walk up to see her. Or Anna would walk down and meet her for lunch. She climbed into the front seat and turned to Adolph.

"It's time to retire, Anna. Oregon American Lumber Company has been a wonderful place to work. It has provided for us well. We now have the means to buy a farm. I have saved as much as I could, despite the Great Depression. The property we are going to see is about five miles out in the country."

Anna knew already she did not like it. No point in seeing it. She was going to stay right where she was. That was her home. Her *last* home. "We don't need another house, Adolph. We have one."

"We're retiring, Anna. I want to quit working in the lumber business, retire, and do what I want when I want."

"I'm already doing that," Anna said.

"Anna! The *least* you can do is *look!* That won't cost you anything!" Anna sat in silence.

"If you don't like it, I will move there and you can stay in town." Adolph drove a little faster.

"I go where you go, Adolph." Anna was silent the rest of the trip.

The first thing Anna noticed was that the style of the farmhouse was Swedish.

Adolph parked the car. The young couple came out to greet them and escorted them inside.

"We want to move into town. It is too isolated for us out here," the young girl told them.

"Yes, I know," Anna said. Silently, she looked around. Despite her reservations, she liked what she saw. *Another move. New friends. Isolation. Loneliness.* Anna had known those things all her life. Yet if her Adolph moved here, that would mean she would also. God taught the woman to follow the man and be his helpmate, not his rebuttal.

Adolph took Anna around the eleven acres. At the back of the field was the Nehalem River. That meant his own private fishing spot. A gravel road beside the house led the way down. There was plenty of pasture to raise a cow and a steer. There was room for a garden. A small garage sat at the end of the long gravel driveway, leading from the main road. Behind the farmhouse and garage sat a huge red two-story barn. It was perfect.

"Anna, what do you think?" Adolph gave her a determined look.

"It's up to you, Adolph." *It always is,* she thought.

Adolph and Anna returned to the house. Adolph made the owner a substantial offer.

"It's yours, Adolph!" He extended his hand in final agreement.

Anna was silent all the way home.

Adolph didn't care. He had the farm and retirement. Anna would adjust. There would be plenty to do. She didn't need people. There were animals and canning and plenty to keep her busy.

Anna called Phyl. "Do you have a minute?" Anna sat down at her kitchen table. She looked around and felt an empty heart. She had worked so very hard and now had a home she was proud of.

"What is it, Momma? You sound despondent." Phyl listened for a response.

"We're moving," Anna said.

"Where? Why? Has something happened to Papa?" Phyl was very concerned, especially because of the depressed voice at the other end.

"Adolph wants to retire from the lumber business and move to a farm," Anna said.

"That's not retiring, Momma. That's just a different job!" Phyl laughed. Anna did not.

"You're serious, aren't you, Momma? Have you seen it? Tell me about it. When will you decide?"

"Adolph made him an offer. He accepted. Adolph will list our house tomorrow. It's done, Phyl. I have not told Peggy. It's a Swedish-style farmhouse on eleven acres with a river in the back of the property and a pasture and a huge two-story barn. For a farmhouse, it's lovely."

"Momma, if Papa has already bought it, it does not sound to me like you have time to protest. It's done! Can you be happy there?" Phyl did her best to encourage Anna in a decision that was already a done deal. You do drive, don't you, Momma?"

"Yes, I can drive. I would be able to go into town and visit my friends and see Peggy."

"Mig and I will drive out this weekend—Sunday—and go there with you and Papa. Then, we'll talk, Momma. I'll bring out a dessert."

"Yes, I would like your opinion. See you Sunday?"

"Sunday, Momma. Should I bring old shoes?"

"That might be a good idea. There is a cow pasture in the back." Anna hung up. She felt some relief that Phyl would give her opinion.

Anna wondered what kind of history the place had.

Adolph met with his men from the lumber company.

"I'll make sure your jobs are secure. The only change will be a new boss. He will begin in two weeks. I am proud of all of you, every single one. It is you who have seen me through difficult times. Each of you did your job to the best of your ability."

"Where will you be moving, Adolph?" one of the guys inquired.

"An eleven-acre farm out on Timber Route. It has the Nehalem in the back, a pasture for cows and a steer, plenty of room for crops, a two-story barn. It even has a small root house."

"Is that the house that used to be next to the dance club during the early twenties?" one of the guys asked.

"I have no idea." Adolph said. "Why?"

"It has ghosts! You haven't heard the stories?" The guys started laughing.

"Come on, gentlemen. I don't even believe in ghosts. Who knows? They might be nice to have around. I'll need helping hands!" Adolph was tired of being the butt of the joke.

"Not *those* hands, Adolph! They'll grab you when you are least expecting!" The guys laughed again.

"Mind if we tell you the stories, Adolph?"

"Go ahead. It is not going to change my plans."

"There used to be a dine and dance place next to the farmhouse—back in the early years of the century. It burned down one Halloween night. Shortly after that, cars were heard driving up and down the farmhouse's gravel driveway, with crowds of people laughing and cutting up. Yet in reality, no one was there."

Another worker chimed in. "Art and Lulu Lamping told about their three-year-old grandniece, who was playing in the living room. She told LuLu she saw a young boy who wanted to play with her. She went to the stairwell and said the boy was at the top, holding out his arms and wanting to come down to play. She held out her arms in response and invited him down. He never came down because there was no one there, LuLu said."

"Here's another. One day the doorbell rang. When someone answered the door, no one was there."

"One resident had Hepatitis B and, being very ill, went to bed. A hand reached out and touched her. There was a lady in a long black dress who tiptoed and looked down at her, touching her forehead to comfort her. The hand put a wet cloth on her forehead, and then crawled in bed next to her to comfort her. Her husband came out of the bathroom and started to crawl into bed. The woman of the house said, 'I need to tell you that there is already someone here beside me.' He could not see anyone but said to his wife, 'Tell 'em to move over 'cause I'm going to bed!'"

"A train was heard roaring by. Yet there was no train because there are no tracks anywhere nearby."

"I have one," one of the men piped up. "The piano keys played by themselves. That happened multiple times."

"A priest visited the house to exorcise it. He saw someone sitting in the corner playing the guitar. He left and never returned."

"Adolph," Harvard began, "is there a long gravel road that runs beside the property and pasture leading down to the creek?"

"Yes, there is, Harvard. Why?"

"Many years ago a team of horses was pulling a wagon down that road by the farmhouse. Something spooked the horses, and the driver fell and was killed. His casket was brought into the farmhouse and placed in the corner of the living room for viewing. A memorial service was held. Some of the mourners sat on a settee at the corner by the casket, weeping. Their tears left wet stains on the settee. The spot never dried—ever!"

Now they had Adolph's attention. They had described the very property he had purchased!

"A friend went to visit and saw someone come downstairs and look at him."

"A man was called to come out from the store to make some repairs and brought a friend with him. The floor installer saw a guy in front of the refrigerator watching him. When the other store man returned to finish his portion of the job, the first guy would not return."

"The same man saw a man in his forties who was wearing jeans and a plaid shirt, standing in front of the bedroom window with a cup of coffee. Yet no one by that description ever lived there."

"A neighbor man brought over his tractor to do some work at

the farmhouse, looked in the farmhouse window, and saw a man standing in the bedroom window, wearing blue jeans and a plaid shirt and drinking a cup of coffee. It was the same description and same place where the other man had seen him. Yet no one by that description was ever seen in that farmhouse. The neighbor refused to return and plow."

"Upstairs the people had gone to bed and noticed a fog hovering over them. Someone came and wiped their foreheads with a wet towel. Yet no one was there."

Adolph laughed. He would never let them know that it had gotten his attention. There was no way he was going to let someone's belief in ghosts affect his decisions.

"Well, Adolph. Do you still want to move there?" the guys laughed.

"You're darn right I do, gentlemen. If it is good enough for all those ghosts, it is certainly good enough for me. Nice to know we'll have some extra hands." Adolph stood up. "It's time to go, gentlemen." He shook each man's hand. "I'll see you for a couple of weeks. Then, I will only see you when I come to town."

"How does Anna feel about the move?" The men studied Adolph's expression.

"She'll adjust. She has good training at moving and fixing up a new place. It will be good for her. She needs something to do." He looked over at Harvard. Harvard looked away.

The Farm

Two weeks later, Anna had everything packed. Adolph had hired some guys to move their belongings. The house had been sold. As Adolph drove away unconcerned, Anna looked back as the tears trickled down her cheeks. She wiped them away quickly so Adolph would not tease her. *Lord, I thought this was my final home. My resting place. Now, here I am moving again to unfamiliar territory. Will this be the last, Lord?* She did not hear the Lord answer.

Once again, Anna scrubbed and cleaned. She arranged and rearranged the furniture until it looked just right. The kitchen had a little breakfast nook and a wood stove. The dining room was huge. It also contained a wood stove. The living room was comfortable. She arranged the wicker furniture. The piano looked nice against the wall, as did the Victrola.

Adolph had set up the old wringer-washer on

the inside covered porch. Anna gathered the weeks of clothing and began to run each piece through as the electric ringer drained the wash water from each piece.

Suddenly, Anna screamed in pain. Adolph heard her clear out by the barn. He came running onto the porch. He pulled the plug and helped Anna remove her tangled and gnarled fingertip from the ringer. Anna passed out cold on the floor. When she awoke, he helped her up to her feet.

"I have the car going, Anna. I'm taking you to the doctor. Your finger is badly mangled."

"I need to finish the laundry, Adolph. I don't want the clothes to mildew." Anna walked to the washer.

"Anna, don't be dumb!" He put her arm around his neck and walked her to the car.

The doctor examined her. He gave her some medicine for the pain. "Other than that, Anna, there is nothing I can do for your finger. I might try surgery. Your fingertip and nail will be mangled unless I can apply skin grafts and surgery."

"I will manage, doctor. I must get home and finish the laundry." Adolph escorted her out the door.

"Adolph, would you help me with the last load?" Anna turned to him for his answer. She was in a great deal of pain.

"I have chores to do, Anna. I'll get you some medicine, if you like." Adolph headed for the kitchen.

"No, Adolph. I'll be all right. Go do your chores." Anna was so tired.

"What's for dinner?" Adolph asked.

"Leftovers. I'll see what I can get together. Would eggs be all right tonight?"

"Anything, Anna. I'm getting hungry. I'll be in soon. Take it easy with that hand."

The farm work was never done. Anna brought in the old butter churn with a wooden handle. With three hundred strokes, she had butter. The cow's milk was placed in a huge refrigerator pan. When it separated, she had rich thick cream.

Adolph raised a steer for six months. He attempted to raise a pig. Adolph did everything possible to keep that pig clean. Finally, he made it into bacon, pork chops, and ham.

Phyl and Peggy's daughters were born two months apart. They loved the farm.

Anna would crawl between them at night and tell them stories. Their favorite was *The Little Match Girl* by Hans Christian Andersen. Anna recalled the story. She loved telling it to the little girls.

Anna always hugged the girls goodnight. They would sleep peacefully and request the same story the next night. Anna would then slip back into bed and whisper to Adolph about her nightly visit.

Anna always saw Phyl, Peggy, and the granddaughters after their yearly summer trip to the beach for a two-week stay. They would rent a cabin on the beach and shop for groceries. Always, they would stop in Seaside to get the girls paper dolls. It reminded them of a song they used to sing called "Paper Doll."

"Paper Doll"

I want to buy a paper doll that I can call my own.
A doll that other fellas will not steal.
And, when those flirty, flirty guys with their
Flirty, flirty eyes…
Will have to flirt with dollies that are real.
When I come home at night she will be waiting.
She'll be the sweetest doll in all the world.
I'd rather have a paper doll that I can call my own
Than have a fickle-minded real live girl.

❧

"Mickey, do you remember the time we came to the beach when you were about five years old? I was reading and watching you play. I had taken my eyes away from you for just a moment when I heard yelling. A man raced down to a little tide pool. He was removing a young child who was facedown and struggling to get out of the water. I ran down to see what was wrong. It was you, Mickey. It must have been an undertow. I thanked that man profusely. He saved your life."

"No, Mom, I don't remember that."

"The Lord was watching over you, Mickey, just as he watches over every one of us who belong to him."

The farm would always hold a special place in Mickey's heart. She and her cousin Dee found many activities—some good and some bad. It depended on who was interpreting them.

"Mickey," Adolph called from the other room, "if you are willing to go dig your own worms, bait your own hook, and clean your own fish, you can go fishing with me tomorrow."

"Yes, Grandpa." Adolph handed her an old bucket. It was small, but it was perfect for the number of earthworms needed to hook on for bait. Mickey knelt down on her knees in the backyard by the doghouse. She dug and dug until she had a full bucket of earthworms. Satisfied, she covered up the bucket so they would not crawl out.

Before she headed back inside, she noticed the doghouse, left there from previous owners. *That doghouse. I wonder what it feels like to be a dog and live in there.* Mickey managed to squeeze herself through the small opening. *It's awfully cramped in here,* she thought. It was not a comfortable place for a human. The next thing Mickey discovered was that she could not get back out.

"Grandpa. Grandpa!" Mickey yelled and yelled. It seemed like an eternity. Adolph was looking for her, too. Finally, he heard her voice. Taking the roof entirely off the doghouse, he lifted Mickey out of her cramped quarters.

"I won't do that again, Grandpa," Mickey confessed.

"Why did you do it in the first place?" Adolph inquired.

"I just wanted to know what it felt like to be a dog in his house." It all seemed perfectly logical to Mickey.

"Well, now you know. Remember, you need to go to bed early tonight and get up at four in the morning." Adolph opened the screen door and let Mickey go first into the farmhouse with her bucket of worms.

Early the next morning, Adolph woke her saying, "Rise and shine, little girl. It's time to get ready!" Adolph walked into the kitchen to see if Anna had breakfast and their lunches ready.

"Grandpa, it's still *dark,*" Mickey retorted.

"Remember, Mickey, the early bird…"

"Catches the worm," Mickey finished.

Anna fixed a hearty oatmeal breakfast and packed some good lunches and snacks.

Adolph drove for about an hour toward Astoria to his favorite fishing spot on the Columbia. It was so cold. They climbed into the boat with their gear and lunches.

Mickey had brought along layers of clothing and still was not warm.

"Sit very still in the boat when you climb in," Adolph told Mickey. "Better go over to the bushes there and go to the bathroom before climbing in. Once you are in the boat and on the water, there will be no place to go."

If it wasn't for Grandpa, Mickey thought, *I would be awfully afraid on this big river.*

Adolph handed Mickey the fishing rod and showed her how to hook on the worm and toss the line into the water.

"A bite! Grandpa, I have a bite!"

Adolph instructed her how to reel it in.

"Let us play a little. Give it a slight jerk to hook it. Reel it in slowly. Let it play. Get your net ready. When it comes alongside, reach out and place the net under the fish and bring it in. Place it in the wicker basket."

"Grandpa, Grandma will be mad if I drink beer," Mickey told Adolph when he offered her some.

"Grandma does not need to know everything, Mickey. We won't tell her. It is cold out here, and it will help warm you."

Mickey took a swallow. "Ugh! It tastes awful!"

"Take enough to keep you warm. You don't have to drink it all," Adolph added.

Time dragged. Nothing was biting. Then…

"I got another one, Grandpa!" Mickey stood up in excitement.

"Sit down, child. You'll—"

Mickey fell overboard into the icy Columbia and began to bob up and down.

"Help, Grandpa. Help!" The current was pulling her out.

Adolph reached out his hand to her, but she was too far away. He tried to row. He was about to jump in when another boat came alongside.

Two young guys dove in and grabbed Mickey. They swam to Adolph's boat and placed her icy-cold hands onto the boat. Adolph took her hands and pulled her into the boat with the help of the two guys. The two girls who had been left on the other boat paddled over to the young men and helped them climb back aboard.

"Thank you. Thank you so much." Adolph wrapped every extra towel, blanket, and covering he had around Mickey. She was shivering uncontrollably.

The two guys and girls waved as they, too, wrapped up warmly and rowed off toward shore.

"We're going home, Mickey. We caught more than we bargained for. How do I explain this to your grandma? She will never allow you to go again." Adolph rowed toward shore.

"It's okay, Grandpa. We had a good time and caught our dinner. We don't have to tell Grandma everything, remember?"

"But she will ask why you are so wet and cold," Adolph said.

"Very wet fish, Grandpa. Got me all wet and cold."

They laughed as they placed themselves and their gear into the car and drove home, grateful to both be alive.

Anna placed a few strips of bacon into the cast iron frying pan. She added some salt and pepper to the flour and rubbed it onto the cleaned fish. She then placed the fish in the pan to fry. Taking six new potatoes, she peeled and sliced them into some cold ice water to crisp. Patting them dry, she took a little of the bacon grease and placed it into another fry pan. Mickey picked fresh spinach leaves from the garden. Anna washed and patted them dry and placed a little sugar on top. Fresh beets, cooked until tender, added a nice color to the plate. She had made her sunshine salad earlier in the day. When the lemon Jell-O had begun to firm, she had added cut pieces of celery, grated carrot, and thin slices of radish into the dish, returning it to the refrigerator until it firmed completely. She always added a teaspoon of vinegar and a teaspoon of sugar to the Jell-O mix with the water. It was one of Mickey's favorites.

That evening, after the dishes were washed and dried, they sat around the living room. Mickey played the piano. Anna had fixed hot chocolate for the three of them.

Mickey played a few records on the Victrola.

"Mickey, Anna, come into the bedroom and look out the window."

The three of them sat very still and silent as they looked toward the apple tree. After a long wait, they were rewarded. Two deer began nibbling at the fallen apples. They were beauties.

Peggy's daughter, Dee, who was just two months younger than Mickey, would be coming to the farm tomorrow and stay the rest of the week. The girls always enjoyed each other's company. Often, their fun was mischief. Anna did her best to keep them busy and occupied.

Mickey arose early. Anna had fixed some toast, a boiled egg, and some cereal. Coffee, for Adolph and Anna, always came mid-morning, after some of the early chores were done.

Mickey grabbed a basket and headed for the chicken coop. It scared her a bit to reach under those hens. They did not care much for her, either. One by one, Mickey gathered each egg into the basket. Then the rooster crowed and came charging at her. Scared, she nearly dropped the eggs.

Mickey took the basket into the farmhouse and handed it to Anna. Those eggs not only fed them; they gave Adolph and Anna some spending money when Adolph took them into town to sell.

The day was going to be really hot. It was already seventy-five degrees at noon!

Peggy arrived with Dee. Anna had prepared a picnic basket full of fruit, sandwiches, and beverages. The girls donned their swimsuits, and the family walked down through the cow pasture to the end of the property out back.

"Careful, girls! Watch out for those cow pies! You won't smell too good once you step in them!"

Reaching the Nehalem River (just a creek behind the pasture), they spread out a blanket at the river bank.

"You girls better go swimming first before we eat so you don't get stomach cramps," Peggy yelled.

The rocks were slippery and covered with bits of moss. The girls swam in the shallow creek.

"Ouch!" Dee yelled. "A crawfish just pinched me!"

"Here, girls, take the buckets and place the crawfish into them. We'll take them home and cook them." Between the two of them, they were able to find about ten.

They lay on the blankets in the warm sunshine and dined on Anna's delicious feast.

Back at the farm, Anna placed a large pan of water onto the wood stove. Adolph stoked the fire, placing a few more pieces of kindling under the top cover. Soon, the water began to boil. Peggy dropped each crawfish live into the boiling water. It seemed cruel to the girls. Anna explained that it didn't really bother the crawfish.

Anna had baked an apple pie that morning. With some rice and fresh green beans, they enjoyed a delicious meal. The crawfish tasted like miniature lobsters.

The girls looked around the farmhouse for buckets of all sizes. Tomorrow, they would drive up to the highway to the Oregon coast, walk up the trails from the road, and pick wild blackberries.

It was time to accompany Adolph out to the barn. First, Bossie had to be coaxed in from the pasture. Once in the barn, she was fed hay. When she was chewing her cud and content, Mickey placed the small stool Adolph handed her to the rear. Mickey grabbed each teat and squeezed spurts of milk into the bucket. A small dish was filled and placed beside the stool. A tiny kitten happily came alongside Mickey and slurped into oblivion. Her purrs and mews were balanced with the cow's moos. It was a chorus unlike any other.

Dee and Mickey recalled the time they took Anna's clothes out to the barn and covered them with hay. Worse, they decided to try smoking there, too. An ash fell from one of the cigarettes and set some straw on fire. Mickey took Grandma's clothing and put out the flame. Grandma never could understand why her dresses smelled so funny.

Then there was the time they had broken into the root cellar and drunk a beer. Or the time they had gone across the street to the trailer and grabbed pipes. Smoking them had made them ill all day.

After breakfast, each of them donned their old grubby clothes, grabbed their buckets, and set out for Hwy 26. They were already halfway from Vernonia to the highway at the farmhouse.

En route, they each thought of old songs and sang to their hearts' content.

Stained and dirty, they had filled their buckets to the brim. There was just no more room to put berries. They gently placed each bucket into wooden boxes Adolph had placed in the trunk to keep them from spilling.

Each one took turns soaking the dirt off in the tub. Anna immediately went to work making a fresh wild blackberry pie. Adolph had picked up some ice cream in town. Peggy washed and placed berries in jars, adding a little sugar, to stack into the cooler for future use.

Adolph had taken the six-month-old calf into town for butchering and packaging. That night Adolph brought in a steak for each of them. He again stoked up the fire in the wood stove. Anna placed some potatoes in the oven.

Mickey and Dee had churned butter the day before. Anna then had taken the churned ball of butter and made it into a huge square, patting down the top and sides. Then, with a big knife, she had sliced it into butter cubes.

Anna took the big pan of fresh milk and dipped the ladle into it. She scooped enough out so each of them would have a full glass of fresh milk. Mickey and Dee thought it tasted peculiar. They were used to "city milk."

Anna sat down at the piano in the living room. Memories flooded back about her fingers being hit with a ruler when she made mistakes. She only knew a few songs. It had hurt too much to continue her lessons.

It was time for the girls to return to their homes. Summer was nearly over. School supplies and new clothes needed to be purchased.

With the girls back in their own homes, Adolph decided to do a little local fishing. Fishing season had officially ended, but he had a built-in fishing spot right at the end of his own property! Adolph grabbed the familiar, well-worn wicker basket, placed in it some bait, and prepared his favorite rod for the trip.

Anna handed Adolph a sandwich, piece of fruit, and a thermos of coffee and waved goodbye from the farmhouse doorway. Adolph grabbed his worn denim jacket, put on his fishing boots, and walked down the long gravel road to the property's end. It was a beautiful day, and it had rained the day before. A perfect day for fish to bite. Sitting along the bank, it was so peaceful and quiet. There was not another soul in sight. Just the way Adolph wanted it. All to himself. He threw in the line and teased it back and forth. An hour later, he had caught five nice trout.

He was just getting ready to eat his sandwich when he heard a voice behind him.

"Afternoon, Adolph! How's the fishing?" The tall gentleman stood beside him, his old car sitting on the gravel road.

"Doin' yust fine, Gunter. How are you?"

"How many fish did you catch today, Adolph?"

Adolph knew he had been caught. He could not sit there beside his catch and lie to the fish and game warden.

"Five, I believe, Gunter. Want me to count them again?"

"One would be enough, Adolph. I have to give you a fine, you know."

"Yeah, I know. How much?" Adolph just wanted his peace and quiet returned. He did not want to visit with Gunter.

"Twenty-six dollars." Gunter wrote out the ticket and handed it to Adolph.

"Isn't that a little steep for five fish?" Adolph retorted.

"Not during off-season, Adolph. That is reasonable. Complaints will raise the price."

"Here's thirty dollars. It will pay for your gas." Adolph ignored Emil and began to pack up.

"Goodbye, Adolph. Better wait until the season begins again." Gunter put the thirty dollars into his wallet.

"Do I get to keep the fish? Or shall I throw dead fish into the river?" Adolph retorted sarcastically.

"Keep the fish, Adolph—this time!"

Adolph gathered his belongings and walked back home—satisfied with his catch.

"Adolph, how was the fishing? What did you catch?"

"Very expensive fish." Adolph shared the story about Gunter's appearance.

"It will make the trout that much more enjoyable!" Anna laughed.

Spring and summer had passed. Fall had arrived. Anna was preparing for the holidays.

Adolph walked to his property across the street and found a six-foot pine tree perfect for the farm's living room. Placing it in the stand, he placed a little water in the bottom.

Anna walked upstairs and searched for the old-fashioned lights they had used for their entire marriage. They remembered using a fresh tree that had been put up Christmas Eve when they were children, and decorated with candles, which were lit the next morning. Now, trees were put up earlier. To place the traditional candles upon them would be a fire hazard, they knew.

Anna offered to do the tedious job of stringing cranberries and popped corn. When she had finished, Adolph strung them layer by layer on the tree limbs. Anna looked lovingly at the old-fashioned Christmas balls handed down from each generation. Gently, she placed them one by one onto the tree, evening them out to be distributed until the tree seemed to smile back at them.

Adolph wound up the old Victrola, placed the needle on the record, and played Bing Crosby's *White Christmas.* They sat together with a cup of hot coffee and some slices of cardamom bread Anna had toasted in the oven. Adolph dunked his slice into his coffee, sat back, and admired the tree.

"The family will be here in a few days, Anna. What do we need from the store? I'll be going into Portland tomorrow morning. I'm going to the meat market in North Portland to buy meat and skins to make Potatas Korv. Do you have time to ride along?"

Anna made a list of all the things she needed to do.

"Yes, I do. I have a few things I can purchase from the farmers market in downtown Portland." Anna circled these on her list. Purchasing a turkey from the meat market was her number one priority.

Every year Phyl and Anna traded places for Christmas Eve and Christmas Day. This year it was Anna's turn. Swedish mints were placed in the compote on the buffet. In the window was an electric candle always on to greet the welcomed guests.

Christmas Eve would be the traditional smorgasbord. Anna prepared head cheese. She decided not to use the brains. The granddaughters would not touch it. Adolph pulled out the electric oven and placed it on the stand. He wheeled it into the dining room and put it near the buffet.

Anna prepared the sweet dough for cardamom bread, kneading and adding a little more flour until it felt right.

"Anna, would you give me the recipe?" others would ask.

"I don't have a recipe," Anna said. "Just watch me and write down what I do. Recipes are for people who do not know how to cook."

Anna took the plump dough and divided it. Taking two sections at a time, she braided them together. Cinnamon topped each loaf. She buttered a cookie sheet and placed the braided loaf on the sheet.

Adolph stoked the fire in the kitchen stove. When the wood burned down to embers, Anna placed the sheet into the oven for baking.

The aroma permeated the farmhouse. Saliva tingled atop her tongue as she waited for the bread to be done.

Stale bread was cubed and placed into a plastic bag. Anna placed a little salt, pepper, and sage into the bag, shaking it to cover each cube. When it came time to stuff the turkey, she melted a little butter in the fry pan, add chopped celery, onion, and broken walnuts and, last, some chicken broth. Stirring these all together, she then poured it atop a bowl full of bread cubes. The mixture was put in the turkey cavity. The turkey was then placed in the portable oven and left to bake. Drippings, giblets, and flour with salt and pepper would be stirred until crumbly. Then Anna added milk to make thick gravy.

Greens from the garden plus a fruit salad accompanied the dinner. She placed the candied sweet potatoes and mashed potatoes made with a little garlic into serving bowls. In a small dish, Anna placed the cooked and sugared cranberries.

Adolph called the family to dinner.

"Mig, would you give a toast?" Adolph looked across the dinner table as Mig nodded in affirmation.

"I will say the blessing," Adolph said, after Mig gave his toast. When he finished, he looked over at Clarence, Mickey's husband, concerned. "Clarence, you have not said a word! Are you always this quiet?" he asked.

Clarence chuckled. "I'm just a quiet man, Adolph."

When everyone had had their fill, Anna spoke up. "Now that we have finished dinner and while we have our pumpkin pie, I want to read a letter from Earl." Anna smiled at her guests.

Phyl and Mig looked to Anna, surprised.

The Navy Seabees/Bikini Atoll

Anna opened the welcomed letter from Earl and read it aloud.

"What are the Seabees?" Anna said.

"Anna! You are so dumb! Let *me* explain it!" Adolph grumbled, and Anna fell humbly silent.

"Papa! I have listened to that for the last time. You will not ever call her dumb in my presence again. Momma is *not* dumb. She married you, Papa! Would someone dumb marry you? She has achieved many goals. She was the first nanny to the world-famous Davenport family of the historic Davenport Hotel in Spokane, Washington. She achieved her own millinery business. She is an outstanding cook. She is very wise. How is it you can call her dumb, Papa?"

Adolph was silent. He did not apologize. He rose and suggested everyone retire to the living room.

Anna followed the family into the living room and continued reading the letter.

> Shortly after joining, I learned that the Navy was seeking volunteers to do a study for undersea photography during the testing of the nuclear bomb and its effects.
>
> After World War II ended, the United States War Department ordered two atomic tests to determine the effect on war ships, equipment, and materials of atomic detonations above and below water. The Bikini Atoll, located in the Marshall Islands about 2,000 miles southwest of Hawaii, was chosen as the site. Nearly 42,000 people, including military personnel, civilians, scientists, and United States and foreign dignitaries, traveled from all over the world to help stage and witness the test. In the spring of 1946, twenty-two photographers of the Pacific Fleet Camera Party at Pearl Harbor responded to the Navy's request for volunteers to train to become qualified Navy deep-sea divers and use underwater cameras specially constructed to photograph the target ships that would be used during Test Able and Test Baker at Bikini. When the intensive program ended, only seven photographers out of the twenty-two volunteers qualified for the title of Navy Deep Sea Diver, Second Class. I was one of those chosen.
>
> At age eighteen, after graduating from Klamath Union High School, I began a ten-week stint at the navy boot camp in San Diego, California. On the sixth week, naval officers arrived at the camp, seeking volunteers for the Seabees, a division of the navy with personnel who operated heavy equipment for rebuilding airfields and roads in liberated war zones. As I had long lost my enthusiasm for boot camp, and since volunteers would be relived at once from finishing their boot camp training, I immediately volunteered. They

transferred me then to Camp Parks, fifty miles east of San Francisco, where I served for six months as a yeoman in the Seabees before the navy reassigned me to the Fleet Camera Party at Pearl Harbor, Hawaii. My only qualification was my experience during my senior year as a part-time photographer at a newspaper in Klamath Falls, Oregon, under the auspices of the head photographer, Wes Guderian.

During World War II, many ships damaged in battle were sent to Pearl Harbor for repairs, including the recalibration of their guns. Our main duty in the Fleet Camera Party was to photograph the accuracy of those guns after their battle damage had been repaired. We accomplished this by photographing with high-speed cameras. The shells were fired from the repaired battle ships toward a twelve-foot, square, upright target towed on pontoons 400 feet behind the tugboat we photographers were on. Sometimes, the whistling noise of a sixteen-inch shell came too close for comfort as we were photographing the shell's trajectory from the tugboat. Luckily, we escaped the friendly fire while helping to realign the warship's guns!

Later, twenty-two of us were selected to train as underwater photographers for the upcoming Bikini atomic bomb tests. We began our initial training in the 100-foot submarine training tower in Pearl Harbor, which was ordinarily used to train submarine personnel to escape if their submarines sank. Our training consisted first of classroom sessions to acquaint us with the proper use of the diving equipment and the underwater cameras. Later, we sometimes practiced dives in Pearl Harbor's shallow waters where ship movements constantly churned the harbor into a black, mucky void.

One literally breathtaking test required a free descent from the top of the 100-foot training tower, swimming down twenty-five feet to the first safety air chamber hatch with no breathing equipment of any kind. Our six-week final test and graduation dive was a 165-foot dive, in 200-pound training gear, to the ocean floor near Barburs Point, off the coast of Oahu. The crystal-clear water was a beautiful sight after Pearl Harbor's black waters.

After the seven of us who were chosen finally finished our training at Pearl Harbor, we were transferred to Bikini in the Marshall Islands. Shortly after arriving, we were issued the use of a sixty-foot Landing Craft Medium (LCM) to use as a storage and diving platform for our shallow-water work. We needed to have an air-supply line, which would supply air to and from the air compressor on the LCM, attached to our lifeline. We had the Navy carpenters build a roof over our LC and paint 'Underwater Photo Unit' on both sides.

Our initial shallow-water dives were less than 100 feet, and we only used a lightweight belt with a facemask. Those dives in the crystal-clear waters of the Bikini Lagoon were magnificent, as most of the time we could see clearly things that were more than a football-field length away. Currents sculpted the white sandy sea bottom, which resembled an underwater desert. Beautiful mountains of pastel coral rose here and there, on the rock outcroppings. Multicolored fish of every size were as curious about us as we were about them.

It was during this camera testing time that we discovered that the triggers on our $30,000 cameras were useless. The designers hadn't realized that the water pressure at 80 feet would force the triggers to close. As the cameras were operated electrically, the only way we could take an underwater photo was by using the phones in our helmets! So, when a diver said, "Shoot!" a crewman topside pulled the plug out of the camera's battery on deck, and then pushed it back in, thereby firing the camera's shutter. Ironically, we eventually improved by mounting German-made wind-up, 35mm cameras in

150 mm shell castings! After that, there were no further unexpected surprises from our equipment.

To dive over 100 feet, we used a diving ship equipped with a compression chamber, in case we got the bends, which means, in medical terms, a condition that develops when the gas bubbles expand in the blood stream or enter joints, causing pain. We usually suited up and dived in pairs. Whether a diver wore his full diving suit or just his helmet and a pair of shorts depended on the depth of the dive. Our main task was to photograph the parts of the ships that had failed enough after the atomic explosion to cause the ships to sink. We stayed down no longer than necessary, because the more time we spent diving and the farther we descended, the more time we'd need to ascend and decompress at various depths under the surface before we could safely reach normal topside air pressure, which is 14.5 pounds per square inch.

If we dove 150 feet down and stayed fifteen minutes, we could climb the lifeline to fifty feet from the surface and stand on an underwater platform for maybe forty minutes. A winch raised the platform to thirty feet and we'd stand there for thirty minutes. Then the platform was raised to twenty feet and we'd stand there for twenty minutes, after which we and the platform were pulled out of the water, so the crew topside had to move us from the platform to a dressing chair and remove our diving suits, so we could breathe fresh air again. Next, they removed our eighty-pound belt, our diving shoes (eighteen pounds each), and unscrewed our helmet from our brass breastplate. Finally, they removed the breastplate and then the suit. They also delivered our cameras to the laboratory that processed the film.

In April 1946, we seven divers, with our diving equipment and six $30,000 underwater cameras, left Pearl Harbor for Bikini Atoll and the atomic tests. They went from twenty selected men to Bikini, then to seven men to Bikini Atoll. At 9:00 a.m., July 1, 1946, the Test Able atomic bomb was exploded 520 feet in the air above the target ships at Bikini Lagoon. Observers on ships fifteen miles away viewed through dark glasses the bomb's awesome 12,000-foot mushroom cloud. Located on the islands surrounding the target area were many different cameras, all designed to record as much information as possible. All the cameras were mounted on towers, with doors that closed automatically after the photos were taken, to prevent radiation from damaging the film by fogging it. One movie camera could take 1,000 photos per second. Over 10,000 instruments of all kinds were located on the ships and on the shore. After the test, radiological surveys proved the lagoon surprisingly safe to enter the same day, since most of the radiation had dispersed harmlessly into the air.

On July 25, 1946, the Test Baker atomic bomb was exploded ninety feet below the waters of Bikini Lagoon. Observers watching from seven miles away were astounded as a column of ten million tons of water, 2,000 feet across, rose 6,000 feet into the air. Test Baker caused substantially more residual radioactivity than Test Able, as surface radioactive water had doused the target ships, so re-entry by the photographers was delayed until the ships were washed down to eliminate radioactivity.

Anna finished the letter and spoke first. "I cannot even begin to tell you just how proud I am of every member of my family. You have all set goals and accomplished them. You have achieved your dreams and passed on to your children the desire to set your standards high and not recognize defeat. Earl is a prime example of this. I am so proud of him."

"We are proud of you, Anna. You began the process. You set goals. You set your standards high. You achieved. You passed these principles on from generation to generation. You set biblical standards. You are our godly example of what God can accomplish through anyone who is willing to follow him," Clarence said.

Anna had never heard such praise before from her family. All she had heard from Adolph lately was how dumb she was. *"Let me tell it, Anna. You never get it right. You're so dumb, Anna."* She had begun to believe and accept it as true. Now, her family was telling her that *she* was the example the generations followed because she followed the Lord and taught them to do likewise.

Do they really think that? Anna thought to herself, as the tears welled up in her eyes. Adolph chimed in. "I'm grateful that the wars are over, that our children and grandchildren are back home, and that they have served their country well. That is not only a credit to our family and our country. It is a credit to God who directed their paths, protected them, and provided for them."

The women gathered in the kitchen to wash the dishes. When they finished, they took their tired bodies into the living room. Phyl, Peggy, and the girls insisted that Anna be seated in the living room. She had done enough.

The presents were waiting under the tree.

"Mickey and Dee, will you distribute the gifts?" Adolph asked.

After the gifts had all been distributed and opened, Adolph stood up and looked at his gathered family. "I have an announcement." Everyone looked up from the paper trash pile.

Adolph continued, "Anna and I are finding it too difficult to keep up the farm any longer. We're thinking about selling and moving to Port Orford. We have looked at property there and will build a home."

Phyl said, "We will miss you. When will you make your decision?"

"We have made our decision. I list the farm tomorrow. We'll move as soon as it is sold."

"Now, who would like Tom and Jerrys?" Mig asked.

Adolph and Mig excused themselves into the kitchen. Mig

heated a pan of milk while Adolph beat the egg whites into foam and the yolks to a smooth yellow and added sugar. Stirring slowly, he added the hot milk to the yolk mixture. He added one teaspoon of rum and one teaspoon of whiskey to each coffee mug, then poured in the hot milk mixture. He then topped it off with the beaten egg whites and topped that with nutmeg.

They brought each adult a fresh Tom and Jerry and a plate of Anna's delicious Spritz cookies. The girls would have to be content with the alcohol-free beverages until they were older.

Anna said, "Peggy, we are all so grateful for the way God saved you and Dee from the Vanport Flood in 1948. Mig and Phyl drove us to the site. Mickey and Dee were only twelve years old. You lost your home, your job—everything." Anna looked at Peggy with compassion. She understood suffering, moving, and loss from a personal standpoint.

"That was one of the worst years of our lives, Momma. The river just rose and rose. It would not stop. Yes, I believe God divinely intervened to warn us to get out. A whole community was wiped out that day, never to be rebuilt. I never again heard from those people. I don't know if any survived." Peggy walked over and hugged Anna. "Thank you."

"It was our pleasure, Peggy, to take you and Dee in with us until you could find a job and a home in Vernonia," Anna said.

In the spring, Adolph listed the farm for sale where they had lived for the last twenty-five years. They distributed many of their valuables to the family and sold the rest. A young couple bought it to use for their home and her business of selling antiques and collectibles.

Adolph and Anna moved into their Port Orford home by the lake. At least they had a glimpse of the ocean.

Shortly after their move, Peggy and her husband, Rusty, moved nearby. Rusty found work in the mill at Sixes.

Next to join them were Dee and her husband, Reggie. Reggie also found employment at the mill.

Dee gave birth to a son, Charles. Her marriage to Reggie was declining. One day, in a drunken rage, Reggie came home and threw out all of Dee and Charles's clothing and pushed them outside, locking the doors behind him.

Dee took Charles and drove over to Peggy's. Peggy wanted them to stay and never return to Reggie.

Just as they were ready to return to their home, Reggie phoned.

"I have a rifle. It's loaded. I am going to kill all of you. I am just calling to warn you." Reggie again was in a drunken stupor.

Peggy and Rusty drove over to Anna and Adolph's, taking Dee and little Charles with them. Adolph called the police.

Reggie called their house too. Adolph answered the phone.

"My rifle is loaded. I plan to kill all of you. You will never leave that house. One by one, I will get each of you." Reggie slurred his words. He stumbled his way to the car and drove off, peeling out of the driveway. First, he arrived at Rusty and Peggy's house. Finding no one home, he called Adolph again.

"Where are Rusty and Peggy? And where are my wife and child? I demand an answer. Now!" Adolph was terrified of Reggie's voice. He decided to act calm.

"You will never harm any one of us. You're crazy, Reggie. Crazy in the head!" Adolph yelled into the phone.

Anna, Peggy, Dee, and Charles sat frozen in their places.

"They're all there—at your house, aren't they, Adolph? They're all there!" Reggie was screaming into the phone. Everyone could hear him. Adolph hung up. He telephoned the police again. A patrol squad had been sent out to canvas the town for his whereabouts. One was staked at his home and one at Rusty and Peggy's house.

Anna managed to get up and close the drapes. Adolph checked the doors to be sure they were locked securely.

The phone rang again. Adolph let it ring. Everyone sat frozen, staring at it. The doorbell rang. No one moved.

"It's the police."

Finally, Adolph decided to peek out through the drape. He saw the officer's car near the yard.

Adolph gently opened the front door.

"I have an officer staked out at the street. I wanted to tell you that we just received a phone call from the mill at Sixes. Apparently, Reggie returned there for some reason. They had received our warning about his absurd and dangerous behavior. Before he left the mill, he had a heart attack. I'm here to tell you that we did not have to apprehend him. He's dead. No one can harm you anymore. You're safe to go home." The officer stayed a moment.

Adolph thanked the officer and shook his hand. Closing the door behind him, he dropped down onto a chair.

In the quietness of that moment, they began to sob, releasing their tension. They were free and safe.

One of the men who had worked at the mill had known Reggie. He name was Chuck. In the next few months, he began to court Dee, expressing his love for her and desire to adopt her little boy. They eventually married, and after a few years, Chuck decided to move his family to Klamath Falls.

Growing Old

Adolph and Anna were grateful for Peggy's presence with them in their old age. Peggy had sold her home without any problems after Rusty, her husband, died of a heart attack while working in the woods one fateful morning.

Peggy awakened one morning with terrible pains near her stomach. When they became worse, she decided to visit a doctor in Coos Bay. She wanted to drive alone. Adolph and Anna insisted on going along.

The doctor told her, "Peggy, I want to send you over to the hospital for some additional tests. It is just routine. I want to be certain that it is not anything more serious. I will have you do a CT scan. Do you have someone with you, or are you driving?"

Peggy assured him she had a ride home. She prepared for the CT scan, had it, and then went back home and waited for the results. She did not have to wait long.

A phone call came the following day from her doctor. "Peggy, I am sad to inform you that you have liver cancer. I will need to put you into chemotherapy treatment every two weeks beginning next week. Two weeks on, two weeks off. It will be a lot of driving. You'll feel nauseated after each treatment, and you will be very tired. I hope we have caught this in time."

Peggy was devastated. She began the treatments and continued them for nearly a year. When Mickey came down to visit them once, they went out for a drive.

"I cannot continue living like this, Mickey. I am so sick of cancer and its treatments. I am tired all the time. I am taking care of Momma and Papa. I cannot do it any longer. I don't want to. I am going to stop the treatments. I cannot see that I am getting any better." Peggy sat in silence.

"Yes, I'll die," Peggy said.

"You will be in heaven." Mickey wanted to be certain.

"Yes, Mickey. I accepted Christ into my life. I will be with Jesus."

"Please, reconsider this, Peggy. God may not be through with you here on earth. Dying is his timing, not ours," Mickey insisted.

"I have made up my mind. I am concerned about Momma and Papa. I will make arrangements for them."

Shortly after Mickey returned home, she received word that Peggy had gone to be with her Lord. "She's home."

Adolph and Anna would have to get along as best they could. Dee, Peggy's daughter, and her family had moved to Roseburg. The rest of the family was living near Portland. Adolph and Anna would have to call on the help of their church family and community for their needs unless family members came to visit.

Anna had Adolph. Though they were now elderly, he would take care of her.

It was the spring of 1969.

"Anna, get a lunch ready—some sandwiches, fruit, and a beverage—maybe a couple of cookies. I'd like to go down along the river and do some fishing."

Anna, ever obedient to her husband's demands, packed a healthy lunch for the two of them. She did not enjoy fishing, but she loved to ride along with Adolph. Whenever he hooked a fish, he always put up his index finger to let her know he had a fish on the line. She would smile and wave.

It was a beautiful day. The sun was shining. The rain was done for a day. Adolph always said that the fishing was best the day after a good, hard rain. They drove south to Gold Beach and inland a little way to the bank of the Rogue River.

Adolph found a good spot and parked the car. He baited his hook and walked to the river's edge. He threw out the line and played with it for a while, whisking it back and forth. He tried without any luck for an hour and decided to stop for some coffee and lunch. He returned to the car. Anna opened the thermos and put out two cups. She spread out each sandwich on a napkin and placed an apple out for each of them. They ate and talked, enjoying the breathtaking view of the river and the new spring foliage.

After eating and visiting for another hour, Adolph returned to the riverbank. He tossed out the line with some new bait on the end, hoping that would change his luck. A bite! He began reeling it in ferociously. It was going to be a real struggle; he could feel the weight of the fish on the line and wondered if he would even get it at all. He reached up his index finger to let Anna know that he had one on. He eventually reeled in the huge fish. It plopped around on the ground, trying to break free.

Then Adolph fell to the ground. Anna sat and waited for him to get up. She waited and waited. Adolph did not move. Anna opened the door and stepped out. She walked toward where Adolph lay unmoving. She called his name. No response. She called again. Still no response. Anna cradled his head in her arms and began to wail and weep. She looked out toward the water. There, in the distance, was a boat. Inside were three men with their fishing rods dangling out the side. They waved. They had seen Adolph fall and Anna kneeling. They rode over to the bank where Anna knelt beside Adolph.

The men stepped out and walked toward Anna. Anna's tender brown eyes looked up at the men. "He reeled in this fish. Then, he fell. He did not get up. He is not moving or responding."

One of the men knelt down and felt Adolph's pulse. He held Anna in his arms, ever so gently, and whispered to her, "Your husband is dead."

Anna began to sob uncontrollably. She held Adolph, rocking him back and forth. The other two men knelt and lifted Adolph up. They carried him to the backseat of the car and placed Anna in the front passenger seat. The fish was unhooked and placed into the fishing bag. They then gathered up the fishing gear and put it in the trunk.

They each introduced themselves and asked her name.

"Anna, we will take you home. Is there anyone there to be with you?"

"No," Anna replied. "Adolph and I live alone."

"We will take Adolph to the county morgue and help you with the arrangements. We will stay with you until you can find someone to come and be with you. Who is your nearest relative?"

"I guess that would be my granddaughter, Dee. She lives in Roseburg. My only living daughter, Phyl, lives near Portland."

One of the men helped her make the call. Dee said she would leave right away and come to stay with Anna and help her with the arrangements. The man insisted that Anna call her physician. The doctor came over and administered a shot to help Anna stay calm.

Anna called the church. Someone would be right over and bring a meal and stay with her. Then, she called Phyl. One of the men helped her with that call, too. The other man had taken Adolph's car and driven it to the county morgue. He asked them to call Anna the next day, after Dee would have arrived, to make arrangements. They also placed the fish in the freezer and waited for someone to arrive from her church.

The couple from the church brought Anna a meal, but she wasn't hungry. They helped get her into bed. With the help of the shot, she went right to sleep, tears streaming down her wrinkled cheek onto the pillow. Death had found her again.

The next morning arrived. Anna awoke and looked for Adolph. She was in such deep grief, she had momentarily forgotten the previous day's events—until she walked into the living room and saw the lady from the church.

"Where's Adolph? Did he go out?" Anna looked around. "It was nice of you to drop by. I'm sorry I was asleep when you arrived."

"Anna, sit down. Let's have a little breakfast and coffee and talk." She reminded Anna of what had happened, bringing it step by step back into Anna's tired mind.

"Oh, Adolph. Adolph!" Anna cried. The lady put her arm around Anna to comfort her.

"Dee will be arriving soon to stay here with you and help with arrangements. You have a lot to do. She will help you."

"What will happen to me now?" Anna became fearful.

"That is up to you and Dee," the lady said.

"I want to stay right here in my home. I am *not* going anywhere!" Anna slammed her fist onto the table.

"Your doctor wants you to call him," the lady said.

"What for? I don't need a doctor. I need Adolph!" Anna insisted.

"Anna, your body has suffered a tremendous shock. Your doctor wants to give you another shot to help you through this difficult time. I think you should let him come over, Anna. It will help you relax while you make difficult decisions." The lady poured them another cup of coffee.

"No, I don't want any more shots. I want to *think!*" Anna said.

Dee arrived and hugged her grandma. Phyl called and said she would be taking the bus down and would arrive that evening.

Mig insisted they could not take Anna into their home. It was up to Dee now, he said.

The funeral arrangements were made; the obituary was in the paper. After the service, all gathered at Anna's home, and they shared a meal and fellowship.

Phyl would return home after the service.

Dee insisted Anna spend a few days in Roseburg with them.

Anna looked behind her at her home, her memories. She thought of Adolph and accepted. She would see her beloved Adolph again someday. There would be a family reunion up in heaven with those who had gone before her.

"You served your family well, Anna. You were the beautiful and faithful bride." The reverend had spoken these words. Anna looked out the car window, up to the sky, and smiled appreciatively.

Epilogue

It was 1984.

The Port Orford home had been sold.

Anna had been moved to a care facility in Klamath Falls, where Dee and her husband had moved.

Phyl stopped by to visit her. "I will be going home soon, Phyl. The house should be all ready for me to move back in. I think Dee has been getting it ready." Anna looked trustingly up at her daughter.

"Sure, Momma. Home. Soon." Phyl looked away. Anna had unwittingly signed everything away when Dee had taken her to the bank.

Anna's health began to decline rapidly when she learned she would never leave the care facility.

"Momma, I have a letter here for you from Spokane."

Anna looked up at Phyl. "Who is it from, honey?"

"I don't know, Momma. Why don't you open it and read it?"

"My eyes are too old and weak, Phyl. Would you do that for me?"

Phyl opened up the letter and read its contents.

Dearest Anna,

I am writing to thank you for your influence in my life. I was just a baby boy when you knew me. You read to me every day from a book. Thank you for leaving that book—your Bible—in my mother's care when you went away. Perhaps you did not intend to leave it there. I believe God meant it to be so. It began my journey and now influences my vocation. It has changed my life thanks to you. I believe it is the reason God placed you on this earth, Anna. I am serving God now in a pastorate position in a little Swedish church. I pray that God has continued to bless your life as he has my own.

With deepest joy,
L.D.

"Who might that be, Momma? Who is L.D.?"

"Someone very tiny from a long time ago." Anna clutched the letter to her heart and went to sleep.

Phyl and Mickey received their phone call from Dee.

It was May, 1984.

"Anna has moved again. Heaven is her home."

Anna's Recipes

Cardamom Bread.

1 quart milk, scalded

¾ lb margarine (1 ½ cups)

2 eggs, beaten

2 cups sugar

1 ¼ tsp salt

¾ tsp ground cardamom *(best to use the whole cardamom and pound it until it appears ground—for flavor improvement)*

5 cups flour for first rising; 9–10 ½ cups for second addition *(all together uses all but about 1 ½ cups of a 5-lb. bag of flour.)*

Scald milk, add margarine, cool temperature to add yeast. Add yeast and eggs. Put flour, sugar, salt, and cardamom in bowl. Add milk mixture. Let rise. Add remaining flour to make dough. Let rise. Make into rolls or loaves. Bake at 350 degrees for about 30 minutes or more, depending upon size of loaves.

SWEDISH MEATBALLS.

1/3 pound each: ground round, ground veal, and ground pork

Shred one medium potato into meat.

Add 1 beaten egg

Add bread crumbs enough to tighten meat balls

Add allspice, salt, and pepper to taste

Lightly brown meatballs on all sides. Lightly flour meatballs and add milk to cover bottom of meatballs. Simmer, covered until meatballs are cooked. Cook rice or noodles. Place cooked meatballs thickened with the milk gravy over rice or meatballs.

POTATIS KORV.

Two pounds pork, ground

One pound beef, ground

Measure meat and add as many coarse, ground potatoes as you have meat.

1 Tbsp salt

1 tsp pepper

1 small can condensed milk

1 large onion, ground fine

Mix well and fill casings, which have been soaked in cold water and washed thoroughly. (This is easily done by attaching the cold water faucet, letting the water run through them.) Cut to desired lengths. Have salted water boiling in kettle and place the rings in it and boil slowly for one hour.

5 large potatoes

1 large onion, coarsely chopped

½ tsp white pepper

½ tsp black pepper

2 tsp salt, to taste

¼ tsp allspice

¼ tsp ground mace

3 cups chicken broth

Peel and boil potatoes in lightly-salted water for 10 minutes. They should be very firm in the center. Allow to cool before proceeding to the next step. Cut the potatoes and mix with onion. Put through the fine disk on the grinder and mix well. This mixture will be quite sticky. Stuff and twist into 12" lengths. With cotton butcher's twine, tie two separate knots between each link and one knot at each end. Separate the links by cutting between the two knots between each pair of links. Bring the ends of each link together and tie to form rings. Boil in well-seasoned chicken broth for 45 minutes. Eat warm…or serve cool.

Fruitopia. (Old Fashioned Swedish Fruit Soup)

¾ C dried apricots

¾ C dried prunes

6 Cups cold water

1 cinnamon stick

2 lemon slices

3 tbsp Tapioca

1 Cup sugar

2 tbsp raisins

1 tbsp dried currants

1 tart apple, peeled, cored and sliced

Soak apricots and prunes in 6 cups cold water for 30 minutes, in a large enamel pan. Add cinnamon, lemon, and tapioca, and bring to a boil. Reduce heat and simmer for 15 minutes, stirring to prevent sticking. Add raisins, currants, and apple slices until apples are tender. Pour into bowl and cool to room temperature. Remove cinnamon stick and serve at room temperature.

Wine, rum, contra could be added in small quantity. This is served as a light, but nourishing dessert.

Rice Pudding. (8 servings)

8 Cups milk, scalded

¼ Cup sugar

1 Cup raisins (or any other dried fruit)

¼ Cup rice

¼ tsp salt

Wash rice. Combine milk, rice, sugar and salt. Pour into shallow baking dish. Bake in slow oven about three hours. Stir frequently. Add dried fruit.

Photographs

Seattle to Spokane Run—Northern Cascades

Adolph and Anna

The Vernonia Home on Corey Hill

Harriet, at Age 4—Spokane

The Lindquist Home in Moscow, Idaho (Anna—Far Right)

John Albert and Wilhelmina Lindquist

Anna in Spokane—Davenport Nanny

Anna—Millinery Entrepreneur

The Chetco River Bridge and Supervisor Adolph Nelson

Phyl and Harriet

Phyl and Peggy

The Mullan, Idaho, Home and Newlywed Anna